IN THE SHADOWS OF FREEDOM

C & C SPELLMAN

Rosemont Books

We wish to thank the following people for their invaluable help and wisdom in the writing of this book.

Elizabeth Birch

Carlee Collins

Nicholas De Falco

Matthew Gaul

John David Kudrick

Lisa Nicholas

Louise Schrecongost

Cindy Spellman

David Spellman

Mary Spellman

Peter Spellman

To our children

They see only their own shadows,
or the shadows of one another, which the fire throws....

Plato

(from *The Republic*—Book VII)

CHAPTER ONE

COMMENCEMENT

"Mom would be so proud of you today. You know that, right?"

Amanda froze. Beaming at her from the doorway where he stood, her dad appeared misty-eyed. She quickly turned away. Of course references to her mom would happen today. It was her college graduation—a milestone event. Today *should* be celebratory. But it wasn't. Her mom could never be here. She was dead.

Ignoring her dad's comments, she glanced around her empty dorm room. "I should check again to see if I packed everything."

Chiara, her younger sister, burst out laughing. "Amanda, you checked the room *three times*. What you need to do is let me fix your hair." Pulling a brush from her purse, Chiara stood behind her and began gathering the mass of black curls. "Think about how few people get to graduate from an Academy! You're the first one in our whole family!" Chiara finished braiding. "You should look beautiful."

"Well, *I* think Amanda always looks beautiful." Their dad laid his strong, rough hands on a shoulder of each girl, looking from daughter to daughter with affection in his blue eyes. "Oh, I knew I'd almost forget. I got a little something for you … just a sec." He fumbled in his coat pocket for a moment and pulled out a white corsage. "Go ahead and turn around. I'll pin it on your robe, okay?"

Stifling a sigh, but not wanting to hurt his feelings, Amanda obeyed.

"That did the trick!" Her dad nodded.

Chiara tilted her head to the side. "And, you know, the corsage really distracts from the fact that you didn't iron your robe."

Outside the chapel bells began to toll.

"Gosh, we better get moving." Her dad ushered them toward the door. "Remember to smile when you walk across the stage!"

Amanda rolled her eyes. "I'll smile when this is over."

Her dad and Chiara went in search of their seats; Amanda joined the long procession line. It was a perfect May morning: the sun shone in a cobalt-blue sky. There couldn't have been more ideal conditions for an outdoor graduation ceremony. The various schools processed in, heralded regally by bagpipers. Amanda sat on the outer fringe of the graduates. Through the rows and rows of students ahead of her, she could just barely make out the stage. She spotted her dad and Chiara in the crowd behind her, beaming and waving.

The procession thus completed and the national anthem sung, everyone sat down. The first speaker was a biology professor who began by offering typical clichés and generic life tips. Amanda ignored him and started making a mental list of what art supplies she would need to pack for the Graduate Academy of Fine Art.

The crowd around her applauded politely, signaling that the professor's droning was done at last. She awoke from her stupor and sat up a little straighter in her metal folding chair. She didn't know how many speakers they had on tap, but at least they were one closer to diplomas being handed out— and then she could clear out of here.

At the podium, the Academy president cleared his throat and, in his monotone voice, announced, "I now have the privilege of calling forward the Most Reverend Bishop Stephen Fisher."

Amanda heaved a quiet sigh. Her dad would be sitting on the edge of his seat now; she slumped in hers and gritted her teeth. She had chosen the Academy for its art program, not its religious affiliation. Considering her strong aversion to the latter, it was a testament to the quality of the art professors that she'd even enrolled here in the first place.

The bishop walked across the stage, the sun playing upon the gold cross that hung against his black robe. That gold could probably feed a lot of the Unfit. The church was always giving handouts to the starving masses; it seemed surprising they had any wealth left for their leaders.

His hands now grasping the edges of the podium, the bishop looked out into the crowd, his expression somber, lines of age marking his face. His voice, powerful in its force and passionate in its emphasis, reverberated and boomed through the microphone. "Graduates of Valor Academy, I come before you this morning with no professional or academic advice to offer. Instead, I bring you a grim admonition. The time has come for you to make a choice. I don't refer to choosing a Graduate Academy or professional future. No, I am referring to your freedom."

The bishop paused and leaned forward, then continued, his words still commanding. "In this time of unprecedented, so-called liberty in our nation—when so little is restricted or outlawed or punished—you have a choice: What will you do with this freedom? How will you charter your course in a world with no boundaries? Will you seek a *'freedom from'* or a *'freedom for'*? Why have you been given this free—"

It happened in an instant. An ear-splitting, deafening sound of destruction silenced every other noise. A thunderous explosion came from the stage, obliterating everyone and everything in its immediate environs, and then cascaded outward into the defenseless crowd.

The ground beneath Amanda shook from the force. Her body was ripped from the chair, and she crashed into the ground a few feet away. Everything moved rapidly, like a movie on fast-forward, and she struggled to maintain consciousness. Dense, black smoke filled the air. Past that, massive flames reached into the sky. The fireball roared, and tiny bits of shrapnel slashed through the air, only halting when meeting the defenseless flesh of the victims.

Then came the terrified, panicked screams—a high-pitched, spontaneous chorus of shock and pain … a melody of death.

The spot where the bishop had been mere seconds ago was now vacant, save for the consuming fire. The rows of graduates closest to the stage were also gone, their fragile bodies no match for the explosive shock wave.

Gasping, coughing, and wheezing, Amanda struggled to get up. She had to get out of here, as fast as—No! She had to find her dad and Chiara. They were behind her, somewhere in the frenzy. She started to sit up, but a fellow graduate, his arm pouring blood, plowed through the chairs and trampled her right leg. Amanda fell back to the ground, stifling a cry and clutching her leg. The heat of the flames drew ever closer, and she screamed as her heart raced and chest clenched, her voice joining countless others.

Another person raced by her, this time shoving chairs out of his way. Amanda ducked, covering her head with her arms. Several metal chairs crashed on top of her. Dozens of students emerged from the thick black smoke, racing toward her, entirely blind and indifferent to her in their panic. She stared up at them, paralyzed with fear and horror. If she didn't die from the blazing fire, she might still get trampled to death.

"Stop!" Amanda yelled. She tried to scramble out of the way, but her movements were clumsy and she fumbled to even stand, pain running up and down her body.

At that moment, two strong hands seized her, pulled her up from the ground, and supported her. Amanda found herself half-stumbling, half-walking. Dazed and wincing, she turned and looked at her unexpected rescuer.

He stared back, the lightest of blue eyes watching her. "Follow me."

She asked no questions, but let him guide her away from the wreckage. He must have been one of the graduates too. He wore neatly pressed khakis and a crisp white dress shirt with a navy-blue tie. It was distracting to think about him— a good distraction. In fact, there was something about him, something very familiar. She must have taken a class with him. Maybe freshman year?

They kept walking, farther and farther away from the main quad, the sound of sirens now wailing all around them. Her companion strode with determination, as though he had a set destination in mind.

At last, the crowd thinned, and they stopped outside one of the administrative buildings on the fringe of campus.

The other graduate gestured for her to have a seat on the steps. "You will be safe here."

Amanda swallowed hard. She looked down at her hands: they were shaking. "Wh-What just happened?"

"Evil."

"Amanda! Amanda!"

She jumped up at the sound of her name: it was her dad calling. Forgetting any pain, she hobbled toward him, falling into his arms. Chiara walked just behind him, and she rushed forward, grabbing Amanda and sobbing.

"Oh, thank God!" Her dad's voice trembled as he clutched her.

Amanda stiffened in his arms. Thank *God*? Where was *God* in all of this?

Her dad stepped back a moment, looking Amanda up and down. "Are you hurt at all?"

"No ... I don't think so. Nothing really serious at least. What about you and Chiara?"

Chiara took a breath between her cries and tried to get the words out. "We were ... far enough away ... but we saw everything. The bomb exploding, the fire, the ..."

Amanda could finish the sentence: the victims.

"Let's get out of here." Their dad put his arms around both of them. "I'm sure the Justice and Protection Division will be here soon." His face hardened with a look of disdain. "Unless they've already executed their justice."

Wanting to thank the other graduate for saving her life, Amanda turned around, but he was nowhere to be seen.

CHAPTER TWO

THE ROOMMATE

Nikki took a long swig of coffee. Third cup so far and the day was young. She cracked a few knuckles with satisfaction and flipped through the prints she had scattered on the small space of kitchen counter not already filled with dirty dishes, sticky notes to herself, or magazines.

Now *this* one … this picture was the stuff she wanted. She picked it up and studied it.

Great lighting, asymmetrical balance, good use of the frame.

She had snapped the photo at a fundraising event for the National Citizens Party last week. Senator Caroline Crauss of Virginia, the party's newest rising star, had been there, beaming from the podium. Nikki had lucked out and even scored some conversation with Caroline after her speech. They were on a first-name basis now—always a good thing. Nikki drummed her nails on the counter in rhythm to the dance hall music blasting from the nearby speakers. Maybe … just maybe, one day *she* would be that star.

At least one day. Right now, she'd stay behind the camera and keep building her contacts. She had work to do. The NCP kept her busy, and that's the way she wanted it.

They would put up some big bucks for her snaps of the fundraiser: more money in her pocket and another step closer to her dreams. Money meant influence; influence meant power. She would never be a victim again. The NCP had given Nikki her freedom, the greatest gift she had ever received.

She drank the last mouthful of coffee and glanced up at the empty pot. Damn it, she'd have to make more. She shoveled a few more spoonfuls of coffee into the filter—who even bothered with measuring?—and the bracelets on her wrist jangled with her movements. Her favorite bracelet was the turquoise beaded one that Chloe had given her last year after she went to Greece. *Greece.* Now that was a dream: getting out of the South Bronx and exploring the world.

The fluorescent lights flickered overhead, and she rolled her eyes. *There goes the circuit breaker … again. Well, who really cares?* The coffeepot still worked, and that was all she needed. One day, though … one day, she'd bust out of this hole in the wall. It was a crime how much she had to pay for this dump. At least she was getting a roommate.

Roommate! Nikki stopped for a moment and stared ahead. When was the new girl getting here? Putting down her mug, she picked up her cell phone and searched for the messages they'd exchanged. Here was the original alert from the Graduate Academy of Fine Art, connecting them. The school was a good source for roommates: that's where she'd found her last two. Ah, she found the right message: *Amanda Burrow.* Right, that was her name. And Amanda would be arriving …

Wait, what was the date today? She checked her phone. Amanda was coming today!

Nikki took a deep breath. She had work to do. She rushed into the bathroom and began to adjust her makeup. She had her priorities after all. She smoothed her cropped auburn hair (she had better schedule an appointment to get another coloring soon) and applied some more mascara.

Soon afterward, Nikki was clearing file folders and papers off the spare bed when a faint buzzing sound reached her over the blaring music. Throwing everything into a heap on the floor, she paused the song and bolted over to the front door, pressing the Talk button. "What's up?"

"Umm … it's Amanda. Amanda Burrow … your new roommate."

"Fabulous!" Nikki clicked the button, unlocking the front entrance door downstairs, and then waited in anticipation.

A faint knocking sounded. Nikki swung the door open wide and smiled at her new roommate.

The girl was short. Or maybe it was more that Nikki was exceptionally tall, especially wearing her stilettos. Either way, Amanda looked up at her, her face pale and blue eyes wide. She fidgeted in the hallway, shuffling her feet about and twisting her hands together. And, wow … those curls. They were seriously out of control! The girl didn't do a single thing to even attempt to make her hair look attractive.

Nikki remembered her manners and put on her most encouraging and welcoming tone. "Well, come on in! How was your trip? Sorry I didn't have time to clean up. I totally forgot you were coming today! But you might as well get used to it." She stepped aside and gestured for Amanda to come in. "I'm not a *complete* slob, really. Look at me—I didn't even introduce myself. I'm Nikki King."

She held out her hand. Amanda extended a limp hand and gave a lifeless handshake. A corpse probably would have shown more enthusiasm.

Amanda murmured something that sounded like, "Nice to meet you," and then stood there, staring around the room and avoiding eye contact.

Nikki was not impressed. Amanda's plain T-shirt and worn jeans weren't helping matters any either. Nikki walked over to the kitchen and filled her cup again. She'd need some caffeine to stay awake during this hardly gripping conversation. "So, you a coffee drinker? Can I pour you a cup?"

Amanda shook her head and returned to studying the room decor. Nikki was so used to it that she forgot how striking it looked. She had plastered the walls—ceiling included—with photographs: black-and-whites, neon pinks and greens, people, animals, and random objects such as flaming toasters and foaming pigs ... all of them together creating a slew of colors and images. And, of course, the best part was the familiar *I Stand With the NCP!* bumper stickers, which stood out among the swirling visual noise.

Amanda's eyes continued to rove about the room. "Wow."

"I know, right? That's what everyone says. I like it. It's my own personal wallpaper."

"It's impressive."

"It took forever to design. I wanted it to be like a mosaic that never creates a unified picture. I wanted it to unsettle people, to make them think."

"Yeah ... you succeeded. You took all of these pictures?"

"Each and every one." Nikki paused for a moment, and inspiration hit her. "So, you know, since this is your home now, feel free to put any of your pictures up."

Amanda raised her eyebrows, but looked down. "I'm not really into photography, but thanks."

"You paint, right?"

"Mostly. Sometimes I sketch."

Amanda set her book bag and small suitcase down on the floor beside her. There wasn't really anywhere else to put them. The apartment was tiny to begin with, and the explosion of clothes around the room didn't help. Nikki didn't care, though. She had more important things to do besides folding laundry.

She went over and picked up Amanda's suitcase. "We can stick these in the bedroom if you want. Come on, I'll show you." As they walked, Nikki shook her head in wonder. "Two bags! Are you for real?"

"I travel pretty light. But I had some art supplies shipped here. I hope that was okay. Did you happen to get them?"

"Oh ... yeah. Let me find that." Nikki went to the corner of the bedroom and picked up a cardboard box. She peered at the return address in the corner. "Fort Christopher? That's where you live?"

"Where I used to live."

"Huh. Where the heck is that?"

"It's upstate ... in the Adirondacks."

"Sounds familiar."

Amanda cocked her head. "It does? Not many people have heard of it. It's pretty small. The only thing of note is Valor Academy, and that's about an hour's drive away."

Nikki's stomach churned. "That must be what I'm thinking of. Did you go to Valor?"

"Yeah."

Nikki waited, hoping for some elaboration. Amanda surely must know Nikki's allegiance: she had to have seen the

NCP stickers everywhere. Nikki decided to probe her for more information. "What did you think of it?"

"I liked the art program. That was about it."

"I hear there are a lot of religious activists and protesters up there." Nikki tried to keep her voice neutral.

Amanda's face darkened, and she crossed her arms. "I wouldn't know. Or care. That's not my thing. I'm glad I'm not there anymore."

"Well, if that's the case, welcome to NYC! You'll be happy here." Nikki grinned. Maybe Amanda Burrow would be a good roommate after all. She would require some work, but she had potential.

Amanda opened the box and began checking her supplies. Nikki glanced at her from the corner of her eye. Amanda seemed really quiet, though. Maybe too quiet … it was unsettling. But that could change as she loosened up and felt more comfortable.

Nikki walked toward the doorway. "Hate to take off so soon, but I've got to run for a meeting. The extra key to the apartment is by the coffeepot. You have my number, right? Just give me a ring if you need anything."

"Yeah, thanks." Amanda gave a timid, close-lipped smile. On the heels of that success, Nikki grabbed her photos from the kitchen counter and left.

~ ~ ~

Amanda sank onto the bed, more exhausted from the conversation than from all her traveling. She loathed introductions: they exacerbated her normal social awkwardness. She never knew the right thing to say. Now that it was thankfully over, she would replay everything in her mind and see how badly she had done.

She untied her worn sneakers and pulled them off. What had Nikki thought of her? She couldn't have been impressed. Nikki personified glamour. The taupe-colored dress that hung long and loose on her tall frame, the numerous piercings in her nose and ears, her gel-styled hair that was sleek and sophisticated … Amanda couldn't be more of a contrast.

But she liked Nikki and her welcoming, bright personality. *Maybe* they could become friends. It would be nice not to be so alone.

Amanda unpacked her few possessions. There was only one of value: a small painting carefully covered and tucked safely inside her book bag. Brown wrapping paper covered all of her creations—she never showed them to anyone, not even to her dad or Chiara. This rule applied most of all to the particular work now before her: one of her earliest paintings and, more importantly, her favorite. She hid the masked image under the bed.

Her inspiration piqued, she unpacked her brushes and oils, wanting to capture this moment. This was a turning point: she needed to mark it through art—the only way she could express herself anymore. The strokes of the brush were the beats of her heart, her life story; the varying colors were the dimensions of her personality. Her personal art was her diary in image form.

She opened the tiny window in the living room. She was used to the pungent scent of her painting medium, but Nikki probably was not. She set her wooden palette on the cardboard shipping box, and on the other side, she placed her tackle box, which held her tubes of oil paints. Thus situated, she began.

As soon as her brush touched the canvas, she lost herself in the realm of thoughts and dreams. Even the noises from outside—traffic, shouts, blaring hip-hop music—failed to disturb her. She relished the first few strokes, the colors dashing across the expanse of the white gessoed board—the start of a new creation. Time escaped her as she delved into the deep space where she kept her most private self locked away.

The hours passed, but she continued her work. That was her one definitive rule when it came to her creations: leave nothing unfinished. For her, an incomplete painting felt like a story with no final chapter or a song with a missing coda. She just couldn't put a piece of herself in her work and walk away from it undone.

The sun slipped past the tall frames of buildings and then finally set. Sighing with contentment, Amanda put down her brush and, stepping back and stretching, surveyed the result, the transformation from *tabula rasa* to accomplished picture having been fulfilled.

The painting was, naturally, of a city. Yet the buildings in her painting began as trees, a complete garden of them. As they stretched upward, their wood trunks gradually became steel, transforming themselves into looming skyscrapers. On the ground, wandering amid the roots, stood amorphous gray shadows of people, uniform in their anonymity. In the forefront of the picture loomed an imposing figure of a person—dark and mysterious. A sole billboard displayed the only object of color in the painting: a glistening crimson apple.

The piece was an enigma to her, which didn't surprise her. Following an inner impulse when painting, she often couldn't understand her own creations. She stretched and yawned. Tomorrow would be her first class at the Graduate Academy and she wanted to meet the day refreshed. After cleaning up her art supplies and rinsing her brushes, she crawled into bed and closed her eyes. Maybe it was the unfamiliar bed or the curious figure from her painting or the screams of the bombing victims that still filled her head in the stillness—whatever the reason, she couldn't ignore the foreboding heaviness that filtered through her restless dreams.

CHAPTER THREE

FIRST DAY

"Hey! Come on over and have yourself a nutritious breakfast. You can't skip the most important meal of the day!"

Amanda jumped at the sound of Nikki's voice. She had just gotten ready (with uncommon alacrity) and, leaving the bedroom, found Nikki perched on one of the stools by the counter in the kitchenette. Nikki patted the stool next to her and waved Amanda over.

Normally, Amanda would have chugged a glass of orange juice and grabbed a banana. But, not wanting to be rude to her new roommate, she decided to take a seat beside Nikki. She had a few extra minutes until she had to leave for the Masters Academy anyway.

Nikki slid a box of cereal in front of her. "I also have the cocoa kind that turns your milk all chocolatey, if you want that instead."

"Thanks, but this is fine. I didn't think you would be up so early. Didn't you get back pretty late last night?"

Nikki looked up at the ceiling, squinting her eyes. "About 5:00 a.m. So ... around two hours ago."

Even after rolling out of bed and lounging in a lime-green bathrobe, Nikki looked like she belonged on the cover of a fashion magazine.

"That must have been quite the meeting."

"It wasn't just the meeting. A bunch of us hung out afterward and got some food and drinks. I completely lost track of time. Happens like that when I'm around them. Sorry for leaving you alone for so long on your first day here! That's a big roommate fail."

"It's okay. I'm used to being alone."

"So … you excited? Big day for you, right? The first day at the *Graduate Academy*." She spoke in an exaggerated, fake British accent.

"Actually … yeah, I am excited."

"Word on the street is that they have some cool exhibits on display. My friends and I were just talking about that last night."

"Oh. Did you go to the Masters Academy of Art too?"

"Me?" Nikki laughed dryly. "No. I didn't make the cut. Not all of us are that smart. But I don't need a Masters Academy anyway. It's all about connections and knowing the right people. Ask any artist and they'd tell you that."

"You mean a degree doesn't actually mean that much?"

"Eh. It's impressive, obviously. I mean, how could it not be? Only one hundred students across the country get accepted into that art program! But it's not the be-all and end-all of everything. You've got to get out there: meet the people, get your art into the venues, learn techniques from the up-and-coming artists. People care about what you can do … and who you know. Sometime you'll have to come around and meet my friends."

"Yeah." Amanda swirled the cereal around in the bowl, her appetite gone.

"Okay!" Nikki stood up and cleared away Amanda's bowl. Grabbing Amanda's hands, she pulled her up, handed Amanda her bookbag, and then steered her toward the door.

"Time for school, young lady! You can't be late on your first day. I've got to be honest—your outfit leaves *much* to be desired. Seriously, you're making first impressions today. But I'll let it go for now. We'll discuss that later."

Amanda cringed: she could hardly wait. She waved goodbye to Nikki and began the trek to the subway. It was a lengthy ride into Manhattan, but she didn't mind. She had waited, worked, and hoped for this day for years, and the immensity of the occasion gave an air of grandeur even to her long commute in a jam-packed subway car.

Arriving in Manhattan, she exited the dark, stuffy subway station and walked up the stairs to the street. She waited at the crosswalk, where a nearby street vendor, shouting and cajoling, peddled some sunglasses—"Twenty-five percent off, today only!" Bright billboards stood out among the grays and silvers of gargantuan steel buildings. A man walking in the crowd in front of her spoke into his cell phone in a language she didn't recognize. She turned the corner and caught the aroma of bagels, hot out of the oven.

Her pace quickened and her stomach fluttered with anticipation. There, straight ahead, stood the large building that was her new art school. *Her* art school: she belonged here. She bounded up the steps and presented her acceptance letter to the doorman, who opened the entryway for her. She found herself in an open foyer with hallways branching in different directions. Art exhibits filled the space. Following Nikki's suggestion, she started to investigate them.

First, she viewed "The Devil's Playground" and then "Genetic Gems." She ambled from display to display, observing the technique and medium. But one series in particular captured her attention.

The title of the display was "Passions." She cocked her head, trying to make sense of it. All the paintings looked identical, save their varying colors. They lacked a clear image, any symbolism, or a definable shape; they were just erratic color. Did the artist take a can of paint, throw it on the canvas, and walk away? Paint-by-number seemed like the simplest way to paint, but this might beat even that. Repulsion, as opposed to admiration, filled her.

"What do you think?" A girl stood next to her. She had long, greasy black hair, and her eyes stared at Amanda from behind thick glasses.

"It's ... different ... I guess."

"Care to elaborate?"

"I guess I just don't understand nonrepresentational art, that's all."

"Do you have any idea the technique this requires?"

Amanda shook her head no.

"That's what makes it so challenging, obviously. The artist has to create her painting in a way that gives the impression that it was simple, casual. The ordinary observer can't even grasp the effort and honed skills necessary to accomplish this. This is the final capstone project for the graduating students, the culmination of all their studies. We work our whole career here to be able to accomplish something of this caliber." She peered at Amanda. "Is this your first day here or something?"

"Yeah."

"Good luck. Looks like you have a lot to learn." Without waiting for Amanda's response, she spun on her heel and strode down the hallway.

Amanda glanced back at the art exhibit, biting her lip. To think that all of her studies here would culminate in *this*

... there had to be some mistake. Maybe it depended on which professor you had your final year.

She took a deep breath and checked her class schedule. It was time to go to Studio Painting I. Actually, it was past time. She rushed down the hallway, but it was the wrong one and she had to turn around. She scanned the room numbers, gritting her teeth. This was *exactly* what she'd wanted to avoid.

Opening the door, she slipped inside. A stout man with some wisps of gray hair on the top of his head stood in front of the room. "Okay, everyone! Welcome to the painting studio. My name's Michael. Let's begin with a few preliminaries ..." Glancing up, he spotted Amanda. "Go ahead and take a seat." He pointed to an empty easel on the far side of the room. "Next time, I expect everyone to be punctual."

The eyes of the whole class fell upon her. Her cheeks burned, and she scurried over to the empty easel. The girl she had just spoken to by the art display—the condescending one—happened to be standing at the easel next to her. Perfect.

Michael paced back and forth. "So, as I was saying, next class we'll talk about the syllabus and the schedule for projects, along with the supply list. But for now, let's hit the ground running. I want you to do an impromptu ninety-minute sketch of this large sports drink bottle." He gestured to the plastic bottle he had set up as a still life, with a bottle next to each easel. "I realize not everyone brought their materials today, so I have some Nitram charcoal you may use, and as you see, there is already some paper taped onto your drawing board on each easel. Remember: you have ninety minutes, not a second more, so get to work!"

Amanda smiled to herself. This wasn't the most inspirational of tasks, but she could do it with ease. She would show them how much she belonged here. She had earned her seat in this studio.

She focused her mind and efforts on the yet inchoate image. She paused every few minutes to gaze at the bottle, double-checking her proportions. She made some initial markings on the paper and then squinted, getting a good sense of the values and contrast. Then she picked up her charcoal and began sketching with intense focus, using the side of the stick to block in the dark values first.

Over the years, she had perfected her art skills, honing them through disciplined tasks just like this. Amanda would ask Chiara to pick an object in the house for her to sketch, and then she would get to work, challenging herself each time to make it more and more realistic—she was a perfectionist. It was a game to her, and eventually, Chiara lost interest because she could find nothing Amanda was not able to sketch. She always sought to create another reality, an extension of the present existence, seemingly as authentic as this one.

Once she succeeded in capturing this world on canvas, then she began to venture into her inner world of thoughts, sensations, questions, feelings. But *that* way of painting was usually unpredictable and always very personal—those were the paintings she covered and masked.

"Charcoal down!" Michael looked up from his watch.

The students put down their charcoal. Amanda had finished five minutes ago. She sat on the edge of her stool, ready to go. Her discerning eye looked over her sketch once more: a model representation with all the right dimensions, shades, and textures. She dared anyone to produce something more realistic than hers.

"Now this is how we're going to do it." Michael rubbed his hands together. "Starting on this side of the semicircle, I want you to stand up, tell us your name, and turn your easel around so everyone can see your work."

Michael began at the other end of the circle, farthest from Amanda. The first girl stood up and revealed a cartoon bottle, its outline grossly exaggerated and stylized.

Nodding, Michael said, "Nice! Very, very nice! Great contrast in this one."

Amanda furrowed her brow.

The next student had drawn his sketch from an entirely different perspective, as though the viewer were inside the bottle looking out at the class.

"Brilliant! I love it!" Michael even stepped closer to study the image.

The creativity only increased with each following sketch, causing Amanda's pulse to quicken. Had she missed something? What had Michael's original directions been again? She glanced at her sketch, a perfect representation … yet so bland when compared to the others thus far. She massaged her temples: a headache was coming on.

The girl next to her was up. "I'm Leila, and I created my image as though I were one with the liquid inside the bottle."

Bold, wavy lines and ripples of haphazard bubbles filled her drawing. Her work prompted audible exclamations of praise from some students.

"Wow. Just wow. Great work!" Michael shook his head, eyes fixed on Leila's piece.

Leila smirked. Then, tossing her slick hair behind her shoulder, she looked at Amanda.

"And last but not least, you!" Michael walked in front of Amanda.

Her stomach churned. … That's all she needed right now: to vomit on the professor. Twelve pairs of eyes stared at her. She swallowed and stood, trying to hide her trembling hands. She turned her easel around. A long, painful silence ensued.

"Now *that's* original." Leila snickered under her breath.

Michael cleared his throat. "Okay, thanks." He almost reached the front of the classroom, but then turned back around. "You didn't tell us your name."

She had already sat back down, defeated, on her stool. "Amanda."

"Alright, thanks. So that's it for today. Next class we'll be discussing the semester project. For now, just finish up any final details on your sketch."

Everyone filed out of the room, chattering in groups, but Amanda lagged behind. She couldn't understand. How was it possible that here, at an art school, she might not belong? Art was the one thing—the *only* thing—she was ever good at. But somehow it failed to meet the standard today.

Wanting to escape, she raced down the stairs to the first floor, where she came upon a study lounge. She sighed with relief: the overhead lights were off. This was exactly what she wanted. She pulled open the door and flicked on the lights— a room all to herself, a refuge from other people.

She was wrong. Someone was looking at her as soon as she entered.

He sat at one of the several wooden, circular tables, a closed laptop in front of him. Something about his look made Amanda's breath catch in her throat. He didn't even appear surprised at her entrance. The way he stared, though … it was almost as if he had been watching the door, waiting for her.

Brushing the thought aside, she looked down at the floor and scurried to the table farthest from him.

"Hey."

Of course he had to initiate a conversation.

"Umm. Hi." Bending her head, she opened her book bag and rummaged through it. She didn't want to talk to anyone else today.

"I'm Ethan."

Seriously, couldn't this guy take a hint? She let go of her bag and gave him a sidelong glance. "My name's Amanda."

"You must be new; I haven't seen you around here before." He nonchalantly stretched his arm over the chair next to him.

"Yeah."

"Nice. What brought you here?" His baritone voice sounded friendly and inviting.

"I paint. … It's my passion."

"You're at the right place. A degree from here will help you make a career doing what you love."

"That's exactly what I was hoping." She put her book bag down and studied him a little more. He had black hair, which he had styled so the front pieces curved upward ever so slightly. His face was long and slender, with a sharp chin and Roman nose. A neatly trimmed goatee framed his mouth. "So … how about you? Are you working on a degree here or something like that?"

"I'm taking a couple of classes in graphic design … which, by the way, makes me wonder: If you're here for painting, what brings you near the graphic design studios?"

"Oh … I was just looking for a quiet place."

He smiled for the first time, a wide, enchanting grin. At the sight, her social barriers, normally so rigid and impenetrable, began to weaken. He had no idea what he was doing. Or maybe he did?

She reactively stood up. "I better get going to my next class."

He leaned forward on the table. "It was nice to meet you, Amanda. I'll see you around."

"Yeah, thanks. Bye."

She turned and did her best to walk out the door like a normal human being. A few yards away from the lounge, she picked up her pace and took the stairs two at a time until she returned to the second floor again. She stopped and leaned back against the cool concrete wall, trying to still her racing heart.

There was something distinctly peculiar about Ethan—maybe more than just the fact that he'd been the only person to welcome her thus far today. She actually would want to talk to him more, if she had the chance. But a lot of students attended the Masters Academy, and he wasn't even in the same discipline as she was. The likelihood of them bumping into each other again seemed slim. She could hope for it, but realistically speaking, she would probably never see him again.

At least running into Ethan ended up as the silver lining for what otherwise turned out to be an abysmal first day.

CHAPTER FOUR

LIVING NIGHTMARES

"Roomie!" Nikki breezed through the doorway wearing an ankle-length suede coat. "What's new and exciting?"

"Nothing." Amanda sat cross-legged on the sofa, fingering the soft bristles of a paintbrush.

Nikki cocked her head, looking at the blank canvas in front of Amanda. "Very original. Is this your specialty?"

Amanda tossed the paintbrush onto the floor, lying back on the sofa and letting a clipped sigh escape her lips. "No, it's not. I can't do anything today." She felt zero motivation to paint. The rest of her week had been as disappointing as the first day. Attending the Graduate Academy had been the dream that motivated her for so long. But now? She was living that dream, and it was a nightmare.

"Ah, I see." Nikki pursed her lips. "Have you been sitting here all day?"

"I'm trying to do my assignment."

"Amanda, it's Friday. You know you have the whole weekend to finish your work, right?"

"I figured I might as well get it out of the way."

Nikki didn't reply. Instead, she gazed in another direction, her eyes betraying a hint of mischief.

Amanda eyed her. "What? … What is it?"

"It's so perfect and—Hold on." Nikki strode over to her purse. "I can tell you need inspiration, and have I got the solution for you, missy."

"When I can't paint, I usually find it helps if I just spend some time alone, thinking."

Nikki swiveled, her hands on her hips. "You've been home all day, and so far, all you managed to do is that." She pointed at the blank canvas. "I rest my case." Nikki gave a cry of triumph and pulled a piece of paper from her bag, thrusting it in Amanda's face. "Take a look at this!"

Amanda did as ordered, straightening out the crumpled paper before reading the flier. The headline, in bold bubble letters, proclaimed: *Living Nightmares—Mixed Media Sensations at Little Pete's.*

She looked up at Nikki and said, "Living nightmares? That's the theme of the art display? That sounds pleasant." She returned the flier, shaking her head.

"Pleasant—just like you, right? Always so chipper and optimistic. A ray of sunshine!" Nikki raised her eyebrows and stared at Amanda.

Amanda gave a sheepish half smile. "Well, what's Little Pete's?"

"It's a club downtown. My friends and I are regulars. The owner supports local artists. You can buy the art on display, so artists make a few bucks, but, better yet, you never know who's going to spot you."

Amanda bit her lower lip. How could she forge a career as an artist with her inspiration and drive to create mired in disappointment and dashed expectations? "Will your friends be there too?"

"You better believe it! We were just talking about it last night. They'd love to meet you! I'll introduce you to all the right people."

She sighed, shoulders sagging. "Okay ... I'll go."

"Well, don't get too excited now." Nikki glanced at the clock on the microwave. "Ooo, crap, we've got to move it! Come on—off the couch! It's time to get ready!"

"But the flier said it doesn't start for another three hours."

"Tell me about it! Let's go!" She grabbed Amanda's arm and started pulling her toward the bathroom.

"What's going on?"

"If you're planning on going dressed like that, you will not be going with me." Nikki gestured at Amanda's jeans and long-sleeved T-shirt.

"You won't do anything really wild?"

"I promise: no purple eye shadow or green lipstick."

Amanda nodded and shuffled toward the bathroom.

Nikki pumped her fist into the air and dashed into the bedroom. "I'll be there in just a sec. I'm getting all my stuff!"

A full two hours later, Amanda stood in front of Nikki's tall mirror, hardly recognizing the reflection staring back at her. If clothes made a person, who was she becoming? Her black curls, normally bobbing every which way, now weaved their way below her shoulders. Black eyeliner outlined her eyes, while the red lipstick contrasted her white skin. The short dress she now wore caught the light in its tight seams, highlighting royal-blue hues.

She never used makeup or took much interest in clothes. She didn't have some inherent opposition to them. She just pretended not to care. ... It didn't hurt as much that way.

"And now for the finishing touch!" Nikki placed a purse in Amanda's hands.

"Thanks, but I don't really use purses."

"Oh, come on. First off, it's a *designer evening bag*. Get it right. Secondly, every woman needs one. Didn't anyone ever teach you these things?" Nikki pulled a dress from her closet. "Give me a chance to change and freshen up, then we're outta here."

Nikki, of course, was not to be outdone. She exited the bedroom wearing a teal dress, the hem zigzagging above her knees as the chiffon material cascaded in varying lengths. A black pendant formed the center, where the material gathered low on her chest. She slipped on a pair of ankle-strap dress sandals, easily gaining another inch; Amanda felt a dwarf next to her in black flats.

Soon enough, their taxi sped toward Manhattan. Slouched in the back seat behind the driver, Amanda crossed her legs, squeezing them together, and then pulled the hem of her dress down as far as possible. Her legs and arms were naked … leaving her feeling vulnerable and exposed. She shivered and rubbed her arms up and down. They must be getting pretty close to the club now. … Her breathing quickened.

"Just chill." Nikki bent over a pocket mirror, applying some mascara. "Tonight will be awesome."

Amanda gripped the edge of the seat with white knuckles and just stared out the window.

A thumping bass sound made it clear that they had arrived. The taxi pulled to the curb in front of a three-story brick building nestled off the beaten path. Upon getting out, Amanda spotted the flashing neon sign that read *Little Pete's*. A long snake of people lined the sidewalk, mingling and laughing in the night air. Nikki was exactly right: Amanda at once felt stimulated by the rush of what her senses drank in—a fluorescent green straw resting on the rim of a cocktail glass, the scent of hot wings as a miniskirt-wearing waitress carried them to an outside table, the obnoxious guffawing of a man probably on his fourth beer.

Nikki was busy paying the driver, so Amanda waited for her on the sidewalk. From her position, she could just make out the side of the building where a massive mural spanned the space. This was no graffiti done by the Unfit, but the serious work of a trained artist. She walked closer to investigate. One massive figure dominated the wall: a brilliant red dragon. Its wings spanned the broad expanse of brick, stretching from one end to the other. The beast arched its back and twisted its head to glare at the viewer. Its eyes were fire, and Amanda marveled at the strength it conveyed, even as a two-dimensional image. She would like to know about the artist and the meaning of the work.

Upon turning around, Amanda saw that the taxi was gone—and so was Nikki. She swallowed and stared at the sidewalk. Her whole consolation with this escapade was that Nikki would help facilitate conversation with these strangers. Now Amanda had lost her critical link. She walked inside, scanning the room for Nikki. Her eyes fell upon a group of people at the far end of the bar. They sat on bright red stools, laughing and talking with sweeping hand gestures. Several of them sat there, but she paid attention to only one of them: *him.*

He wore a navy-blue shirt, the top button casually undone, and dark blue jeans, the latest design. The man next to him said something, and they both laughed. She once again felt mesmerized by his smile, and her heart began to pound. He was here—really here.

His green eyes turned from the table and looked at her. She met his look for a second, taken aback, and then turned away. Her cheeks burned and her body froze. He had caught her staring at him. How rude could she be? Maybe she could disappear into the crowd …

"Hey!"

Her head shot up at his greeting. He stood before her, stretching his arm out to lean against the wall. The booming bass pouring down from somewhere above made his greeting hard to hear, but his voice still sounded as appealing as the first time she had heard it.

"Hi." She was certain he couldn't hear her tentative reply.

He moved closer and her heart began beating even faster. For the first time, she could observe all his finer features. She was not disappointed.

"Amanda, right?"

He remembered her. Her stomach fluttered … and everything else besides him faded into the distance.

"Right. And you're Ethan."

He nodded, a pleased smile on his face.

She wanted him to stay here, interested and engaged. She had to keep the dialogue going. "Do—Do you come here often?"

"Definitely. I wasn't originally planning on coming tonight, though."

"Oh." She couldn't think of anything else to say. How profound …

Ethan shifted his body, inclining his head closer to her. "To tell you the truth, I only came tonight because I was hoping I might see you."

31

She nearly gaped at him. No, this was too much. Knowing her name was one thing. That was unexpected, but still fairly credible. But to think that he came with the explicit desire to see *her?*

Complete shock took over, and skepticism emboldened her. She crossed her arms. "Yeah, sure you did. You've probably been looking all over for me."

Ethan's eyes widened, and he seemed uncertain how to respond to her sarcasm, which came so natural to her.

"I'm sorry … I …" She floundered. "I didn't think you were really serious. It sounded like a one-liner you'd use on a girl you wanted to pick up."

"I'm not like that."

"I guess I'm a classic cynic. You'll just have to get used to it."

He raised his eyebrows. "Get used to it? It sounds as though you're implying we'll be spending some time together."

"I didn't mean that. … I mean, you don't have to …"

Ethan gave a little smile. "I know I don't have to. But I'd like to. How about over dinner?"

Now Amanda's eyes widened. Could this be too good to be true? He was asking her on a date?

He stood there, watching her and waiting.

"That would be good. I'd like that."

He grinned. "So what day would be best for you?"

"I have a pretty open schedule." In other words, she had no social life.

"I have a conflict tomorrow, but would Sunday work? Maybe around six?"

"Yeah, that's fine."

"Great. Can I get your phone number? I'll give you a call tomorrow, and we can work out the details." He pulled his phone from his pocket—he had the Axis 13-S, which she knew hadn't even been released on the market yet.

"Nice phone."

"Thanks. It's useful."

He entered her contact information and tucked the device back into his pocket.

"I'm guessing you must be into technology?" she asked.

"You could say that. I have a very scientific mind. I like understanding how things work. ... It's a sort of puzzle to me. I unravel something—undo it and take it apart—so I can see its internal functioning. Then I challenge myself to create it anew ... create it better."

"What brought you to the Masters Academy, then?"

"My employer sent me to take some courses in graphic design."

"Oh. You work in the city?" She couldn't stop asking questions: she wanted to learn everything about him.

"Yes. But, you know, I've been talking a lot. Why don't you tell me about yourself?"

"There isn't much to say. What you see is what you get with me."

"No. You fascinate me."

"Me? Why?" How could this rich, attractive, successful guy be so interested in her?

"You just fascinate me ... in many ways." He shrugged. "Like, for instance, this whole time I've been trying to figure out the color of your eyes." He moved even closer, until his fingers brushed against hers.

A powerful adrenaline burst began pounding within her. She looked down, diffident beneath his unrelenting stare. "I guess you'll have to wait until Sunday, then."

"Right. Well, the best things are worth waiting for." He stepped back and put his hands into his pockets. "I should probably get back to my friends. I'll give you a call tomorrow."

"Okay, thanks."

"Good night, Amanda."

She walked toward the stairs at the other end of the room, her mind still reeling in disbelief and confusion. She glanced once more behind her. She expected to find him returned to his friends. Instead, he remained there, cemented in the spot where she'd left him—a dark, solitary figure among all the others, still watching her with his analytical gaze. Goosebumps ran up and down her back as she headed upstairs.

A DJ and a large dance floor glutted with sweaty, entangled bodies filled the second floor of Little Pete's. The floor shook from the bass, and she turned away from the flashing neon signs and disorienting strobe lighting.

Continuing up a back staircase from there, Amanda reached the top floor, where a large poster advertised the "Living Nightmares" exhibit. Her eyes had to adjust to the darkness in the large, open room. Red beams—the only lighting—eerily illuminated the display lining the walls.

The nearest painting was a take on Norman Rockwell's *Freedom from Want*. It showed a bounteous Thanksgiving dinner. A man, presumably the patriarch of the family, sat at the head of the table, a blank expression on his face. Surrounding the table, instead of people, were coffins. Amanda turned away, not wanting to sink into the painting's depressive and familiar tone.

"You finally made it! I thought I'd lost you!" Nikki jumped up from behind, throwing an arm around Amanda's shoulder, the scent of alcohol distinct on her breath.

"Yeah, sorry."

"Come on over here. My friends are dying to meet you."

Nikki steered Amanda to the other end of the room, where three women gathered around another painting. A brunette wearing a purple sequined miniskirt waved at Nikki. Adjacent to the brunette, pushing her bangs to the side, stood a girl clad in a black leather jacket and wearing an animal-print dress that hugged her figure. A tall dirty blonde finished the trio. Her thick burgundy lipstick matched her stilettos perfectly.

"Ladies, this is Miss Amanda Burrow." Nikki pushed Amanda into their inner ring.

"Hi." Amanda glanced at each of them in turn, then stared at the floor. She ran her thumb across her clenched fingers, back and forth, back and forth.

"So ... I have yet to see Amanda's art," Nikki said, "but I feel quite confident that she's a potential comrade of ours. She's going to the Graduate Academy."

Amanda almost smiled to herself: Nikki actually seemed somewhat pleased to have her as a roommate.

"And what about her outfit? Isn't it hot?" Nikki asked.

"It's fab! Great hair too. That must have been a job." The brunette nodded.

"It's all in the products. I got to try out the new gel." Nikki paused for a brief moment, then slapped her forehead. "Crap, here I am, going off and I forgot to introduce you. Amanda, this is Chloe." She gestured to the brunette. "And then we have Heather and Kate. There are a few more, but I think they wanted to get back to the dance floor." She looked at Amanda. "Do you dance?"

"No."

"Amanda, did you check out some of the paintings over here?" Chloe gestured to the wall behind her.

"Not yet."

"Check it out!" Chloe stepped aside so Amanda could see better.

She stared at a huge painting, filled with monstrous, terrifying creatures of various shapes and sizes, their hands disfigured and reaching out toward the viewer in a groping manner. Their eyes were sometimes blazing red, other times black, in a few instances completely absent. Some of them wore hideous grins, revealing a set of sharp, fang-like teeth. Their skin—if you could call it that—dangled from their bodies, sheer in its lack of density.

Amanda's gut reaction: repulsion.

"So wicked." Kate grinned.

Heather burst out laughing and flung her arm around Chloe. "Of course Chloe wants you to see this one. It's her work, naturally."

Chloe shrugged, unaffected, and took a sip from her glass, looking at Amanda. "I'd appreciate any feedback."

Amanda was now under examination, with the spotlight on her. "You made good use of the space. I like the complementary interplay of light and shadows. Great chiaroscuro." She searched her mind for what else to say. Her lack of exposure to horror movies left her ignorant when it came to classifying creatures she would call "Things from the Deep." Stalling, she asked, "What's the title?"

"*Demons in Your Dreams.*"

"Well, it seems right at home in this exhibit, then." Amanda could feel sweat on her palms. The overwhelming attention of all four girls started bringing out the worst in her social abilities—or lack thereof. The time had come to escape. "I think I better get going."

Chloe raised her eyebrows. "So soon? Aren't you coming to the after-party?"

Kate smirked. "That's when the real fun starts. You've got to know about the Pleasure House, right? It's just a few doors down from here. Pick whoever suits your fancy—guy or girl— and have a very *pleasurable* night. If you aren't familiar with anyone there yet, I can give you recommendations."

"As long as it's not Alex. He's Kate's favorite." Heather chuckled and drained her glass.

Amanda squirmed. "Oh ... I'm fine, thanks. I have a lot of work to do for my classes."

Nikki took her by the arm. "There's always next time. Come on, roomie, I'll head home with you. I've seen all of the exhibit, and I'm too beat to hit the dance floor. Unless you might reconsider?"

"Uh ... no thanks."

Amanda followed Nikki out of the room. At the doorway, she glanced up and spotted some strange lettering written across the top of the doorframe. It had to be another language, since she didn't recognize the characters. Intrigued, Amanda opened her mouth to ask Nikki about it, but found that she was already halfway down the stairs.

Outside, they waited on the sidewalk for a cab, and Amanda began to relax, relishing the fresh night air after the humidity of the club.

"So ... what'd you think of Little Pete's? Bet you're glad I dragged you here."

Amanda looked at Nikki and reflected on the consequences of her invitation. Thanks to her, she now had a date with Ethan. "Actually, yeah. Thanks so much for inviting me, Nikki."

"Ooo. That's high praise coming from you! And I think that's the first time I've seen you smile. Alright, now tell me: What'd you think of my friends?"

"Mmm, I don't think I made a very good impression."

"Just give it some time! You'll loosen up around them, just like you have around me."

Amanda wasn't so sure, but didn't argue. Nikki kept herself busy during the cab ride home by sending a flurry of messages on her phone. Amanda appreciated the silence. When they reached the apartment, Nikki declared that she was exhausted and headed straight to bed. Disregarding the late hour, Amanda picked up her paintbrush.

The images and ideas now burst into her imagination one after another. She savored the emotion behind each stroke. When she had finished, the cryptic image somehow seemed a perfect expression of her thoughts. She stood back, nodding.

There was a small arm, constructed of tiny particles of dust—light in color, almost translucent in its weakness. On its own, it appeared petty and unimpressive, save for one fact: the hand of that small arm feebly grasped another arm. This arm, in sharp contrast, epitomized strength and power. Strips of veins protruded from underneath its skin. The arm stretched upward, breaking the links of a silver chain that sought to constrain it. The liberated hand—the forearm muscles bulging—crushed a miniature Earth in its grip, the continents of the world spilling forth.

Amanda's world was changing too.

CHAPTER FIVE

WOMAN'S PLIGHT

Amanda painted one last stroke and completed her latest work: a heart. She considered it tacky, ridiculous, very pink, and something she would never want to show anyone. She had been daydreaming and doodling with her brush ... and that's what happened. She didn't care, though. She was going on a date with Ethan. It was one day away: close enough to be exciting, but far enough to keep any serious anxiety at bay.

"Get it through your thick skull: they're going to keep being a problem until we do something!" Nikki was in the bedroom on a private call, which wasn't private at all. Her booming voice and the paper-thin walls made overhearing the only option. "You said that already. ... I don't care! Everything they stand for is an obstacle for us and what we're working toward!"

Amanda turned back to her art and tested the paint on the canvas. It was still wet but couldn't stay out to dry. This was definitely *not* the first piece of art she wanted to show Nikki. She slid it under the couch—and just in time too.

Nikki flung open the door and marched over to the fridge. "Damn it, I need a beer."

"Is everything okay?" It seemed like the right thing to say, though Amanda didn't want to get involved.

"Yeah, yeah, yeah. It's fine. Work stuff." Nikki waved her hand around. "I have a really dense coworker."

"People can be a hassle." Amanda swished her paintbrush in a cup of water.

Nikki sighed, pacing back and forth. "It doesn't matter anymore. I've got things under control." She took a long swig and then looked at Amanda's array of brushes and tubes of oil paint. "So whatcha workin' on?"

"Well, nothing right now."

"Paint me!"

"Okay."

Nikki eyed her. "You serious?"

"I mean, I should prove myself. Then you can honestly recommend me to your friends." Amanda picked up a fresh canvas and positioned herself on one of the kitchen stools, her easel before her.

Nikki crashed onto the couch, her purple-striped toe socks propped up at the other end.

"You don't need to sit in one position. You can read … take a nap … tell me your life story." Amanda studied Nikki and began to block in the shapes.

"Good. I couldn't sit still for more than five minutes anyway. Oh yeah! Awesome! There's a new issue of *Liberated Woman* out." Nikki fished under the closest pile of clothing for her magazine.

Amanda had mastered the painting of objects. People, on the other hand, were a different matter altogether. Inorganic objects were straightforward: basic dimensions … specific textures and colors. An individual, however, was not just a height, weight, and eye color; a person had an inward expression. To paint someone, she had to go beyond the outward appearance, past Nikki's brown eyes or sleek auburn hair; she needed to somehow reveal Nikki's inner self.

The time passed, but Amanda hardly noticed. Nikki moved from reading her magazine to making another call. When she wasn't thus occupied, she chatted away.

"So I grew up here in the Bronx, in a high-rise just a few blocks away. When I was twelve, my father took off with a girl he met in a bar." Nikki checked the nail polish she'd just applied and then waved her hands back and forth, trying to get her nails to dry. "You can imagine the type: blonde, flirty, naïve. At first, I wasn't that sorry to have him gone. He mostly just sat on his lazy ass, watching football and smoking cigarettes all day. Well, at least when he wasn't gambling our money away and sleeping around, of course. Yeah, he was a real gem of a father."

"Sounds like it." Amanda leaned closer to the canvas, inspecting her last stroke.

"He died a couple of years ago. He got sick, and no one gave a crap to foot his medical bills. So he went to Hoboken, New Jersey. That's the closest quarantine area for the sick and dying who can't afford treatment. It's one of the smartest things our government has done: ending any welfare or aid to these 'hobos,' these bottom-dwellers."

"Your dad died in quarantine?"

"Maybe. Or maybe he acted on his freedom to die and went to Hoboken's Dying with Dignity Center. I don't know. Don't really care. He sucked as a father, but sometimes I wish he had stuck around, if only because those who came after him were even worse.

"I spent my whole childhood watching my mom trying to pull things together and failing completely. After Dad left, she had a long string of boyfriends—all of them much worse than my father. And that's saying something, believe me. But, no matter how bad things got, my mom would never kick anyone out or fight for something better for us. She needed that guy in her life, even if it meant bruises on her arms and increasing disappointment."

"Can you turn to the right for just a sec?"

"What? Oh ... yeah. I learned my lesson well: a woman cannot rely on a man. At some point, he will let you down—use and abuse you. I've come to realize the misery of every woman's plight: men have completely abducted our rights ... from the workplace to even our bodies. But times are changing. We're making great progress. For the first time, we have a woman president. The National Citizens Party is making incredible strides for freedom—women's freedom especially."

"Yeah, that's great ..." Politics interested Amanda as much as advanced calculus.

"Just think what we've accomplished in such a short time!" Nikki sat up straight, her face lit with zeal. "The federal government is probably a quarter of the size it used to be, maybe even less than that. We've trashed all the enslaving and unnecessary laws and regulations that have been beating down our liberty. Public education is done. Now private academies with entrance exams make sure only bookworms—like yourself—are enrolled. We have a flat tax: Why rob the rich from the income they rightfully earned? When I'm making boatloads of cash, no one's taking a cent away from me! No more government aid to the Unfit—those who aren't helping advance our society. The JPD protects against the only crime the state should concern itself with: treason. And if someone is seeking justice, private police can take care of the job. Soon we'll be the land of the free once again."

"You sound like an ad for the NCP."

Nikki sat back against the couch cushion, her face pensive. "The NCP changed my life. I didn't score high enough on the exams to get into an Academy. I didn't know where to go. Waitressing was staring me in the face, but that was my mom's life. I didn't want that for me, you know? But I didn't know how to escape it. Then Chloe invited me to an NCP meeting. The idea of freedom ... of nothing holding you back from reaching your potential ... that was *exactly* what I was looking for. They offered me a job—bottom rung of the ladder, of course, but I got my foot in the door. I've been climbing that ladder ever since. The NCP sees my abilities and values me for them. And I can use my talents to advance the cause of freedom. I wouldn't want to do anything else with my life."

Amanda grunted. She needed a darker shade for this corner ...

"Well, can I be done here?" Her monologue over, Nikki stood up and stretched.

"You can go. Let me just take a picture of you on my phone. I can work from that."

Amanda kept painting, barely aware of Nikki's movements about the apartment. At one point, Nikki left and Amanda just waved wordlessly, her gaze not leaving the canvas.

Much later, she set down her brush. She had finished. She slid off the stool and stepped back, examining her work. She nodded with satisfaction: it looked professional. The lines and shape, the color, the light and value, the balance—it was perfect. She wouldn't change a thing.

Or would she? Technically speaking, this was outstanding. But the meaning of the work? She had followed the interior instinct that drove all her personal paintings. It was a sure guide, though most times ambiguous. She bit her lip and cast a closer look at her piece. This time, the meaning was very clear … frighteningly so.

A deep burgundy filled the background, giving an ominous feel to the picture. In the foreground, Nikki stood with her back to the viewer, though her head was turned, looking over her right shoulder. She wore a sleek black top, and her auburn hair was slicked close to her head. Her facial expression was the most striking—and alarming—facet of the painting.

It was not the bright, welcoming face that Amanda met when entering the apartment for the first time. Instead, Nikki's black eyebrows slanted inward, drawn together in a deep, low crease. Her eyes squinted in fury and hate. Her crimson lips snarled underneath flared nostrils. This Nikki in the portrait looked nothing short of sinister.

What went wrong? Amanda had followed her inspiration, just like she always did. But the portrait in front of her seemed the inverse of the Nikki she had come to know. This was anything but flattering; it was disturbing.

She clenched her jaw. Why did she ever agree to paint Nikki's portrait in the first place? Now whatever growing friendship she had with Nikki would be ruined. She rubbed her chin, debating. Maybe she could fix it somehow? Or paint a new one? She glanced at the clock. … How much time until Nikki returned?

But footsteps were already coming down the hallway … closer, closer. Amanda froze, hoping the person would stop at another door, enter another apartment. Yet they kept approaching: *clickety-click*. Those were Nikki's heeled shoes.

Amanda dove for the portrait and made a beeline for the bedroom. Outside the apartment door, Nikki's keys jingled, probably as she fumbled for the right one. Amanda shoved the portrait underneath her bed and then sprinted for the sofa.

She had just landed on the cushion when the door opened and Nikki breezed through. "Well it's about time! I was going to kill you if you were *still* working on my portrait. Let's see it!"

"I don't think it turned out very well."

"Look, I totally get it: it's scary to show someone your work for the first time. Don't worry! It's just me. I'm sure it's amazing." Nikki took off her peacoat and flung her purse on the counter. "Now come on. You know I'm not a patient woman."

"Right …" Amanda avoided Nikki's stare. "So I did it kind of symbolically."

"Very cool. Let's see it!"

"I—I just want you to be prepared. It's not really an exact replica of you."

"Seriously, it's okay. Just show it to me!"

"Okay. Hold on." Amanda reached underneath the sofa, pushing pieces of clothing aside and trying to grasp the canvas.

Nikki cocked an eyebrow. "You hid it?"

"Well, you know, suspense and all …" Amanda found it. She pulled the canvas out, keeping the image from Nikki's eyes. "So just remember—"

"Yeah, yeah, I got it!"

Amanda turned the canvas around, revealing the jovial pink heart she had painted much earlier in the day.

Nikki's mouth dropped open. A vein in her temple began to throb, and she put her hands on her hips. "That's bull. You couldn't *possibly* have worked on that all day."

"It seemed too predictable to just paint you." Amanda hoped her voice didn't sound too shaky. "Everyone knows what you look like. So I went with an emblematic image."

"Do I look stupid to you? Just because I didn't go to an Academy, you assume I'm some kind of an idiot? You didn't spend six hours working on that!" Nikki's voice rose in a growing crescendo of anger.

Amanda began to sweat, though her stomach felt like an icy pit. "How do you know?" Her words sounded feeble, and her plan, unsurprisingly, was unraveling fast.

"I don't care how bad of an artist you are, it wouldn't take you so long to paint that." Nikki stepped forward, eyes slit. "Where's the real portrait?"

"I'm sorry." Amanda rose from the couch, the heart picture toppling to the ground. "The truth is … I don't want to show you the real one."

"Why? It didn't turn out well?"

"No, not really."

"What, you painted me as fat as an elephant? You chose the wrong color for my hair?"

"No, nothing like that. It just isn't very flattering."

"Show me. You agreed to paint a portrait of me. I wasted three hours of my afternoon posing for you. Show me the stupid thing!"

Amanda shrank before Nikki's fury. For the first time, she glimpsed a shadow of the Nikki in her portrait.

"Okay, alright, I'll get it." Amanda hurried to the bedroom and came back with the canvas, no longer sure what would make Nikki angrier: withholding the portrait or showing it. "Here it is." Holding her breath and bracing herself for the worst, Amanda revealed her work.

Nikki's face was an emotionless mask at first. She walked forward toward Amanda, her eyes wide in disbelief, her voice hushed. "How did you do this?" Nikki reached out, then hesitated, and finally took the portrait to hold it in her hands and examine up close.

"I … I don't know. I just paint. I never meant for it to look so bad, honestly." Amanda hung her head. "I'm not really good at getting close to other people. I never had any close friends at Valor Academy. I like you. I feel like, you know, we were getting along." She stopped for a moment. This degree of disclosure was painful. "I'm sorry about the portrait. I don't know what happened. Clearly, I need to learn a thing or two at the Masters Academy. I didn't mean to hurt your feelings, and I'll paint you a new one, a better one. We can get rid of it." She grabbed the canvas from Nikki's hands and walked toward the garbage can in the kitchen.

"No!" Nikki jumped forward, reclaiming the portrait.

"What … you *like* it?"

"It's …" She seemed to struggle trying to find the words. "The Nikki you painted is powerful. She's somebody no one would take advantage of."

"You don't have to be nice. You can call it trash. It's fine."

"No one has ever painted a portrait of me like this before. You've done something incredibly unusual." Nikki studied Amanda, a strange admiration in her eyes. "Is it okay if I hang on to this?"

"If you want to …" Amanda shrugged. "Yeah, I guess so."

"Excellent!" Nikki propped the portrait on the floor in the corner of the room. "I think it'll be better in the bedroom eventually. Until then, I want to leave it here where I can see

47

it." She grinned. "I'm starving! Do we still have that leftover Chinese food?"

Without waiting for a reply, Nikki turned on her music and began taking two plates out of the cabinet.

Baffled, Amanda watched until something subtle caught her attention—a monophonic beeping. She looked around the kitchenette for the source, then asked, "Do you hear that noise?"

"Sounds like an ancient cell phone." Nikki spooned a heaping pile of noodles onto one of the plates.

Amanda gasped. "That's my phone!" She raced for the bedroom, practically careening into her bed, reaching the phone just at the end of its ring.

"Hello?"

"Amanda?"

"Yeah, and this is Ethan?"

"You got it."

She could detect a smile in his voice, and it made her grin in return.

He went on, "I was thinking of what we could do tomorrow, and I wanted to run my plans by you, to make sure you're okay with things."

"Alright. Thanks."

"There's this great restaurant that I'd like to take you to, and then, afterwards, maybe we can go for a walk. It'll give us an opportunity to talk and get to know each other better."

"That sounds great."

"I'll pick you up around six, then?"

"Sure, thanks. I live in the Bronx at 875 Dawkson Street. It's apartment 406."

Pause. "Did you say apartment 406?"

"Yeah, 406."

Silence.

She checked to make sure her phone was still working. "Umm ... did you get that?"

"Oh ... yeah, sorry." He seemed distracted. "Just jotting it down."

"Do you need directions or anything?"

He laughed. "That won't be necessary. Thanks, Amanda! I look forward to seeing you tomorrow."

"Me too." He had no idea just how much ...

CHAPTER SIX

MRS. RAMSEY

"Ugh! What's that nasty smell?" Nikki came out of the bedroom, wrinkling her nose.

"Oh. Oops. Sorry." Amanda hurried to turn off the stove. She had burned her grilled cheese sandwich black as night. Flustered, she reached her hand toward the loaf of bread, knocking over her glass of water.

"What's gotten into you?" Nikki tossed a dish towel to Amanda.

She fumbled it and stooped to pick it up off the floor. "I kind of have a date in a little while."

"*What?* And you didn't tell me? Come on!"

"I'm sorry."

"Yeah, you should be. I mean, come on! So what are you wearing?"

Amanda chewed her lip. "I ... don't really know."

"Alright, let's get to work. Hair and makeup first. What would you do without me, huh?"

Amanda smiled shyly and followed Nikki into the bathroom. She had been toying with telling Nikki about her date all morning, but couldn't seem to get the words out. Now she sighed with relief. She appreciated Nikki's wisdom when it came to fashion. She did want to impress Ethan.

With the primping and preening complete, Nikki steered Amanda toward their bedroom, where she rummaged through her stuffed closet. "I'm thinking something provocative. At the very least, you definitely want to show some skin."

"You know, conservative works for me." Out of habit, Amanda reached up to twirl a curl, but only grasped the air. Nikki had put her hair up in an intricate design, leaving nothing for her to fidget with.

"Don't be ridiculous. It's your body: show it off!" A few minutes later, Nikki's muffled voice called triumphantly from the back recesses of the closet: "This is *perfect*." Emerging, Nikki handed Amanda some clothes. "You're going to look fabulous! Put them on and then come out into the living room."

She had chosen a tight black miniskirt and a silk gold top. Neither would have been Amanda's preference, but Nikki was the designer, so she yielded to her choice. Amanda dressed and left the bedroom.

Nikki smiled, then began clapping. "What did I tell you? Stunning! Here, put on these heels to complete the ensemble."

"These don't seem comfortable or safe."

"Who cares? They look so good!"

The only thing left to do was wait. Amanda glanced at the clock: five minutes until six. Walking over to the window, she stared at the street below, tapping her bitten nails against the sill. A sports car turned onto their street—a cherry-red Anaconda. The coupe looked polished and waxed to perfection. It would stand out anywhere, but most of all here among the outdated and dented jalopies. She knew, even before he exited, that it had to belong to Ethan.

She swallowed. "My date's here."

"Have a great time! And promise to tell me all the juicy details."

"Okay. Thanks for all of your help, Nikki. I really appreciate it."

"Of course!" Nikki hugged her. "I like you, Amanda Burrow. You're growing on me."

The intercom buzzed.

"Go get 'im!" Nikki said.

Amanda took a deep breath and pressed the button. "Hello?"

"Hey! Mind if I come up?"

"Yeah, sure."

Amanda retreated to the couch to wait, wanting to bite her nails again but resisting. She imagined Ethan stepping into the elevator and then walking down their hallway. A few minutes later, she heard a loud rapping on the door. She could barely move: her feet felt like stone. She seemed paralyzed.

"Here, I'll get it." Nikki walked over and opened the door.

There stood Ethan.

"Nikki!" He smiled, his face lit with amusement.

Nikki staggered back a few feet. She looked back and forth from Amanda to Ethan. "Wait, what? *You?* You're Amanda's date?"

Amanda just stared at them: They knew each other?

Ethan walked into the apartment and over to Amanda. "Hey again. Wow, you look amazing!"

"Thanks. The credit all goes to Nikki."

Nikki leaned against the kitchen counter, her eyebrows scrunched. "Whoa, whoa, whoa. Amanda, when did you meet Ethan?"

"I met him at the Graduate Academy—my first day there. You know Ethan too?"

Nikki's face turned white. Ignoring Amanda, she turned to Ethan. "You met Amanda at the Masters Academy?"

"That would be correct."

"She's the one—"

"The one I asked on a date, yes." Ethan's composure was a great contrast to Nikki's growing agitation.

"But ..." Nikki sputtered, a sickened expression on her face. "You knew she was my roommate?"

"It became pretty apparent after she told me her address last night."

"And you didn't tell me immediately?"

"I thought a surprise would be much more fun. But I guess not."

Amanda glanced from one to another, lost in the conversation. "So ... how, exactly, do you two know each other?"

"We both work for the National Citizens Party." Ethan hooked his thumbs in his pockets. "We're coworkers, actually."

"Unfortunately." Nikki spat out the word, her bewilderment changing to fury.

So they weren't past lovers, which had been Amanda's first assumption. That was a relief. Nikki had complained about her "dense coworker" just yesterday. Perhaps she had been referring to Ethan.

"We have a reservation to keep, so we better be going." Ethan gestured toward the door. "Ready, Amanda?"

"Yeah." Amanda paused at the door, turning to Nikki, who glared at the wall, her jaw locked. "Bye, Nikki."

Nikki moved her head to stare at Amanda with a look full of disdain and disgust. Amanda sucked in her breath like she had been kicked in the stomach. Without another word, Nikki strode into the bedroom, slamming the door behind her. Bewildered, Amanda gazed at the closed bedroom door, her spirits sinking. All this because Nikki didn't approve of her going out with Ethan?

Ethan touched her arm. "Don't worry. It's me she's upset with, not you. Nikki has a volatile personality and tends to overreact. But give her a few hours and she'll be back to normal."

It was true: Nikki's moods fluctuated from one extreme to another. For now, Amanda would have to forget about Nikki and just hope she would cool down. Taking a deep breath, Amanda followed Ethan into the elevator and outside.

His car was even more impressive up close. "That's quite the vehicle."

Ethan opened the passenger door for her. "Thanks. It does the job."

In the few seconds that it took him to walk over to the driver's side, she observed the interior of the car: black leather seats, immaculately clean floor mats, the smell wonderfully masculine. He slid into his seat, put on his shades, and spoke the command to start, the car roaring to life. He darted out of the spot and began weaving his way through the city.

She glanced at him. He appeared completely at ease, even with taxicab and other drivers beeping, cursing, and gesturing all around. "You don't seem to mind all the traffic."

"I know where I'm going."

"Yeah, but you still have all these other vehicles to deal with."

"They'll move over for me." He swerved ahead of a taxi to their left, leaning back in his seat, unperturbed. "I live what Hannibal said, crossing the Alps with elephants: 'I'll find a way or make one.'"

She cringed and clutched the seat cushion, preparing for what looked like an inevitable fender bender. Instead, he expertly maneuvered his way in front of another taxi, forcing a space for himself in the adjacent traffic lane. She laughed at his audacity.

He gave a look of surprise, pretending to be offended. "Are you laughing at me?"

"No! No, not at all. It's just … does anything worry you? It seems like the world could be ending and you wouldn't be concerned."

"Right now, I'm in control, so there's no reason to be worried."

"True. But that can't always be the case. What if the world really were ending?"

He shrugged. "My priority would be survival for as long as possible—same as everyone else. When that fails, then, hey, at least I can die knowing that I enjoyed my life. Based on your question, I take it that you would be concerned?"

"You could say that."

"What, specifically, would you be upset about?"

"Some people would say we should fear the unknown … what lies beyond this world."

"You think there is something after this life?"

He stopped at a red light and she fell silent, pondering her response before saying, "I used to believe I'd see my loved ones again someday. I don't think so anymore."

"It's a nice thought, no doubt about it—but not one I want to cling to at the expense of reality. Science shows us that death is a natural, physical process. Life begins and life ends. That ending doesn't have to be bad. No regret, no pain—a peaceful nothingness. That's why the Freedom to Die campaign has been so successful, especially for those whose lives have become miserable. Anyway, I would rather treasure my loved ones here, in this life, than console myself with an illusory 'happily ever after.'"

Amanda frowned. "Yeah … I know quite well that 'happily ever after' is a lie."

"Many people base their entire lives on a whole series of lies." He put the car into park. "We're here."

The restaurant was almost hidden, tucked belowground on the bottom floor of one of the countless skyscrapers. Ethan opened her door and then led her down a few stone steps to the entrance.

Ethan walked up to the hostess. "Good evening. I have a reservation for two under Ramsey."

So that was his last name. Ethan Ramsey. Her mind next jumped to: Amanda Ramsey.

"Of course, Mr. Ramsey. Please follow me this way." The hostess tucked two menus under her arm and led them through the dimly lit restaurant to a quiet booth in the back, where a single candle flickered on the table. "Someone will be with you shortly."

They took their places on either side of the table. He leaned toward her, ignoring the menu in front of him. "What are you thinking about?"

She startled, his words disrupting her daydream of being Mrs. Ethan Ramsey. "Wh-What do you mean?"

"I could see it in your eyes: you were deep in thought about something. I'm fascinated to learn what it could possibly be."

"Oh … I was just thinking about your last name. I didn't know it until you told the hostess."

"We have lots to learn about each other. Your last name is …?"

"Burrow."

"Nice. So we got some preliminaries out of the way. Now tell me about the Burrow family."

The waitress appeared, cutting off her reply. Amanda couldn't stand having to select a dish. Some required special finesse to eat, such as a lobster tail; others were a potential mess, like spaghetti or a stuffed burrito. So she played it safe and went with a basic, no-fuss salad.

Having taken their orders, the waitress left.

Ethan took a sip of wine. "Let's try that again. What's your family like?"

She was prepared for this question and answered with ease. "There's my dad, Kevin, who works in construction, and my sister, Chiara. She's fourteen and just started a trade program for agriculture and equine work."

"Are you close with them?"

She tilted her head, considering. "Well, they live upstate. This is my first time living away from home. I suppose we're close. I'm pretty different from them, though. … We don't share the same interests at all. Or the same values, I guess you could say. What about your family?"

He started buttering one of the warm dinner rolls sitting in a basket on the table. "There are three of us: my parents and me. My dad is the CEO of a large, multinational software company he founded, so growing up, my mom and I traveled with him around the world. It was an unconventional childhood, you might say."

"Did you attend an Academy of some sort?"

"No. I learned more from my dad than from reading any textbook or preparing for a 'standardized' test. My dad taught me all about his new business methodology—stripping away needless bureaucracy within his enterprise and letting people do what people do best without interference or control. He taught me the importance of freedom: to follow one's desires without a 'big brother' watching over you or hierarchical command dictating what is right. And that's how I learned: I experienced things, pursuing my interests and discovering the answers to my questions."

She could picture him as an inquisitive seven-year-old, standing with his mother in front of the pyramids of Egypt, or as a lanky teenager, exploring the palace at Versailles. He was a world traveler, an eclectic connoisseur of knowledge. She, on the other hand, had never been out of the state of New York. Even more pathetically, she'd never left her hometown until she moved to the city.

Amanda plopped her lemon slice into her glass of water. "Why did you end up here in the city?"

"It's New York! This is where all the action is. All the opportunities are here."

She was about to ask what these opportunities and activities consisted of, but the waitress came with their dinners.

Ethan asked the next question. "So what do you like to do when you're not in class or hiding in the graphic design lounge?" He smiled.

If only she could offer him something exquisite, fascinating, or corresponding to his diverse upbringing. If only she could impress him by listing flame throwing or bungee jumping among her skilled and varied pastimes. Yet she had one hobby, one exclusive pursuit. "I paint."

"What do you like so much about painting?"

"I don't normally share things with other people. I find that it's safer to keep most thoughts and emotions to myself. Painting is my way of expressing these things. I take whatever is in my heart and project it onto the canvas. It's like therapy for me, at times. Other times, it's an escape or a sanctuary or even an adventure. You traveled around this world. I travel to other worlds through my art."

He had abandoned his veal parmesan, his eyes now studying her. "Here's a hypothetical for you. Let's say you had a paintbrush in your hand right now. What would you paint?"

"Sorry. I don't share my personal paintings with anyone."

"Why? Don't most artists like showing their work?"

"I guess. It's different for me, though."

"Alright, that's fine. You don't have to explain anymore." He paused for a moment, thinking. Then he leaned closer from across the small table. "Though maybe there might come the time when you would open your heart enough to share your paintings with me?"

She'd already grown accustomed to his intense gaze—his bold, unrelenting stare. Now, though, his eyes appeared soft and supplicating. His regular confidence gave way to a susceptible hope. She stared back at him, her heart divided. The thought of disappointing him felt repulsive. Yet, to reveal her carefully guarded paintings, even to him, seemed like a self-betrayal of sorts.

Amanda decided to mask her indecision. "We'll see. Nikki might have first dibs on the paintings, though. I did meet her before you."

"Game's on. I'm warning you, though: I'm a tough competitor. Be prepared for me to win."

For the remainder of the dinner, she hardly tasted a thing she ate; Ethan consumed her entire focus. She would have sat there for hours, talking with him, but at one point, he cast a quick glance out the front windows of the restaurant. "Shall we go?"

They stood up, and after he had paid the bill, they stepped outside into the city once again. Night had descended. A fluorescent glow lit the avenue, and even at this late hour, the streets were speckled with an assortment of people enjoying a night on the town.

She stared at the bright lights and crowds. "This couldn't be more different from my hometown."

"Let's take a walk so you can soak it all in."

They strolled, and he chatted about his experiences growing up, relating some of his adventures while abroad. He seemed to be leading them in a certain direction, but it wasn't until they had just about reached the site that she could identify the place.

"Central Park?"

"You got it."

Leaving the noisy avenue behind them, they made their way into the park, passing other couples meandering along the wooded paths. Rollerbladers zoomed by, carefree yet rather skillful. The evening had a taste of July in it, nature seemingly clinging to the last crumbs of Indian summer before it gave way to the crispness of autumn.

"Would it be okay if I hold your hand?"

Amanda looked at him, taken aback and touched by his respectful request. He was forward, but he wasn't presumptuous.

"Sure ... I'd like that."

They walked along together, and she marveled at the feel of his fingers interlaced with hers. His hand was warm and his grip firm. They strolled along for a time until they came to a large pond. Gesturing to a park bench, he invited her to have a seat. He sat next to her, close enough so her leg just brushed against his. She looked at him, her breath escaping her. His face was so close.

"Blue ..." His voice was so soft that only she could hear it. "Your eyes ... I can see them in the moonlight. They're an incredible dark blue."

Intimidated by his powerful gaze, she had to look away. Above them, the moon shone against the dark sky. "That's strange. I didn't know you could see stars in the city, considering all the light pollution."

"Only on clear nights can you see them."

A memory came to her, unsummoned and escaping the vault where she repressed such recollections. "I remember, when I was young, I would just sit by my bedroom window, looking up at the stars. They were breathtaking, up in the mountains. Someone once told me that wishing on a star was offering a prayer from the deepest recesses of your heart and that the stars, watching over us, are like the angels."

"Do you agree with that?" His tone sounded altered, his voice slightly sharp and guarded.

"No, not at all." The memory faded like mist—far removed from where she was now and who she had become. "I learned a long time ago not to wish on stars."

He seemed to relax, leaning back against the bench. "I will admit that they're attractive balls of plasma."

"Very true."

61

"I have a childhood memory to share with you too. I remember when I was young, my dad invited me to his office and showed me some of the awards and accolades he had earned throughout the years. He told me something then that I never forgot. In a way, it has directed my life ever since. Do you want to know what he said to me?"

"After that introduction, you better tell me."

"My dad advised me to tell myself in times of hesitation or doubt, 'If it's meant to be, it's up to me.'" He looked upward at the night sky again. "I don't wish on stars to make dreams come true. I am where I am today because of my own hard work. *I* had to make it happen."

"That's how I feel about being at the Masters Academy. It's important to be self-reliant. You can't really depend on other people."

"You're very much a loner, aren't you?"

"It ends up that way most of the time, yes."

"For the majority of my life, I was a loner. It was kind of inevitable, with moving around so much. I still revert to that sometimes."

Amanda gave a small nod. "It's hard to shake the demons of your past. As much as you grow up and try to move on, the experiences of your childhood are always there, haunting you."

"Your past is part of you; it's shaped who you are today. That's not necessarily bad. But it's the present that matters. It's in the here and now that you can become whomever you desire." He squeezed her hand. "And neither of us is alone right now."

They were still, listening to the sounds of the night: the rustling of the water, the harmonious movement of trees around them, the melodic undertone of the slight breeze. In that simple yet profound moment, a sense of bliss filled Amanda—an overwhelming happiness that she had been convinced was permanently gone.

But she had been wrong. He made her feel alive again.

"As much as I regret saying this, I think we should head back." Ethan stood up. "I know I have class tomorrow, and I'm presuming that you do as well."

She had forgotten about her class on Monday. Actually, she had forgotten about everything but him.

They walked hand in hand back to his car. They reached her apartment building much too soon, and disappointment filled her at the thought of leaving him. He opened her door and, taking her hand, helped her out. They stood on the empty sidewalk, looking at each other.

Ethan smiled. "Thank you for a wonderful evening."

"Thanks. ... It was ... great." She regretted the words immediately. "Great" was such an understatement. If only she could find the right combination of adjectives to describe what this night meant to her, a night she would replay over and over again in her mind.

"So I'll see you tomorrow at the Graduate Academy. Until then ..." He brought her hand toward his mouth, pressing his lips against her skin. "... I wish you good night."

After getting back into his car, Ethan drove away. She raised her head once more and looked at the night sky. The stars were gone, masked by cloud cover. She smiled to herself. As if she needed stars ...

CHAPTER SEVEN

AT HELL GATE

She reached the subway stop. A moment later, while she stood on the platform for the green line train to arrive, her phone began to ring. Could it be *him*?

Amanda thrust her hand inside her bag, seized the phone, and answered with breathless anticipation, not bothering to check caller ID. "Hello?"

"Well, hi, stranger!" Not Ethan, but a decidedly female voice spoke, one instantly recognizable.

"Oh. Hi, Chiara."

Hearing her sister's voice was itself an experience of home: the feel of the fuzzy carpet lining the staircase, the creaking of a certain floorboard in the hallway, the sight and scent of pine. It all seemed so far away now ... and that wasn't a bad thing. Amanda was creating her own home.

She slung her bag back over one shoulder. "Why are you calling?"

"Gee, why could I possibly be calling? Hmm. I don't know ... maybe since Dad and I haven't heard from you for more than a week now, we just wanted to make sure you were alive and breathing?"

"It was a busy week."

"How's the city? Do you love it?"

"Yeah."

"And your roommate? What's she like? Do you get along? She's okay?"

"She's nice."

"What about the Masters Academy?"

"It's alright."

"Cool! Dad and I are doing good. Same old, same old. You know how things go around here." Chiara laughed. "Oh, actually, there is one thing that happened. I think it was last Tuesday. Or maybe Wednesday ..."

"Last week sometime—I got it. What was it?"

"Do you know the Connollys? They have a son, Joe, and they live on Pinewoods Avenue, right past Supermarket Saver."

"Yeah, I remember them."

"Their dad, Dr. Connolly, was my orthodontist."

"Yeah, yeah, I know. What about them?"

"I rode my bike past their house, and it's completely empty. No one has seen them for almost a week now."

"Maybe they went on vacation or something."

"But they never go away, Amanda. Dad couldn't believe it when Dr. Connolly didn't show up for the pancake breakfast at church last Sunday."

"Maybe a family member got sick and they had to leave suddenly." Was Amanda's life this mundane before too? Time to change the subject. "How's Boots doing?"

Chiara adored her horse and launched into the details of her upcoming horse show. "I'm pretty sure I can place in the top three. If Elise doesn't show up—you know, the tall girl from Westport—then I might even have a shot at the trophy."

"Good."

"Dad wanted to talk with you too, but he's at one of his opposition meetings. He's had one almost every day. He wants you to call him this week so he can hear how things are going in the Big Apple."

"Okay."

More and more people were gathering on the subway platform, and it was getting hard to hear Chiara. Two bright points of light appeared down the tunnel: the subway was approaching.

"Hey, Chiara, I gotta go. My train is here."

"Oh. Alright. I guess I'll talk with you soon?"

"Sure. Bye."

Amanda arrived at the Masters Academy and began searching for Ethan among the students loitering about the building. Some sprawled across the front steps, sketching, while others conversed over lattes. She didn't spot Ethan anywhere, and in the end, she had to give up and go to Michael's class.

"Today we're going to start by reviewing the syllabus." Michael put on his glasses and peered at his notes. "Let's talk about the semester project. This is the real meat and potatoes of the class. It will count for more than half of your grade, so it would behoove you to pay close attention.

"One of the most effective methods of fine-tuning your technique is to study the masters. That is, in fact, the whole focus of this task: to complete a master copy. Each one of you will be assigned a painting in the Metropolitan Museum of Art. I want you to visit the Met before our next class and make a preliminary sketch. You will then work on that sketch throughout the semester, eventually painting it, until you have emulated the master's work as closely as possible. The syllabus spells out the deadlines and expectations. So if there aren't any questions, I'll hand out the assignments."

Amanda once again had the misfortune of sitting next to Leila, who pursed her lips before saying, "I'd better not get some lame landscape."

Michael stopped in front of her. "Actually, Leila, I think you'll be happy to have *Blue Green Red* by Ellsworth Kelly. It's in the modern art section."

Leila took the slip of paper from his outstretched hand. "I know. I've seen it plenty of times."

Michael came to Amanda. He stood there for a moment, staring at the dozen papers left in his hand. "I think that this will be most beneficial to you." He handed her one, stuffing the rest in his pocket and walking away.

She turned the paper over and read the words written in Michael's sloppy handwriting:

Portrait of a Mother, Anonymous, ca. 1570

Amanda frowned. This was the one subject she would *least* like to explore. She would just ask for another assignment. It wasn't like there weren't a thousand other works of art at the Met. She raised her hand, but Michael had already moved on and was now discussing the supplies required for the course. She would have to wait.

He at last dismissed the class. Amanda approached his desk, the slip of paper clenched in her hand. "Umm, excuse me? Michael? Can I ask you something?"

Rifling through some papers, he paused for a moment. "Go on."

"Would it be possible to have another assignment for the semester project?"

"No, I'm afraid not."

"I … I can't do another painting?"

"I've already handed out the assignments. Either you choose to do the one I gave you or you don't. Simple enough?" Without waiting for her reply, he turned his attention back to his papers, one elbow leaning on the desk and his hand cradling his forehead.

The conversation had ended. She was stuck with *Portrait of a Mother*. She left the classroom, hoping to see Ethan in the hallway, but he wasn't there. Her classes were done for the day, and she had no other reason to stick around. Yet he had said they would see each other, right? Had she been wrong? Maybe he hadn't enjoyed their date after all. In fact, he probably regretted even asking her out in the first place. He just wasn't interested in her, of course, and now he was avoiding her. No surprise there. People had a way of disappearing from her life.

Dejected, she hurried out the front door, her despondency driving her anywhere but here.

"Amanda?"

With her right foot on the lowest step of the staircase, she turned around, though she knew who had spoken to her.

"Ethan!"

He met her at the bottom of the stairs, his expression puzzled. "Are you in a hurry?"

"Not especially. Why?"

"You kind of walked right past me."

"Oh shoot … really?"

"I remembered that your class got out at this time, so I waited for you by the front door. I guess you didn't see me? Or maybe you didn't want to see me?"

"No! No, not at all! I just figured you didn't want to see *me*."

"If I didn't want to see you, I would have told you so last night. I don't sugarcoat things, Amanda. You'll always hear the truth from me."

"Thank you. I'll remember that."

He pulled his keys out of his jeans pocket. "How about we take a drive?"

She nodded, and hand in hand, they walked toward his car.

"So where to, m'lady?" Ethan opened the passenger door for her.

"Well, I usually go back to my apartment after class."

"To the apartment it is, then. Whatever you would like." Flashing his brilliant smile, he revved the engine. "How was your class today? You seem deep in thought. Though, I'm beginning to understand that's normal for you."

"There's just a lot on my mind."

"You can unload some of those cares on me. Class didn't go so well?"

"I don't like the professor or other students too much."

"Who's the professor?"

"Michael Williams."

Amanda saw instant recognition sweep across Ethan's face, his frown revealing a shared dislike for the art teacher.

"Did you have him before too?"

Ethan put the window down and rested his arm on the car door. "No, but I've heard a lot about him. What's your problem with the guy?"

She pretended to ponder the question while grasping for a credible answer. She couldn't tell him about *Portrait of a Mother*. It would introduce a whole conversation she wasn't ready for, one she avoided at all cost. She couldn't talk about it because the truth still hurt too much. "It's his style. I don't care for his technique at all. I wish he were more like the other professors who are contemporary in their methods."

"That makes sense. Michael is without a doubt the black sheep of the faculty. I can't imagine how he's been able to hold on to his job." Ethan pulled into an open space across from her apartment building and turned off the car.

What should she do now? Invite him upstairs? "Umm … so do you have something going on today?"

"That depends."

"On what?"

"On you. I was hoping we could hang out together. Of course, if you have to go now, I'll understand."

"You can come upstairs."

He rewarded her with a broad smile. They exited his car and entered the building. The blasting music coming from inside her apartment told her that Nikki was home. They hadn't spoken yet since Nikki stormed off yesterday.

Standing in the hallway outside the door, Amanda poised her key halfway to the lock. "I forgot that Nikki is home. Maybe we better not go in."

Ethan waved dismissively. "This is your apartment too. Who cares if Nikki is home? Maybe she should be the one to leave."

Amanda took a deep breath, unlocked the door, and walked in. Ethan followed, tossing his coat on the couch. Nikki sat on a stool at the kitchen counter, typing on her laptop. She glared at both of them, her face turning red. She apparently hadn't cooled off yet. Amanda stared at the floor and took a few steps behind Ethan.

"Hey, Nikki. How are things?" Ethan sat on the arm of the couch, crossing his arms.

"Don't waste my time. I'm busy on an assignment."

Ethan looked at Amanda. "She's working on our new project for the National Citizens Party. We're doing a billboard. You see, Nikki and I are both in the public relations department. She does photography; I do graphic design."

Amanda smiled feebly in Nikki's direction. "I'm sure you'll do a great job."

Nikki scoffed. "Tell your boyfriend to stop fooling around and get me some graphics."

"Leave her alone, Nikki." Ethan's playful tone carried an undertone of threat. "I'll have them to you by tomorrow."

"I'll believe it when I see it."

Unruffled, Ethan turned back to Amanda. "Have you seen the NCP's new website? They just launched it a few days ago."

"I ... I don't think I had a chance to check it out yet, no."

"Of course *you're* a member of the NCP, right?" Nikki's voice dripped with sarcasm.

Amanda stared at her, puzzled by Nikki's behavior. She wanted to fix things with Nikki but didn't know how. Nikki obviously had a grudge against her, and it didn't seem to be just about Ethan. "I'm not a registered member." She caught herself. "Not yet."

Nikki nodded, a fake half smile painted on her face. "Why not, Amanda?"

Amanda shifted her weight from one foot to the other. "I'm not that political. I mean, my dad is. But it's never really interested me."

"So your dad must be a member?"

"He ..." Amanda stopped. Her dad despised the NCP and spent most of his free time leading and recruiting for a group opposing the reigning party. "He's not really a member, no."

Ethan stepped between them. "I don't think you would be ambivalent about it, if you understood the NCP."

"Well, why do you love the NCP so much?" Amanda couldn't wait to get the topic of conversation off of herself.

Ethan raised his eyebrows. This seemed to be the very question he had been waiting for. "I've always grappled with the big questions in life. I struggled to understand life's purpose. I did a lot of reading and debating. But I still couldn't find something that articulated clearly and truthfully man's purpose in life … something built on reason and science."

"Right, you told me that you have a scientific mind."

He nodded. "I got my hands on some of the writings of the founders of the National Citizens Party. I realized that here I found like-minded individuals. These people see the world as I see it. I could relate to them. I could help advance their cause, because it's my cause too. That cause is freedom: freedom to be the strongest, the greatest that you can be. And through this freedom, our country will progress in ways we've never dreamed of. I've been working on this graphic I'd like to show you. Nikki, can I borrow your laptop?"

"Just use yours. Usually, it's glued to your body."

"I left it in my car. I'll just be a second."

Pursing her lips, Nikki slid her computer toward him. Ethan searched for a moment and then turned the screen so Amanda could see the bold-print words.

"'Let the Best Rise to the Top.' Sounds Darwinistic," Amanda said, then looked at Ethan.

He nodded. "That's the whole idea. We're building a meritocracy. Today, if you have the ability and drive, nothing

72

will hold you back. Skin color, sexual orientation, gender, income—none of that matters or discriminates anymore. We are each free … free to reach our personal potential."

"Sounds compelling when you put it like that."

"Why don't you come with me to a big rally we're having?" He pulled a pamphlet from his back pocket. "This has all the details."

"Sure—yeah—I'll come." She'd go to a dump with him.

"Hey, what's this?" Ethan walked over to the corner of the room. He pulled a shirtsleeve aside, uncovering Amanda's portrait of Nikki.

No one spoke. Ethan gazed at the artwork, and Amanda's unease grew with each passing moment.

He at last turned to her, his eyes wide. "This is incredible talent."

Amanda exhaled. "Thank you. And now you can relax because you've seen one of my paintings, right?"

"You'd like that, wouldn't you?" Ethan chuckled. "You'd really prefer to keep your paintings hidden?"

Nikki sneered. "She's great at keeping things hidden."

Amanda worked up some courage; it was time to set the story straight. "Nikki, I'm sorry about yesterday. I would have told you my date was with Ethan, honestly. I had no idea you two know each other. I wasn't trying to keep anything from you."

"Okay, Amanda." Her hollow tone and tight lips said something different.

Amanda fell silent, her insides twisted. What had she done wrong?

Ethan picked up the portrait and walked near the window, where there was better lighting. "This portrait is impressive, no argument there. You've got the skills. But this only makes me more eager to see your paintings."

"You wanted to see my art. Isn't this my art?"

"You told me you painted your 'inner thoughts and feelings.' This portrait is an expression of Nikki. I already know Nikki. I want to know *you*. Don't you ever let anyone into your heart?"

She swallowed. "Maybe that takes a little bit of time."

Ethan set her portrait of Nikki down. "Do you want to get out of here?" He grabbed his coat and pulled it on.

"Where would we go?"

"Let's find out."

He stepped out of the apartment and reached for her hand. Amanda clasped his fingers and closed the apartment door behind her, catching one last glimpse of Nikki. Her eyes bore into Amanda, her face cold and body rigid.

They walked outside and were met with a torrential downpour. Making a dash for it, they ran for the car, sloshing through the puddles. Ethan ran much faster, reaching the passenger door and holding it open for her. She got in the vehicle, raindrops trickling down her black curls. His jacket was soaked, and his hair was a little messy from the rain. He looked even more attractive in this somewhat disheveled state.

He pulled out into the road. "Great weather, isn't it? But at least now we can talk, just the two of us. Look, I'm sorry about what happened back there. I get that you're not ready to show me your art."

"It's just so personal to me …"

"As I said, you fascinate me. You're a puzzle. I want to understand you, unravel how you think. I'm not going to give up on you or let your reservation prevent us from growing closer. I want to be the kind of person you can be open with."

She looked out the window. Her heart soared with the idea that he wanted to be closer to her, but she wasn't sure she could do what was needed to make it happen. She had spent so long keeping people at a distance …

The rain pounded on the car roof, frantic and unrelenting, but unsuccessful in reaching them—at least, not yet. The windshield wipers worked overtime, battling the oncoming precipitation.

Amanda decided to return to what seemed to be his favorite subject. "So have you been active in the NCP for a while?"

"Absolutely. It's why I moved here, in fact. I work full-time for the party, and I'm also taking that graphic design class at the Graduate Academy. The NCP pays for any education I pursue, since enhancing my talents can only make me a more valuable leader. They're all about advancing individuals' abilities. You know, it's a good thing I happened to be taking that class this semester, isn't it? If I weren't, we might never have met."

"Definitely a good thing. Someone could almost call it 'made to be' … fate in action."

His brow furrowed. "Fate didn't ask you on a date. I did."

"Right, of course." What an idiotic remark. Why he didn't dump her on the curb at the first opportunity was bewildering.

He remained silent, his face pensive.

Trying to fix things, she changed the subject again. "Do you do this often—drive around aimlessly?"

"It's not aimless; it's a challenge. I like venturing into the unknown, trying to navigate my way back, coming across new places. Some of the best sites are those you never tried to find."

Her window was becoming foggy, so she wiped her hand against the cold glass, clearing her view. They passed through a broken steel gate into what appeared to be an abandoned parking lot. A community of the Unfit stood nearby—staying close to a bevy of rambling shacks and rudimentary shelters constructed of old boxes and pieces of scrap. A middle-aged man sat on a crate, rocking back and forth, looking like he was muttering to himself while the rain ran over his ragged coat and unkempt beard. Amanda's dad often sought out these individuals who existed on the periphery of society. He would even pack an extra sandwich for lunch, which he would share with one of them. He was great at befriending people, regardless of who they were; she had not inherited the trait from him.

"Umm … are we allowed in here?"

"There's no sign specifically prohibiting us. Let me guess: You're one of those people who follows all the rules?"

"I consider myself a law-abiding citizen, if that's what you mean. Aren't you?"

"Of course I am—if the law is just. But some rules are arbitrary. We're programmed by our parents, by societal institutions to believe certain things are wrong. We should be free to question these rules, free to ask why some things are labeled as 'wrong.' Did you ever stop to consider that?"

She shrugged one shoulder. "Not really, no."

"Here, I've got a hypothetical situation for you. You're in the grocery store. You stick a six-pack of paper towels on the bottom of your cart. You go through the checkout line, pay for your groceries, and leave. As you head toward your car, you realize that you never put the paper towels on the counter. You didn't pay for them. Do you go back to the store to pay for them? Or do you continue toward your car?"

"I don't put things on the very bottom of the cart."

"You're evading the question."

"I'd probably go back and pay for them. You?"

Ethan shook his head. "The store employees should have noticed the paper towels. They didn't. It was their error, so I'd keep going."

"You would steal them?"

"But is it stealing? I would've paid for the paper towels, if I had remembered to put them on the counter, or if one of the workers had spotted them. I'd call it negligence on the part of the employees or forgetfulness on my part. I don't think these things are so straightforward, so black and white. The world is full of shadows, of gray areas to be explored and questioned. In fact, there are even some members of Congress proposing eliminating laws against theft. The rationale is that if you're ingenious or strong enough to obtain something, then it's the fault of the one stolen from and it's his responsibility to get it back. Maybe you should think about moving past these conventions others have drilled into you. You can make up your own mind. At the very least, it makes life much more of an adventure."

Amanda had never thought this way before, never even considered these things. What if he was right? She had already rejected her parents' religion. If they were wrong about that, maybe they were wrong about other things too. Ethan was leading her into a new realm of thinking and seeing things. It felt so fresh and unfamiliar, and she wholeheartedly welcomed the change.

He stopped the car and everything was silent, save the pattering of raindrops and their breathing. He placed his hand on his door handle. "How about a little adventure right now?"

She smiled. "Let's go."

They exited the car, and the rain beat down upon them once again, drenching them in mere moments. Through the rainfall, Amanda tried to take in their surroundings. They walked somewhere along the bank of a river, with a red arch bridge just before them. The inclement weather meant that everything was deserted: they were the only people here.

He led her past the looming masonry tower, closer to the edge of the water. A piercing whistle heralded the approaching train, passing overhead. The steel bridge above provided temporary shelter as they stood just feet from the strait, which flowed with particular fury.

"Welcome to the Hell Gate Bridge." Ethan gestured to the structure above them. "Pretty cool, don't you think?"

"I never would have found this place listed on a tourism site. But I like it. I could sketch here."

"We'll have to come back, then." He put his arm around her. "So. Usually, at the end of a date, there is this expectation …"

She froze, her pulse pounding.

"I opted not to pursue it yesterday because I don't want to rush anything with you. I know you've got your walls up."

Without thinking, she grabbed his hand. "Ethan, it's not that I don't trust you. I do."

"Enough to kiss me?"

She didn't need to answer. His lips found hers, and with a sweet, perfect touch, she drew closer to him, the reservations giving way further. Maybe it was only a matter of time … or a matter of kisses … before she would hold nothing back.

Time stubbornly marched forward and they drove back to her apartment, but she didn't want to leave the moment of their kiss. It was something magical, something so real.

Much of her existence to that moment had been a silent numbness. Simply being in Ethan's presence was a beam of light in her darkness, but now his kiss had awakened a new affirmation: he cared about her. Amazingly, she mattered to him. That alone was transforming her from within.

~~~

Nikki waited until Amanda turned on the water in the shower. Then she jacked up the volume on her music and went into the bedroom, locking the door behind her. Amanda couldn't hear anything now. She grabbed her phone. "Call Ethan." She paced back and forth across the small room, listening to the phone ring on the other end.

"Nikki." Ethan didn't sound too surprised. "To what do I owe the pleasure?"

"Cut the crap. I want to know what's going on."

"I think it's fairly obvious, don't you?"

"Would I bother calling you if it were? Look, I don't have that much time. Amanda's gonna be out of the bathroom in a few minutes, so quit playin' around."

"You want the details? Fine. She's my new assignment. I finished tracking the other girl; she's detained now. So they assigned me to Amanda. They told me to find her at the Masters Academy, which I did quite successfully. And since then, I've been keeping my eye on her."

"What did you find out?"

"I don't have to report to you." Ethan's voice grew cold.

"I'm the one who has to put up with living with her." Nikki's voice hissed. The pent-up fury inside her threatened to explode. "If I had any idea I'd be living with some double-crossing, lying bastard, I would've kicked her sorry ass out onto the curb the first day."

"We don't know if she's operating against the NCP. She's just flagged as suspicious."

"Come on. Look what Academy she went to! Look at her background!"

"I need concrete evidence. Indisputable facts. So far, I haven't found any. Don't worry: I'm thorough in my work. If she's working for the opposition, I'll find out."

Nikki curled her hands into fists. "Oh, I'll find out too. I'll make the truth come out."

"This is why the NCP put me on tracking, not you. You should catch flies with honey, Nikki. We're not forcing anything. We're building a relationship. It's all about trust. So you play the role of friendly roommate and leave me to do what I do best."

She hated his arrogance: according to Ethan, he did everything the best. He was nothing but a spoiled brat whose rich daddy gave him everything on a silver platter, like the high-paying, comfy position he had at the NCP. "I'll be her roommate because I have no choice for now. But hell if I'll be friendly."

"She's not that bad. I actually like spending time with her. ... She's different from the other girls I've tracked."

"Whatever. I think she just came out of the bathroom, so I gotta go." Nikki ended the call without waiting for his response. She wasn't going to play Amanda's game: she would make it very clear she was onto her. And forget what Ethan said. ... She would keep her own eye on Amanda. That girl wasn't going to get away with a damn thing.

CHAPTER EIGHT

TRIPPING TUESDAY

Amanda sat perched on the edge of the couch. Every couple of minutes, she got up and peered outside the apartment window. Nikki opened the bedroom door, emerging in full makeup and a glamorous ensemble. Things hadn't improved between them, much to Amanda's disappointment. She missed Nikki. It had been nice having a friend.

"You look great!" Amanda did her best to summon some enthusiasm.

Nikki, however, only grunted in reply.

Amanda decided to persist. "Are you going somewhere special tonight?"

"What, are you keeping tabs on *me* now?" Nikki stared at Amanda, her arms crossed.

"No. I … I was just wondering."

"If you're pumping me for information, I'm going to Little Pete's."

"Oh. Me too, actually."

"Of course you're going there: it's Tuesday. And Ethan's bringing you."

"Is there something special about Tuesday?"

A loud buzzing interrupted them. Nikki rolled her eyes. "Sound the trumpets. He's arrived."

Amanda walked over to the intercom. "Hello?"

"Hey! I'll be right up."

A few minutes later, Ethan came through the door, and despite her best efforts, Amanda couldn't control her smile. He was absolutely addicting. This would be her third date with Ethan, and she couldn't get enough. She craved the happy buzz that his presence produced within her. At first, just seeing him had prompted the pleasant sensation. But then he'd introduced the kiss, which raised everything to a whole new high. Her tolerance was building, leading her to crave more and more. She didn't want to ask herself if this was healthy or what these mounting longings would lead to. … All she wanted was him.

He leaned forward and kissed her on the cheek. Then he turned toward Nikki, nodding a hello. "Hey, Nikki. You off from work tonight?"

"Yeah. What about you? Are you working or having fun?"

"You know I don't usually work nights. You headed to Little Pete's? Want to ride with us?"

"It would be nice if you came too." Amanda gave a feeble smile in Nikki's direction.

Nikki shrugged and picked up her purse. "You're cheaper than public transportation. So, sure."

With that, Ethan took Amanda's hand, and the three of them headed to his car, Amanda in front and Nikki in the back. Nikki ignored them the whole way. Ethan pulled into a parking space by the nightspot, one of the very few remaining thanks to a multitude of cars and taxis.

Amanda couldn't understand it. "It's a regular Tuesday night. This many people go out on a weekday?"

"They go to Little Pete's," Ethan replied.

"Maybe you could be a little less cryptic?" Amanda said.

He laughed. "You're one to talk."

They passed the dragon mural and entered the first floor, which looked even more crowded than Friday night. They weaved through the pockets of people. Ethan had a destination in mind, and she happily let him guide her.

The music blared louder than ever on the second floor. Flashing fluorescent lights flooded the hall as dancers gyrated all across the densely packed floor. She followed Ethan and Nikki to the back staircase, which led to the third floor. A large, muscular man blocked the way. A bouncer? She had no idea about things like this.

Nikki bent closer to the bouncer, whispering in his ear and running her hand down his well-built arm. They were obviously well-acquainted with each other. Nikki and the bouncer had a few more brief exchanges, too soft to catch, and then Nikki moved past the man, up the stairs. His eyes followed her with longing. Ethan led Amanda forward. She could now read the large sign behind the man: NO ADMITTANCE.

"Ramsey! Dude!" The man gave Ethan a fist bump.

"What's happening, Jadyn? Seems pretty crowded tonight."

"Yeah, great crowd. Even better upstairs. You headed up there?"

"I wouldn't miss it. By the way, this is Amanda. She'll be coming with me."

"Don't let me keep you from all the fun. I'll be up soon enough." He moved his large frame out of the way. "Nice to meet you, Amanda." He nodded and Amanda gave a small wave, intimidated by his enormous proportions.

"I thought the top floor was closed." She followed closely at Ethan's heels up the stairs. "I didn't see any lights on up here when we were outside."

"Correct. It is closed—to the uninitiated, that is."

They entered the large room. The exhibit was still displayed, the red lights dancing upon the disturbing works of art. Yet unlike her last visit, couches and chairs now filled the room. Soft light flickered from the many candles placed throughout the space. About fifty people mingled around the room, lounging on the couches or clustered in smaller groups, talking and laughing. Amanda spotted a few people with art supplies, sketching. Large blackout curtains obscured the windows overlooking the street, which was why the floor had appeared vacant from the outside.

"Ethan! So great to see you!" A beautiful woman approached them and embraced Ethan.

Amanda recognized her: Nikki's friend, Heather. Purple streaks colored her long blonde hair. And, of course, she looked like she had just stepped off the runway.

"You haven't been here in a while," Heather said. "We've missed you."

"Thanks, Heather. I've been working overtime, especially with my latest NCP assignment."

Heather's eyes widened. "Oh, absolutely. I'm glad you could get away for the night." She seemed to notice Amanda for the first time. "Hi! It's Amanda, right? Nikki's roommate … I met you on Friday."

"Yeah."

"Welcome to the club, then."

"It looks pretty different in here with all the chairs and couches." Amanda cringed inside: Had she resorted to conversing about upholstery?

"Of course. We need the right set and setting, clearly." Heather tossed her long locks behind her shoulder, but Amanda couldn't stop staring at her eyes. Her pupils were massive black discs with only the smallest circumference of blue around them.

Ethan began steering Amanda in another direction. "We'll have to catch up with you later, Heather."

They walked a few steps, and then another woman called Ethan's name. They turned in the direction of her voice. Amanda hadn't seen her at first, but now there was no mistaking that face and those greasy strands of hair.

"Ethan!" Leila squealed, throwing her arms around him.

Amanda resisted a strong urge to shove her away. Could Leila grip him any tighter?

"Leila! How's it going?"

"Great, now that you're here!" She beamed, but, spotting Amanda, her face soon clouded with displeasure. "Oh, hi, Amanda."

"Um. Hi."

She smirked. "How's your semester project going?"

"I … haven't really started it yet."

"No? I've been to the Met three times already. My initial sketch is finalized for Thursday."

Eyebrows furrowed, Ethan looked from Leila to Amanda. "What's the semester project?"

"It's just this sketch we have to do for Painting I." Amanda began to back away. "Maybe we should go find Nikki?"

"Sure, if you want."

Amanda strode toward the sofa, where she had spotted Nikki. Nikki's other friend, Chloe, sat across from them, her legs propped up on the center table. She was in the middle of a conversation with a short, well-built man who sported a buzz cut and a dragon tattoo on his forearm.

He stood and shook Ethan's hand. "Ethan! How's it going, man?"

"Going great. This is Amanda, by the way. Amanda, this is Pete."

"As in 'Little Pete's.'" Chloe glanced up from checking her phone. "He's the owner of this joint."

Pete nodded his head in Amanda's direction. "Welcome to the club."

He was now the second person that night to welcome her to the "club," whatever that meant. The others continued their conversations, but Amanda watched Chloe pass something to Nikki: a circular golden container, small enough to fit in one's palm.

"Ugh. I'm dying for one of these." Nikki popped a small pill into her mouth and washed it down with a glass of wine.

Amanda frowned. She leaned toward Nikki and spoke under her breath. "Nikki, what was that?"

"Let's just say that it's a little something to get the creative juices flowing." She reclined her head on the sofa and rolled it from side to side.

Amanda took the container in her hands. It was filled with small white pills. Something told her they weren't mints.

"Go ahead, Amanda." Chloe waved her on. "Leila brought them. It's on us tonight, so help yourself."

"Thanks ..." Amanda stared in horror at the pills in front of her. She was in a room full of drug addicts. She scooted closer to Nikki. "Nikki! What are these things?"

"Hey, they don't call it 'Tripping Tuesday' for nothing."

Amanda's mouth dropped open. "That's why everyone is here?" She turned to Ethan, sitting on her other side. "Do you ... do this?"

"I won't tonight, but sometimes I do."

She continued to stare at him in disbelief, and he placed his arm around her.

"Amanda, it's okay. You're just playing into all the fears other people have convinced you to believe."

"What do you mean? We're talking about drugs! These things are illegal." She placed the pillbox on the table.

"Correction: this stuff *was* illegal." Nikki picked up the box and handed it to Pete, who popped a pill. "Thanks to the NCP, we got a bill passed last month that made these fun little things legal. 'Cause, come on … we should have the freedom to choose what we want to take or not."

"Just think back to the way it used to be." Ethan sat back and propped his right foot onto his left knee. "Adolescents in America were raised with the same blanket terminology: 'don't do drugs,' 'just say no,' et cetera, et cetera. Why these prohibitions? It's all because of some inept, daft people who abuse drugs. They're irresponsible and end up doing something incredibly stupid or dangerous."

Nikki scowled. "The Unfit ruin everyone else's fun."

"Then there are people like us." Ethan gestured to the others in the room. "Do you see anyone out of control here? We use drugs for a specific purpose: to reach our greatest potential and to create a more powerful piece of art. Most people use a drug to wake up in the morning. No one has a problem with that. People use drugs for a headache, for a stuffy nose, for all kinds of purposes. We use a drug to enhance our creativity. How is that criminal?"

Amanda had always admired his perfect logic, but now she found it frustratingly simple. Surely, there was something more to it than that. But he was right: she looked around, and everyone appeared rational and self-controlled.

Nikki sat up stiff, her voice sharp. "No one's telling me what to do. This is my body; I can do what I want to. If people want to stuff their bodies with toxic substances … whatever. That's their brainless decision. If we want to spark the artistic genius within us, why should someone stop us? It's our freedom to choose. The NCP respects and upholds that right. Thanks to the assistance of this little pill, I've done some of my greatest work."

Amanda's personal artistic experiences were already a surreal exploration, delving into the deep recesses of her being. What would it be like with some enhancement?

She shook her head, dizzy from this unexpected news. "How do you know you won't do something you'll regret later?"

Ethan shrugged. "Simple: I'm always in control. I never exceed my tolerance level, so the drug never takes over completely. We're human beings: we have physical cravings that need to be satisfied. I listen to my body and its drives. I don't let other people's mistakes hold me back from the thrill of a liberating experience."

Nikki's eyes were already becoming dilated, evidence that the drug was now flowing through her blood system. "Come on! You know you wanna."

Amanda swallowed. Was she conforming to messages drilled into her mind that weren't even true? The allure of an artistic experience, heightened by this potent pill, felt tantalizing. Maybe Ethan was right. Perhaps taking one of the pills wouldn't be so bad after all. *Perhaps …* It was a small, interior whisper of potentiality, of consideration. But not tonight.

"No thanks."

"Well, you never know when you may need the help." Ethan took a drink and set his beer down. "No pressure, of course. Perhaps you'll find that you need the extra enhancement for your semester project."

So he wasn't going to let that slide. "I never needed help before." Amanda sighed. "But maybe this time I will."

"What's the issue?"

"We have to replicate a great work of art. My assignment … I'm just not comfortable with it."

"Too technically challenging?"

"Something like that, yeah …"

The rest of the evening passed without any further incidents. She was oddly at ease in this new group of strangers. Perhaps it was Ethan's constant, reassuring presence by her side or the spontaneous kisses they shared as the night wore on.

But eventually it was time to leave. Nikki didn't need to hitch a ride; Chloe would take her home later. So Ethan and Amanda, hand in hand, walked toward the door.

She again spotted the strange letters etched on the doorframe. She paused. "What's that supposed to be?"

"I think it's called 'room decor.' Interior design isn't my area of interest. Besides, we have business to take care of."

"What do you mean?"

"This is a date, right?"

"That's true. We'd better get to work."

She followed him down the stairs and out to his car. He drove them back to her apartment, anticipation burning within her. After parking the car, he turned to her, unbuckling his seatbelt. She unbuckled hers, and then they said good night … a very slow, wonderful good night.

CHAPTER NINE

FAMILIAR STRANGER

"I think you dropped this."

Amanda glanced up at the person speaking to her: a short, skinny man with black glasses. They were in the same sculpture class, which had just ended. Now she was hurrying to clean up her materials so she could see Ethan. But this guy stood in front of her, holding a piece of paper out to her.

"Thanks." She took the paper, which maybe had fallen out of her pocket or book bag, and started walking away. A few steps out of the classroom, it hit her: her painting class assignment. She removed the paper from her pocket and, unraveling it, read: *Portrait of a Mother.*

Today was Wednesday. The assignment was to make a preliminary sketch of the master painting by tomorrow.

"Hey!" Ethan stood in front of her, grinning. "How's it going?"

"Uh, pretty good, I guess. I just remembered that I have to do an assignment this afternoon."

"The sketch for Michael's class?"

"Yeah, that's the one. It's the semester project, so it's pretty important."

"I'd tag along to the Met with you, but I just got called into work for the rest of the day. There's a special project they want everyone working on. That reminds me … are you still planning on coming to the big NCP rally tomorrow? I'd love for you to join us. It's the perfect introduction to the party. What do you say?"

"Besides Michael's class in the morning, I should be free. So, yeah—I'll come."

"Great! See you then."

They kissed and parted ways.

Amanda buried her hands deep into her jeans pockets, her right hand clenching the slip of paper, and then began her trek to the Met. It was a beautiful day in the city. The sun shone above the skyline, light filtering down to the pedestrians below. White, fluffy clouds dotted the autumn day, and the crispness of fall was in the air. A horse and carriage trotted past her—a telltale sign that she was close to Central Park. A couple, riding inside the carriage, laughed together. Central Park would always remind her of Ethan now. Maybe, as long as she kept him in mind, this assignment wouldn't be so difficult.

The Met was a dominating building, the massive white structure easily noticeable. Its Classical style with tall columns was impressive. She reached the bottom step and looked up toward the entrance. Tourists milled around, taking pictures and reviewing their purchases from the gift shop. A small group of young adults passed her on the stairs, laughing and talking together. She, in contrast, had no one with her. Maybe she should have told Ethan about her mother. At least then she wouldn't feel so alone.

Taking a breath, she marched up the stairs, forcing herself to pass through the front door. She tried to buoy her spirit as she wandered the hallways searching for her destination: "European Paintings, 1250-1800." She saw a sign for the Modern and Contemporary Art section and imagined Leila's gloating face. Amanda had to do this assignment and do it well. She rounded a bend past the Greek and Roman art. There, just ahead, was the sign pointing to her section.

A face passed her on the left, the image flickering ever so briefly in her peripheral vision. The sight, although brief, stopped her in her tracks. Stunned, she began weighing if her eyes had deceived her. Was it him? Or just someone who looked like him? He turned into the European Paintings exhibit and disappeared.

She could let it go; she was probably mistaken anyway. Yet a feeling gnawed at her—she had to know. Without another second's debate, she plunged into the crowd, hoping to spot the stranger who, perhaps, wasn't quite a stranger. She passed through the entrance to pursue her target, ignoring the world-renowned paintings on the walls. She was gaining on him …

"Sorry!" She collided with a school group, gathered in front of one of the Baroque paintings. She emerged from the ruckus, her objective that much farther away. Determined more than ever, she doubled her speed to just short of running. "Wait!"

He didn't seem to hear her calling, but a family a few feet away turned and stared at her. Thankfully, the person she pursued had slowed and was looking at one of the exhibits.

She rushed upon him, his back to her. She grabbed his arm, simultaneously appalled at her own uncharacteristic forwardness even as she blurted out, "Hi!"

He turned around, and for a split second, it seemed like she had the wrong person. Nausea arose within her. Had she done all this, only to find out that she had mistaken him for someone else? Then he fully faced her and she was certain.

"I was right! It is you." She smiled, relief wiping away any social conventions of introductions or explanations.

He looked at her, smiling back.

When he didn't say anything, she continued, "I know you. I mean, we know each other. You probably think I'm crazy. ... We've met before, right?"

"Yes, we do know each other." His voice sounded familiar. It brought memories of home with it.

"Right. We went to Valor Academy together. We were in the same class. You helped me at our graduation—you rescued me. Do you remember?" If he were anything like her, the memory of their graduation was something he could never forget. Maybe the screams of those helpless victims haunted him too.

"Yes, I remember it perfectly. You were there with your father and sister."

They began to stroll together through the exhibit.

"Exactly!" she said.

He looked the same as that May morning. His hair was combed across his forehead, not a strand out of place. His blue eyes were dazzling, so light in color that they appeared almost translucent. He even wore something similar to what he'd been wearing at graduation: brown khakis and a white dress shirt. No tie this time, however.

"This is amazing. I mean, I just caught you out of the corner of my eye." She stared at him, still in disbelief. "When did you come to the city?"

93

"Very recently, actually. I've been here about two weeks now." He was genteel in his manners, his voice soft and peaceful.

"Yeah, me too—pretty much the same." She paused, studying him. "It's strange ... I know I've seen you lots of times at Valor. But I can't remember what class we took together." She laughed. "Do we even know each other's names?"

"Well, you're Amanda Burrow."

"Oh. Okay. That's impressive." She scratched her head, trying to remember his name. Chris? Alex? "I'm not too good at names. Sorry."

"It's alright. We haven't spoken in quite a while. I'm Morgan."

"Oh yeah! Morgan. How did I forget that? Your name fits you."

"Thank you! I like to think so as well. So what brings you to the city, Amanda?"

"I'm attending the Graduate Academy of Fine Art. It was always a dream of mine." Her response came readily: talking to him felt as comfortable as pulling on an old pair of sweats.

"Art is your gift. I always enjoyed seeing your work at Valor. How are your classes?"

"They're mostly good. My painting class has been challenging. That's why I'm here. I was assigned a work of art in the Met that I'm supposed to replicate. I would have preferred any other painting besides this one."

"I know the Met well. What painting are you assigned?"

"*Portrait of a Mother.*"

"That's my favorite painting!"

"Really? Why?"

"If I tell you what the painting means to me, it will prevent you from seeing it with fresh eyes. You have to discover its beauty for yourself. Actually, we're right beside it now. What do you think?"

They had indeed wandered to *Portrait of a Mother*. Amanda turned to gaze at it. The Florentine, naturalistic portrait of a mother and her child was much larger than she had anticipated. It was a landscape: above, the sky in gradient shades of blue—glowing colors made possible with oil painting; below, a flowering meadow; and encompassing the whole image, an early-dawn illumination. The mother was in the foreground, seated on the grass and facing the viewer. Her bright eyes stared forward, and her long forehead gave her a look of intelligence. Her golden hair was swept up and covered with a sheer veil, accentuated with tiny pearls along the edge. Pink hues softened her cheeks of fair skin. She wore a delicate blue brocade gown, embroidered with tiny gold filigree, which draped voluminously to her feet. The sleeves of the dress were slashed, revealing scarlet silk material underneath. On her lap sat her baby—a naked, plump boy. He had light curls on his round head, which he rested against his mother's chest. He stared upward at her, wide eyes and thick eyelashes. A tiny hand extended toward his mother's face, as though playfully trying to grasp her. His whole face seemed to smile with joy.

Amanda sunk down onto a nearby bench, facing the painting. That relationship between mother and child—it didn't matter that this painting was done hundreds of years ago … the bond that existed between the two remained something timeless and unchanging. But it was a bond that had been broken for Amanda.

"You seem sad. Is everything alright?" Morgan sat beside her.

"I just … This is just a subject I don't like to think about."

"A mother and her child?"

"A mother."

He was silent for a moment. "It evokes some strong feelings for you?"

"Yeah. Time doesn't heal all wounds."

"It is hardest when the hurt is very deep." He was quiet for a moment. "Did something happen to your mother?"

"She died."

"I'm sorry." His simple words rang with sincerity. "Did she pass away recently?"

"No. When I was twelve."

"That's young to have lost a parent. How did she die?"

She glanced sideways at him. She could share this with him, couldn't she? There was a wonderful anonymity here, like a therapist perched behind a desk whose sole job was to listen. Morgan was safely distant. Nothing of great consequence hung in the space between him and her. Yet at the same time, it felt like they had somehow known each other for years.

She stared at the floor, and her words tumbled out. "It was my twelfth birthday, the day she died. I remember being so excited. I was going to have a huge party. I went down to the kitchen that morning to help my dad blow up the balloons, and my mom was there with my five-year-old sister, baking my birthday cake. Every year on my birthday, she made my favorite chocolate fudge cake."

"Your mother sounds like a very caring person."

"Yeah, she was. She was my best friend."

"And then what happened?"

A lump rose in her throat. "My mom was mixing the icing, but she ran out of powdered sugar. She gave me a kiss on the top of my head and said, 'Don't worry, birthday girl. I'll run to the store and be back in just a few minutes.' I … I'll never forget those words. It was the last thing she ever said to me." She took a deep breath. "She got in a car accident. Some waste of life ran the red light and smashed into my mom's sedan. She died right there, at the intersection."

"You never got to say goodbye."

Amanda shook her head. The words came more easily now; the hardest part was over. "After that morning, my life changed. I put away everything that reminded me of my mom—the perfume, dresses, pocketbooks. The memories were the hardest. I shoved them away, pretended they didn't exist, repressed them. They just hurt too much. I never laughed or joked like I used to, so I didn't really have close friends anymore. I hated special occasions. I still do. If it hadn't been my birthday, my mom would still be alive, right? I brought everyone else down. Anger, loneliness, grief, pain—they became my new companions."

"So studying this particular painting is painful for you?"

"How can I paint something … the one thing … I did everything possible to forget?" She turned away from the painting and faced Morgan. "I don't expect you to tell me the answer. I didn't mean to dump all of this on you."

"It's alright. Thank you for sharing it with me. I'm sorry you have walked through life with so much hurt in your heart. Maybe doing this sketch will be therapeutic for you."

"If therapy means digging deeper into the wound, then, yeah, I guess."

"Remembering doesn't have to be a kind of curse."

"My memories are all that I have left of my mom. Death is final. She's gone. No happily ever after. These broken fragments of times past—they're beggar's scraps. Death has stolen her from me. Permanently."

"Your mom would want you to be happy, Amanda."

"And I would want her to be alive."

"Consider this, though: perspective in art changes an image in its entirety, giving depth and space. The same is true in life. Maybe your perspective is too shortsighted."

She folded her arms. "Perspective is an illusion, Morgan. It's an art technique that fools the eye into believing that a three-dimensional world is present on a two-dimensional surface. Any perspective that tells me that my mom is somehow still alive, floating on a fluffy cloud surrounded by a choir of angels, is just a delusion."

"All I mean is that remembering your mother shouldn't bring pain and suffering exclusively. There is still sweetness in the bitter."

"I guess that's true." She studied him—his placid face, the neatly pressed khakis, the calm and unhurried gestures of his hands. "It's strange. I don't know … there's some uncanny feeling between us … I'm not certain how to explain it."

"I understand what you mean. We could call it a connection of sorts."

"Right. We have a connection." She smiled at him through her sadness. "You know, I'm really not crazy. I don't go around sharing these personal things with anyone who is willing to listen."

"I never thought you were crazy. I find that it's very easy to talk with you too."

"Don't tell me that you're going to start telling me *your* deepest secrets now."

"Well, everyone has secrets."

"Why don't you keep them to yourself, at least for now. I think I have all I can handle for today." She opened her book bag and pulled out her sketchbook and a charcoal pencil. "I better get to work on my assignment."

"Yes, I agree. Now you must come to know *this* mother—the one in the painting."

She squinted, focusing on the shapes and movement. "That's always the first step. Study your subject: shape, color, design, value."

"It's more than that, though. The greatest works of art all start with an emotional response, not an analytical one. If you're going to paint someone, you have to go beyond his or her exterior: you have to find a way to illuminate the person within. If you are going to paint this mother, you have to try to understand her."

"What, are you an artist yourself?" She drew a sweeping, curved line, approximating the length of the mother's arm that cradled the baby. "You sure have enough recommendations to make it seem like you are."

"No, not exactly."

"What do you do?"

"Right now, I have some temporary work in the city. I don't imagine I will be here too long, but things are always apt to change."

They sat there together, and the hours passed. She blocked in all of the abstract shapes of the painting, carefully proportioning them in relation to each other. It was a simple start, but it was nevertheless an inchoate image of the painting before her. Over and over, through drawing lines, erasing them, and adjusting, she refined the block-in to make it ever more accurate. Renaissance artists often sought the secret geometric design in the natural world; now she was similarly seeking the geometric patterns in this work of art. She was dealing with simple shapes, but she would still have to make it more complex and realistic.

She glanced at her watch. Nearly five o'clock. Only fifteen minutes left until the Met closed. "I'm going to have to be done for today." She frowned. Her sketch was far from being complete. "I can't show up with this tomorrow. Maybe I could stop back at the Met again in the morning, before class, just to make a few more adjustments."

"I come here often. Perhaps we'll run into each other again."

"Yeah, that would be nice. Bye, Morgan. Thank you for everything."

"See you soon, Amanda!"

At the doorway, she glanced once more over her shoulder. He still sat on the bench, staring at *Portrait of a Mother*, a smile on his serene face.

CHAPTER TEN

FAVORITE PLACES

Amanda hurried onto the subway, oblivious of the people jammed in around her. There was no chance of getting a seat, so she clung to the pole in the middle of the car. She wasn't sure if her death-like grip was more for balance or an effort to hold on to her emotional sanity. Talking to Morgan and telling him about her mom had opened a vault in her mind. Memories and feelings poured out now, a tidal wave she couldn't hold back. She paid no attention to the conversations surrounding her or to the announcements for upcoming stops along the line; she could only ponder the long-repressed memories of her mom. It had been so long since she'd allowed herself to remember.

Arriving home, Amanda was in no mood to confront Nikki's passive-aggressive attitude, not to mention she probably couldn't hide her emotional turmoil. Avoidance was in order.

"Look who's back." Nikki glanced up from her computer and scrutinized Amanda. "What have you been doing all day? Painting the town red?"

Amanda scurried past, mumbling, "I don't feel so great. I'm going to bed."

She entered the bedroom, closing the door behind her, and crawled under the covers. She lay there, staring at the bedroom ceiling, remembering ... missing. The microwave beeped and dishes clattered. Nikki was apparently making dinner. The door opened and other voices filled the apartment, most likely Nikki's friends. Amanda watched the digital numbers change on the clock nearby. Late that night, the apartment door closed one final time, all the friends gone. The apartment was almost silent, save Nikki's footsteps and the screaming of the neighbors next door. Then Nikki came into the room they shared and went to bed. Nikki would be the only one who slept.

In her mind, Amanda saw her mother: picking strawberries one June afternoon, her forehead damp with sweat ... visiting Amanda's kindergarten classroom when they made green eggs and ham ... handing her a swaddled, wrinkly faced Chiara and sharing together the marvel of this tiny new person. Amanda could almost see her mother's thick black hair, the mint-colored purse with the gold chain that she brought out on special occasions, her dresser laden with perfume, saint cards, and jewelry.

The room slowly lightened as morning approached. She was still awake, waiting for the night to be over. Her alarm wasn't scheduled to start beeping for another fifteen minutes, but she preemptively turned it off. She tiptoed out of the bedroom, and ten minutes later, she left the apartment. Nikki, thankfully, was still sound asleep.

Amanda got on the subway, her sketchbook tucked in her bag. She yearned for rest, but her mind knew no tranquility. Up the steps of the Met, through the door, throwing in her donation-a repeat of yesterday. The museum had just opened and was almost vacant at this early hour on a weekday.

She had only half an hour to add volume and value to her sketch. She stared at *Portrait of a Mother*, zeroing in on the baby's cherubic face. His eyes were wide, animated with admiration and devotion, as he gazed upward at his mother. She would give anything if she could just see *her* mother's face one more time. It was the first face she ever saw, the one she had known the best. Now it felt so long since she had seen her mother's wide smile, her eyes that seemed to laugh with some hidden joke, her nostrils that flared when she tasted something she didn't like. She spent awhile trying to get the baby's eyes just right.

She then moved to the mother's hand, which grasped the baby. She began shading in the fingers, whose touch was protective and comforting. Her own mother's hand had been marked with prominent veins. Amanda had liked running her finger up and down the blue bumps, like she was tracing a roadmap over her mother's skin.

"You came back!"

Amanda jumped, her heart pounding. She spun around. Morgan stood just a couple of feet away. She hadn't even noticed him approaching. He appeared the same as yesterday—identical clothes and all, though they showed no wear or wrinkles.

"Mind if I have a seat?"

She smiled, sliding over on the bench and making room for him. "Apparently, you weren't lying when you said that you come here often."

"I'll always tell you the truth. How is your sketch coming along?"

"I'm getting there, I guess. I'm trying to add some value and dimension right now."

"What about class this morning?"

Amanda glanced at the clock on the wall. It was now fifteen minutes past the time she was supposed to leave. "I guess I'm skipping today. It's alright—Michael allows one unexcused absence. I'll just spend the rest of the afternoon here, and that way I'll have the assignment done for next class."

Morgan nodded. "It is looking very good."

"Thanks. You know, I couldn't stop thinking about my mom all last night. Working on the sketch, in some weird way, has been helping."

"It is a way of processing."

"Yeah, I guess it is."

They sat in a comfortable silence for some time. Morgan turned from *Portrait of a Mother* to look at her. "Tell me a little about painting. Why do you like it so much?"

Her vault of memories now open, the recollection came easily. "It started the Christmas after my mom died. I dreaded the day. Everything reminded me of her, but the holidays especially so. I convinced my dad to make everything as low-key as possible: no lights, no big family dinner … you get the picture. I didn't ask for any presents, but on Christmas morning, there was a package under the tree with my name on it. It was a paint set. I had never really painted before, and I'm still not sure what inspired my dad to give it to me. That afternoon, I painted for the first time. It's been my window of escape ever since then."

"A window of escape?"

"It's hard to understand." She leaned over her pad, now working on adding depth to the folds of the mother's gown. "Painting puts me in touch with this other reality. Sometimes, when I paint, I'm not even sure why I paint what I do. I begin painting one thing, but when I'm done, I've created something else. My paintings have a symbolism that even I don't understand sometimes. It's kind of magical."

He tilted his head contemplatively. "Another reality ... something beyond this world? Something supernatural?"

"It's just something special, that's all."

"It sounds like it. Do you have a favorite painting?"

"Yeah, I do. It's a painting that I did. I realize that probably sounds incredibly conceited of me. It's not, though: I don't like it so much because of the technique. It's one of my earliest paintings, so overall it's elementary in style." She continued sketching, but her mind roved to the canvas hidden beneath her bed. "I painted it during that first year after my mom died. It's bizarre: it's the painting I cherish most of all, but I don't know what it means."

"It seems to me that most things are much deeper than what appears on the surface. Life is so much more than what mere senses perceive."

Amanda didn't comment. She was visualizing the small painting in her mind. ... She had memorized every inch of it. "There are clouds on the top of the canvas: black and gray storm clouds, very ominous and foreboding. Raindrops fall from the clouds—but the raindrops are really tears. I'm in the foreground of the painting, my head down, and I'm holding something that seems to be an umbrella, but it's formed by three interlocking hands, which protect me from the falling tears. Meanwhile, I'm looking at a puddle formed at my feet. Inside the puddle is a face. It's not my reflection, but the face of a beautiful woman. That's the amazing part of the painting: even though I was just a novice when I created it, the woman's face is perfect in its portrayal. I've never been able to replicate it."

"What does she look like?"

"It's hard to describe her. When I say that she's 'beautiful,' I don't mean what most people consider beauty today. I'm not referring to the women on magazine covers or who win pageants. It doesn't have to do with her eye color or hairstyle. This beauty is something much more genuine and real … powerful and breathtaking."

"It comes from within."

"Exactly."

"Do you know who she is?"

"I don't have the faintest idea. I've never met someone who looks like her." She looked up and stared at him. "Okay. It's your turn now."

"What do you mean?"

"I just told you about the painting closest to my heart. Do you have any idea how huge that is for me? I never reveal anything about my paintings to other people. So now I'm done sharing. You have to tell me something. And I don't mean your favorite color or the instrument you played in the school band. I want something deep."

His light blue eyes widened. "I don't want to tell you something. I want to *show* you something!"

"What?"

"My favorite place." He stood up.

Amanda fiddled the charcoal pencil in her fingers, debating. "You've got me curious now." She had been working on the sketch for a few hours now. It wasn't perfect, but it was just a preliminary sketch after all. "Alright, let's go."

She threw her sketchbook and pencil in her book bag and followed Morgan out of the Met. It was another pristine day in the city, though the cooler air required a coat. Her stomach growled, reminding her that she hadn't eaten all day. She stopped by a street vendor's cart and bought a hot dog (Morgan said he didn't need anything), and then they walked the city blocks, chatting together. She appreciated the casualness of their conversation and the familiarity that they shared. Their connection felt truly remarkable and produced a friendship that, though brief in its duration thus far, was impressively deep.

They walked for about half an hour. He began to slow his pace, and Amanda figured they must be approaching the destination. She scanned the view ahead, hoping to spot the mysterious location. Past the steel grays and flashing signs, two towering spires rose into the air, each bedecked with a cross. She shook her head in disbelief—and disdain. … His favorite place was St. Patrick's Cathedral!

A memory came to her mind: thirteen years ago, on a windy spring afternoon, walking up the steps of the cathedral with her parents. They had brought her along with them on a parish pilgrimage. She had been here before. Even with the time that had passed, the cathedral looked the same. … It had not changed; she had.

Amanda stopped in her tracks. Morgan halted as well, turning to her with a questioning look on his face.

She gritted her teeth. "The cathedral? You're taking me to St. Patrick's?"

"Yes … I said I was taking you to my favorite place."

She sighed. Religion and politics: those were the two things you weren't supposed to discuss in polite company. Politics she didn't care about. Religion she wanted nothing to do with. "I'm not going in there."

"Why?"

"It's an utter waste of time—a tourist trap."

"How so?"

"Come on, Morgan. How many people get sucked into lighting a five-cent candle for five bucks?"

Morgan turned to gaze at the cathedral, while Amanda just groaned within. Why did St. Patrick's have to be his favorite place? Why not Times Square, Broadway, or even the best coffee shop in the Flatiron District? The city held a whole slew of possible locations, but he had to choose a church. Religion now tainted and strained this exquisite friendship. It fueled the fire of her anger.

"You don't have to light any candles," Morgan said, turning back toward her. "Just walk around with me." He didn't seem upset by her refusal, which wasn't surprising. She couldn't imagine him mad.

"If you're looking for inspiration, let's go across the street to Rockefeller Center and see Atlas. One man holding the weight of the world—now that's compelling."

Her vision then strayed to a figure emerging from the massive bronze doors of the cathedral. Something about the woman struck Amanda as familiar, and she watched the individual cross the street and draw near. Amanda recognized the face now: Chloe.

Chloe met Amanda's stare and jumped. "Oh! Hi, Amanda."

"Hi." Amanda squirmed. She didn't enjoy being spotted in close proximity to the cathedral. She wanted no association between herself and the building and everything it represented.

"Did you see the lines around there?" Chloe jerked her thumb toward St. Patrick's. Surrounding the building was a disorderly queue: an aged man shuffling along with a cane, a haggard-looking woman guiding a young girl who drooled and clapped her hands, a teenager who was clearly wasted. "They clog the sidewalk every day at this time."

"Why don't they just go inside?"

Chloe scoffed. "They have to wait for their turn. They're all looking for free food. The church gives it out every day at noon. But really, what's even the point? What can these Unfit even contribute, you know?"

"Doesn't look like they're doing much right now."

"Seriously. I don't know why someone didn't take care of them a long time ago. We have government funding for that, you know? All the way up to two years old."

Amanda shrugged. "I don't know why they can't just go inside the church so they don't hold up the foot traffic."

"There isn't any more room inside." Morgan frowned. "It's already full of starving people."

Chloe scowled. "I'm a little late, so I have to run, but see you later at Little Pete's?"

"Yeah, see you then."

Giving a small wave, Chloe weaved her way into the crowd and disappeared.

Amanda folded her arms and stared at Morgan. "I'm not changing my mind about this. I'm going to go, but I guess I'll just catch up with you at the Met sometime soon."

"No, I'm afraid you won't. You see, I've been the one to find you twice. Now it's your turn. You'll know where to find me." He turned as though to head toward the cathedral.

"Wait!"

He stopped and looked back at her.

She took a step forward. "But I … I told you I'm not going in there!"

"You are free to do as you wish. But I hope to see you soon, Amanda."

She stood alone on the sidewalk, watching him mix in with the crowd of the Unfit. Then she followed his progress up the cathedral steps and through the large doors. He passed out of sight. Rallying her anger to ward off the sadness, she stormed away. Considering the parameters Morgan had set, she probably wouldn't ever see or speak to him again.

It was a welcome relief when the taxi dropped her off at Little Pete's later that evening. The club was the perfect reprieve, and the thought of seeing Ethan buoyed her spirits. She put *Portrait of a Mother* and Morgan out of her mind.

She approached Jadyn, who once again guarded the third floor. "Umm … hi."

"Amanda." He grinned, revealing two rows of white teeth. "Bet you're looking for your man."

"You mean Ethan?"

"Yeah. Unless you've moved on already." He winked.

"No! No … I'm looking for Ethan."

"What's the password?" He stood up, his enormous frame blocking the stair entrance.

She panicked. Password? Ethan never told her a password. … What was she going to do?

Jadyn burst into a deep laughter, bowling over and holding his side. "Your face! Oh man! That was priceless!"

He couldn't stop cackling, but at least he had the courtesy to step aside so she could go upstairs. She hurried past him without saying goodbye. It mystified her as to what Nikki saw in him.

The gathering was small this evening, and she found Ethan right away. He sat apart from the others, typing on his laptop, apparently deep in thought. The red lighting lit the seriousness etched on his face. She plopped down beside him on the sofa and sighed, the stress and agitation of the day subsiding. Being with him somehow made everything alright.

"I missed you."

"Somehow, Amanda, I find that hard to believe." He closed the computer lid and faced her, his brow furrowed.

"Wh-What do you mean?"

"You lied to me."

"What? When?"

"You said you were going to meet me at the NCP rally this afternoon. But Chloe told me that you went—with another guy—to *St. Patrick's.*"

The way he spoke the name of the cathedral produced a shiver up her spine. It surprised her that someone could utter two words with as much loathing as he had managed.

She slapped her forehead. The rally for the National Citizens Party. She forgot ... she completely and utterly forgot. "Ethan, I'm so sorry! I got caught up with my sketch and—"

"You were working on the sketch at St. Patrick's?"

"No. I finished it, and then I went for a walk with my friend—"

"You told me that you didn't know anyone in the city."

"I didn't know Morgan was here. I ran into him at the Met. He went to Valor with me. We're just old friends, that's all."

"And you went to St. Patrick's with him."

"No! *I* didn't go in. And I never will. I'm just so sorry about today. I feel terrible."

He shook his head. "Sometimes I just wonder if I really know you. Just, for a moment, consider things from my perspective. You refuse to let me into your deeper thoughts. You keep yourself so guarded around me, just like your paintings that you won't let me see. How am I not to conclude that there's something else going on?" He sighed. "How about some answers? ... Why? Why won't you ever go into St. Patrick's?"

Her words spilled out, her desire to appease him overcoming any remaining hesitation about disclosing this part of herself. "My family is very religious. Growing up, my parents taught me my prayers, and every Sunday you could find us, without fail, sitting in a church pew. But despite my parents' faithfulness, the God they believed in let my mother die in a car accident on my tenth birthday. My mother's death was the turning point of my life. How could I continue believing in an all-good deity after that kind of tragedy? They say God is our Father, but if so, what kind of a father takes away a young girl's mother? If he's really 'all-powerful,' why didn't he change things? He can't be an all-good God, or any god at all. Any trust or faith I had in religion died with my mother. These organized religions are all empty words and empty practices. It means nothing and does nothing."

He studied her for a long while and then began to speak. "My parents were ambivalent when it came to religion. They never talked about faith or 'God,' so I did a lot of my own personal reading and studying. At first, I was agnostic: not certain if God existed or not. Then I met this girl. She seemed like a good person—intelligent, pretty, fun to be around. She was also a Christian.

"As I became closer to her, I got an inside look into what her religion was like. She was a slave to it. If she didn't say her morning prayers or go to church on Sunday, guilt haunted her. When I asked her questions about God and wouldn't accept her scripture quotes for an answer, she had no reply aside from, 'You just have to have faith.' She had succumbed to this whole system of doctrines, accepting it all because she was told it was the 'truth.' If someone told me from the time I was an infant that fairy tales are real, I would probably believe all of it too. But the real truth is that we aren't born to be slaves to some man they say lived more than two thousand years ago. We are capable of directing and shaping our own lives. She decided it for me. After I broke up with her, I knew that I was an atheist."

He reached over and took her hand. "I'm sorry about your mom, Amanda."

"I would have told you sooner. It's just that it's hard for me to talk about it. It brings up all kinds of painful memories. It's easier to keep my walls up and guard against the hurt."

Ethan moved closer to her and put his arm around her shoulders. "This is the first time you've shared something so personal with me."

"In case you haven't noticed, I really like you." That was the understatement of the year, but there was no reason to disclose everything, most especially the depth of her feelings toward him.

"Oh yeah? Well, while we have this moment of unhindered confessions, let me ask: Why? Why, exactly, do you like me?"

"Isn't it obvious? I was alone in this city and most especially at the Academy. You reached out to me and genuinely wanted to know me. You're bright and intelligent, not to mention very good-looking." Her cheeks grew hot. "And your confidence and self-assurance are what I admire the most about you. You are your own true person, and by being with you, I'm seeing things in a way I never knew possible." She had her own question for him, an enigma that she couldn't comprehend ever since she first met him: "But what about me? I can't understand what you see in *me*."

He sat back, tapping his knuckles against his lips for a moment. Then he leaned forward, resting his elbows on his knees. "You surprised me. You weren't who I was expecting.

I've met a lot of girls in my line of work … but you're different from the others. I suppose that's the quality I find most attractive, as well as the most frustrating. You have this depth to you—there's such a mysterious intensity about you. I feel like others have passed you by because they couldn't recognize the beauty and complexity behind that fortress you've constructed around yourself. Like I say, you fascinate me. You always keep me guessing what you're thinking or what kind of past has formed this person before me. Sometimes, when I get a fleeting peek inside the way your mind works, I think we may actually be very similar. Maybe one day, I'll unravel your whole mystery; until then, I like playing the game."

Standing, he extended his hand toward her. "Come on, I want to show you something."

Hand in hand, they left Little Pete's and got in his car. He was maneuvering through the streets of Manhattan. He clearly wasn't driving aimlessly this time; he had a set purpose in mind. Not that it mattered to her: she would go anywhere with him.

He parked on a quiet street, lined with trees and potted plants. Though they were still in Manhattan, they had left behind the touristy hustle and bustle—and any unwelcome sight of the Unfit. This was the Upper West Side. He strode up the stairs to a four-story brownstone. She grasped the elegant black handrail and observed the bay window, the sharp black shutters, and the sculpted doorframe surrounding the glossy wooden door. He placed his thumb on the small reader above the doorknob, and at once, the door clicked open.

"Coming in?" He smiled at her open-mouthed expression.

"This is your apartment?"

"Not the whole building, mind you. Just the first floor."

She followed him inside and stepped onto a polished cherrywood floor, quite the contrast to the faded wall-to-wall carpeting in her apartment. The walls here were painted deep, multi-shades of gray. A darker gray wall unit lined two walls, providing shelving space from floor to ceiling. The shelving itself was a form of art with contrasting patterns of open shelving, which held everything from books to a Moroccan vase to a bronze statue of the Capitoline wolf.

He had furnished the apartment with modern designs and sophisticated styles. It was contemporary, functional yet dynamic, and entirely impressive. In other words, she seemed out of place.

He placed his phone on the small, metallic table by the door. She wandered through the living room, observing all the details. She didn't want to imagine how much his apartment must cost.

"So what do you think?" He stood nearby, his face attentive.

She smiled to herself. … He wanted her approval.

"To say it's nice would be an understatement."

"It's my favorite place. But let me assure you: I work hard for it. If I can enjoy this place as my home, it's only through my own effort."

"Well, I'm very impressed."

They stared at each other from across the empty, silent room.

"Why don't we have a seat?" He gestured to the black leather loveseat. Everything smelled like him, even the leather. It was tantalizing. He brought two glasses of wine over and placed them on the table in front of them. "We've had a stressful few days. … We're here together, alone." He reached into his pocket and withdrew a small circular box. He didn't need to open it for her to guess its contents.

Nagging fear and energizing adrenaline flooded her body. "What will happen?"

"Your eyes will be opened. Everything will become heightened. The lights will be brighter. Smells will become intoxicating. You'll be able to perceive within and without more sharply and profoundly. And the best part will be when we touch. It will be like electricity running between us." He ran his finger up and down her arm, the delicate caress irresistible. "I want to share this experience with you, Amanda."

The truth was that the anxiety of recent days had worn her reason thin. She didn't want to think anymore, to weigh the possible consequences or to consider the ramifications. She just wanted Ethan, and this was a conduit to being closer to him.

She took one of the pills from the box.

Ethan placed a pill in his mouth, swallowing it with some wine. "You don't have to be afraid. Just follow your desires. … We're only human after all."

Not allowing herself a second's pause, she swallowed the pill.

In just a few minutes, she sensed the overture of something new and unfamiliar coming over her. It reminded her of a lake before daybreak, a misty layer of fog covering the water. The fog was her life: melancholic Amanda, haunted by memories of her past, shunning any close relationship in trepidation of losing another loved one.

Now, though, a new dawn rose within her. The hesitancy and isolation she kept wrapped protectively around her like a blanket were unraveling, giving way to a total liberation. A surging energy pounded through her veins, vanishing the shadows of the past and awakening every joint and muscle of her body with an unrecognizable fire. The fog lifted on the lake, giving way to a blazing sunshine.

Everything changed. The lamp on Ethan's coffee table emitted a light that seemed to visibly flow, weaving its way through the air and wrapping itself in folds around the couch, encompassing both of them in pounding waves of luminance. Every pore of her skin seemed to fill with its heat, her bare arms prickling with heightened sensitivity.

Her body experimented with these attractions of sight and touch. Then she began to explore within herself. The despondency and persistent sorrow underlying all her experiences and thoughts no longer remained. Or maybe they still existed, but this new, more powerful force overshadowed her other feelings. Now came a rush of excitement, pulsing in rhythm with her heartbeat, which pounded inside her like the bass blasting at Little Pete's. She no longer wanted to sit on the couch, for its black leather now possessed so vast a depth that she feared placing her hand in the wrong spot, lest she fall into one of its imposing black holes. Only the man sitting next to her kept her still, despite the overwhelming stimuli of shades, pitches, and scents.

Amanda looked at him through this kaleidoscope, and it was as though she were seeing him for the first time. He had a power about him, unnamable yet definite in its forceful existence. He surely looked right through her, into the very depths of her being. She might have grown hesitant at this intimidating dynamism that he effused, but she was too awestruck by his appearance. Everything about him seemed more attractive, more appealing, more enticing. She took a deep breath and found his scent almost suffocating in its fragrant aroma. Had he worn more cologne tonight than usual? It seemed to waft from him like bacon sizzling in a hot frying pan.

"Amazing, isn't it?" His voice sang to her like a snake charmer playing his flute-like instrument.

She couldn't ignore its hypnotizing melody. He stretched out his hand, placing it on top of hers, and she gasped at the feel. It was as though he had shocked her, but instead of it being a sensation that caused her to flinch away, it pulled her toward him like two magnets drawn irresistibly to one another. He didn't move his hand, and the electricity sparked within her, releasing an exhilarating sensation up her arm: a glorious tingling, numbing her arm with a sweet, sensual euphoria.

"So this is what it's like to be happy …" She couldn't pull her gaze from his bright eyes.

"Happiness is sharing an experience like this with you." He shifted next to her so their bodies touched, the energy now sparking down her torso.

She closed her eyes, overcome by the power of the feel. Even with her eyes closed, images flashed. The darkness was gone; instead, beams of brilliant red light dashed before her like shooting stars. She would have continued to watch them, but the pull of Ethan's handsome face was more alluring.

For the rest of the evening, they played an odd game: he would ask her a question, sometimes of little relevance and other times more demanding of the privacy she had constructed around her. At times, she didn't reply, being too engrossed in observing objects in the room, such as the Oriental rug below them, which seemed to hover in midair, supporting them like a magic carpet.

Sometimes she did answer his questions, and when she did, the memories replayed in her mind with such vividness that she was convinced they were happening again. She returned to that Christmas afternoon when she sat despondent in her bedroom, snow falling outside the window. She reopened the paint set from her father and held the paintbrush again for the first time. Following another one of Ethan's questions, she walked again on Valor's campus for freshman orientation and registered for classes.

The colors swirled around her, a panorama of shades and pigments that reminded her of her paints, and time stood still. She looked at the clock at one point, which proved futile: the digital numbers rapidly changed, not pausing long enough for her to read the time.

"If you're wondering, it's Friday morning." Ethan must have followed her gaze.

Though her mind raced, her body yearned for rest. "I better get to class."

"Are you sure?"

"Yeah, I'm sure." She started to pull on her coat, but then took it right off. She was sweltering.

He drove her back to her apartment so she could retrieve her art supplies. He drove; she reveled in their blissful night. She snuck a look at him, his striking features highlighted by the morning sunlight. They'd had a misunderstanding, but now they were back on track. No, even better than that: last night had been the pinnacle of success. They interacted better than ever, sharing this marvelous, indescribable experience. Maybe, in light of that, it was time to make things official. She longed for the commitment and security of seeing one another exclusively, in a relationship. She didn't want to be just the girl Ethan hung out with; she wanted to be his girlfriend.

He parked the car outside the apartment building. The waning effects of the pill played upon his face, providing him an angelic hue in the golden light of day. "You shared so much with me last night. Thank you for trusting me."

"I'll share more. The more time I spend with you, the more I'll trust you."

Ethan gave her a final kiss, one concluding spark of electricity. "I'll call you later, okay?"

It took all her determination to open the car door. She stepped onto the sidewalk, the sunlight attacking her. Squinting from the painful brightness, she fumbled for the door to the building. Somehow she managed to reach the elevator and make her way into the apartment.

She had taken the plunge. And now she swam freely in a rapturous river taking her speedily toward her goal: Ethan.

Chapter Eleven

Do as You Will

Amanda was weightless and free. The shackles of a haunting past, social reclusion, inward isolation—they were gone. This moment alone mattered … here and now and everything that filled it, both within and without. This moment was perfect. *This is what utopia feels like.* How had she never known it before? How did she ever think it wrong, or undesirable? This was desire.

The past was gone. Time was gone. Days passed, weeks passed. But seconds, minutes, hours meant nothing and held no power over her. Maybe they always meant nothing. Her new way of life didn't need the regular rotation of day and night. Weekend or weeknight—what importance did they hold in this fluid existence of ecstasy? When exhaustion rose within her, she fell into an effortless sleep; when her body surged with adrenaline, she replied with a flurry of action and inspiration.

The agenda belonged to her, and she filled it with Ethan.

He held the key to this new level of reality. He took her by the hand and taught her the ways of this new world, this wilderness of euphoria. Embracing it meant embracing him.

The pill served as their binder, and its adventures blended them together, delving into the landscape of pleasure. How much she owed him for the release and liberation she now recognized …

Thanks to the pill, Amanda enjoyed a level of immediate understanding with Ethan and the elite society she'd now permeated. The pill brought her onto his team, and Little Pete's was their shared playing field. The game had no rules; they were each the champion. The novelty of their dialogue … the extraordinary insights … the audacious dreams that seemed just beyond her fingertips—all while driving with Ethan, crisscrossing the Manhattan grid. Her defenses had evaporated. Together, they were building a cosmos.

Her eyes opened to a ceiling covered in photographs. She stretched out her hand, and her fingers brushed an empty bag of chips, scattering crumbs onto the carpet. Relaxation and elation stirred within her. Warm embers of fire that had ceased producing flames still burned hot. She stoked them within, smiling to herself.

Light broke through the plastic blinds. Car engines roared and horns blared from the street below. She stretched, potential flooding through her arms and limbs. No coat hung on the hook on the back of the door—Nikki was out.

"Ethan?"

Intriguing silence.

The moment was a blank slate waiting to be written by her hand. What future would she choose for this corner of reality she inhabited?

Her shirt was drenched with sweat, and her curls were matted against the sticky skin of her forehead. She welcomed the cold water of the shower pouring over her. And then came another craving to quench: hunger. Three bowls of cereal in, the silence reverberated within her, a summons to action. She despised the safe and predictable; rather, boldness and audaciousness beckoned her now. Her eyes roved about the room until they fell upon her book bag. She checked her phone, pinpointing the day and time. She had Michael's class in an hour.

She put the sunglasses on her face, but not for hiding. With the tight green dress borrowed from Nikki's closet and tall black boots, it was her city and she belonged here. Amanda could be whatever she wanted, and this was who she was right now. She liked this person; it had been so long since she had loved herself.

People drifted about the front steps of the Masters Academy ... so many potential paths to pursue, but Leila walked straight ahead and Amanda jumped at the opportunity.

"Hey! Leila!" Amanda ran ahead and reached Leila, who turned around, wariness traced across her face.

"Are you coming to class today? You skipped again last time." Leila peered at Amanda from behind her thick, plastic glasses.

"What class is that?"

"It's Monday, you freak. We have Michael's class now—in case you've totally lost your mind. What have you been doing?"

"Enjoying myself. It's my life to do with as I please."

Amanda sauntered into the classroom and took a seat in front of her easel. Michael, upon entering the room, looked at her and raised his bushy eyebrows.

"Amanda?"

"Hey there, Mike. Congrats! You remembered my name." She smiled—this was fun.

He frowned. "You were absent last time when I spoke with each student about his or her semester project. Please come up to see me after class."

She smirked: she couldn't wait to show him her sketch. She had visited the Met several times during the past few weeks. Empowered by the pill, she'd spent hours rendering tone to her sketch, building up gradation. Form drawing demanded patience, but the pill helped make the whole enterprise entertaining. Her sketch was now an exact replication of the painting hanging in the Met. Just wait until he saw it. … He would know she belonged here, that she was destined for greatness.

At the end of class, she bustled up to the podium at the front of the classroom, her sketchbook in hand.

Michael peered at her. "Do you have your sketch?"

"Sure do."

She opened the sketchbook and flipped to the key page. Before them appeared *Portrait of a Mother*. The mother wore her royal dress, complete with intricate designs and detailing. She cradled the baby in her arms. The child gazed at his mother with devotion; she in turn stared at the viewer with her penetrating gaze. It was perfect.

Michael took the book into his hands and studied the image for a moment. He shook his head. "It's not right."

She gaped at him, and irritation boiled through her veins. "What's wrong with it?"

"It's a mother. But it's not the mother in the painting. You've looked *at* her, but not *into* her. You have to return to the Met and fix it."

Hands trembling, she snatched her sketchbook back. "I don't *have* to do anything." How dare he … how *dare* he tear down her work again! She turned on her heel and marched to the doorway. "I'll do the sketch if I feel like it!" Her scream reverberated through the hallway.

She left to a stunned silence; her boots made the only audible noise, clicking on the tiled floor, announcing her departure.

Amanda fled the building, her heart hammering and stomach twisted in knots. Confusion and dilemma greeted her outside. The sun shone too bright—and why the hell was it so hot? Like the skin of a snake, the enhancing layers of pleasure and power began to peel off her fragile frame. Yes, she was vulnerable … she was so weak. Now each footstep down the city block brought her one step closer to a sober awakening.

She played her role, spoke her lines. But this wasn't a stage, and no audience applauded. Michael had been silent. What kind of show was this? This was reckless, emotional abandon. *But … no, that's not right.* Why not express her frustration, her disappointment at his misunderstanding of who she was as an artist? She was free to say, to act, as she desired.

Things were wavering … fading within her … and in the vacancy came the old haunts.

How long had it been since she last took a pill? Her head pounded in time with the nearby jackhammer drilling into the pavement; thoughts and ideas spun in her mind with no compass or anchor to direct or ground them. Where was she going again? What was she doing? Too many people pressed all around her … crowding her on every side, waiting on the curb to go somewhere, anywhere—but where?

Panic came toward her like a tidal wave, and her legs shook. She had to keep calm and pull herself together. Ethan … where was Ethan? Maybe he was already trying to reach her, to save her from this downward spiral. She walked clumsily, digging through her bag trying to find her phone. She would have put it here—maybe. Her fingers closed upon the device, and she breathed a sigh of relief: an alert appeared that she had a voicemail message. Soon she would hear the soothing voice that was now the soundtrack of her life.

Instead, another familiar voice spoke in the recorded message, a voice that she had shut into a far corner of her mind because, in the haze of the past few weeks, she had forgotten about him: her dad.

"Hi, honey! Sorry to bother you. I know you're probably extremely busy with all of your classes. I just … I just wanted to tell you how proud I am of you. You already know that, but I can't help saying it again. To have my daughter at the only graduate art academy in the nation—it's just a real honor. Anyway, I know you probably have a ton of projects, and that's why I haven't heard from you in a while. But when you have a chance, just give your old man a quick call, okay? Can't wait to hear all about your classes. I'm sure you're doing great. Well, anyway … Chiara says hi. We'll talk soon. Love you!"

The last car sped by, and the mass of pedestrians began to move, but she retreated in an icy haze, seeking temporary refuge under the cool shade cast by the scaffolding overhead, where construction workers labored. A bedraggled man, eyes closed and graying beard covering his filthy plaid shirt, sat defeated on the sidewalk nearby, an open hat beside him with a few coins inside. A cardboard sign lay on his lap, reading: *Homeless.* What would her sign say—*Lost … Confused … Failure …*?

She rubbed her throbbing temples. The pill's influence was waning, or maybe it was just the jarring effect of her father's unexpected message.

Everything had been so simple, so relaxing. She had been happy … she could still be happy. But her dad. What would she tell him? She didn't have to tell him anything. It was her life, not his. She was her own person.

Who was this person?

Her self-definition began and ended with her art. Or at least it had up until now. She'd had goals and dreams long sought after: go to the Graduate Academy of Fine Art and begin her career as an artist. Were those no longer true and real? How could she have forgotten?

Her father was so proud that she had broken the generational cycle of manual labor and service work. She was the first one in their family to ever be accepted to an Academy, let alone a Graduate Academy. She had been the trailblazer for their family, reaching a new stratosphere of society they had never yet experienced. It wasn't just her dreams in jeopardy; it was her family's hopes and aspirations too.

"I'll do the sketch if I feel like it!" Her words, flung in irritation and resentment toward Michael, ricocheted back to sting her. Her dad seemed so certain she was "doing great" in her classes, but she didn't feel at all confident that was the case anymore. She had started this assignment, had (unwillingly) entered into its mystery. She had to see this through to the end. If she willed it, she could do it.

It was a concrete enough resolution to keep her from drowning in the tsunami waves of the pill's flickering presence. She didn't know where she would be in five hours or five days, but for now she walked toward the Met.

Amanda reached the outside staircase leading up to the Met's entrance, but got no farther than the first step. Surprise and then relief flooded her: a red Anaconda sat parked on the side of the road. She hurried to the passenger door, her heart fluttering in anticipation, and got into the vehicle. Ethan pulled into the avenue, tires squealing.

"Am I happy to see you!" She reclined against the headrest and sighed. "How did you know I was here?"

"Process of elimination. I got a little concerned when I didn't find you at your apartment. I was supposed to meet you there."

"Oh yeah?"

"Yes, but apparently I'm the only one who remembers that." He chuckled. "No worries though: I like a challenge here and there—a little hard to get."

"I'm glad you found me. Paranoia almost got to me first."

"That can be an aftereffect of the pill, if you aren't careful. But what I would like to know is why—out of all the places I looked—*this* is where I found you."

She groaned. "Michael said I have to go back to the Met and work on my sketch."

He took advantage of a red light and turned his puzzled face in her direction. "I thought you told me you finished that."

"Apparently I haven't."

"Is all that time and effort really worth it? The grade you receive in that class is arbitrary. It has little bearing on who you are as an artist. Michael won't determine your career; that power lies in your hands. Maybe your immense talent is better spent elsewhere?"

"I have a rule when it comes to my art: finish what you start. I don't like leaving something undone and incomplete. Plus, doing well at the Masters Academy ... you know, it's really important for me .... for my family. My family isn't like yours. My dad works construction. My sister is probably going to spend her life taking care of horses. This is my only way into a high-powered career."

"It's not the only way."

"What else is there?"

"I could get you into the NCP. They'd love you. You've got the creds. Just having graduated from an Academy distinguishes you. They would be blown away by your artistic abilities. You would be appreciated and affirmed. And they would help you advance."

She mused, chewing on her lower lip. "And I could do art for them or something?"

"Absolutely. We just hired an artist a few weeks ago. We're always expanding, so I'm sure there will be another opening soon."

"I don't think that's the kind of art I'd want to be doing, though."

"It might be a stepping-stone into what you would want to do. The NCP is like a big family. You could network and build connections with other people of influence. You could maybe get an internship there for now. You know, get your foot in the door."

"Maybe, yeah. But first I've got to fix this sketch."

"You're bound and determined to complete it?"

"You like games, so you should understand. It's a challenge I want to meet and conquer. I thought I *did* conquer it already, but I'll keep at it. I can do this assignment: 'If it's meant to be, it's up to me.'"

"I can't argue with that logic, can I?"

"I sometimes have a one-track mind when it comes to my art."

"I just hope that pretty mind of yours still has some room for me."

"Do I detect some doubt in that confident voice of yours?"

"Doubt? Never."

She glanced out the window. A billboard she hadn't seen yet attracted her attention. It had nothing to do with the latest designer clothing or preview of a featured movie. Instead, the billboard displayed a large, stone tablet. The top of the tablet read in bold letters: *THE ONE COMMANDMENT: DO AS YOU WILL.*

They began to drive by and she craned her neck, taking one last look. "Did you see that?"

"The billboard? I did see it. Do you like it?"

"Yeah, of course." She tilted her head, narrowing her eyes at his growing smile. "Wait—did you have something to do with that?"

"It's my design. One of the many projects I've got going right now."

She beamed at him, pride effusing within her. "You certainly made your point."

"I hope so. I want people to realize any religion that chains people to worshipping an empty deity is corrupt. It doesn't matter what name they go by; it's all the same in the end: Allah, Christ, Vishnu … all they do is give people a false idol they can worship and spend their lives trying to please when, in the end, they've forfeited opportunities they were perfectly capable of securing on their own. It's bad enough that these extremists ruin their own lives, but then they try to force their fairy-tale philosophies and laws onto everyone. We're a free nation—not a Christian nation."

"I can't wait to see your next work! Will you be doing another billboard?"

He put his car in park outside Little Pete's. "Not sure. There's talk of some big project coming up soon that they need everyone's help on. I haven't gotten details yet, though." He sat silent for a moment, looking out the window. "Speaking of things we can't wait for …"

"Yeah?"

"If you could have anything at all right now, at this moment, what would you want?"

The answer was easy; divulging it without the pill's assistance was not.

"It's okay." He reached out and held her hand. "Don't start closing up on me again."

"Alright." She sighed. "You really want to know?"

His intense stare confirmed an affirmative.

"I … would want to be in a relationship with you."

He shook his head, a bemused half smile on his face. "Correct me if I'm wrong, but I would venture to say that you and I have a relationship. What else would you call our interactions for the past couple of months?"

"Perhaps that is the *de facto* reality, but it's nice to make things official, you know?"

"I think, ultimately, we're both seeking the same thing: we want to be closer."

"That's the one thing you would want too?"

"Of course. But words aren't going to accomplish that. Some standardized, predictable verbal exchange involving me asking you to be my girlfriend and your assent isn't going to bring us any closer together than we are now. Maybe it's commitment that you're looking for, but a trite, social norm won't satisfy that desire."

"I think, at least for me, knowing that you want to be closer to me is all I require." Even if she never heard the word *love*, just realizing he needed her the way she needed him was all she wanted.

"Don't settle for so little. Aim higher. You want to become closer? Make it happen."

"And how do you propose I do that?"

"Show me your painting."

"Painting? Which painting?"

"You know the one. Show me the painting under your bed, wrapped up." His eyes played upon her face, burning with excited fervor.

When had she told him about her favorite painting? She couldn't place the time. She must have missed a lot during her drug marathon.

"I have an idea." He caressed her hand, running his finger around her knuckles. "How about you and I take a drive to your apartment? Nikki is at Little Pete's, so we'll be all alone. Just you and me … it will be the perfect moment we've been waiting for."

"Waiting for what?"

"Show me yourself. Show me your painting."

"No." Her answer was instinctual and left her lips before she could check it.

He reached over and embraced her, his strong arms wrapped around her. "We both want to become closer, but that's impossible as long as you keep these walls up between us. How can this thing between us work if you keep shutting me out?"

He pulled back and fingered one of her dangling curls. "I'm not asking you to show the painting to everyone. I'm not even asking you to show me all of your paintings. I just want to see that one. It's not that unreasonable of a request: artists show each other their work all the time; it's perfectly normal. It'll be an intimate moment between us."

Revealing her painting to Ethan was an irrevocable act: forever after, he would carry this piece of her with him. Once she gave it to him—once she let him see the painting—it would permanently belong to him too. She could never undo it.

"I still need time …" She mumbled the words and stared at her boots.

"More time? We're running short on time."

"Wh-What do you mean by that?"

"Are you content with the way things are? I'm not. If we don't keep growing closer, we will grow apart."

"Well then … maybe once I'm no longer distracted by this sketch, we can go forward … we can become closer … just like you said."

"If that's the case, you should finish that assignment as soon as possible!"

"That's my plan for tomorrow."

"I've got a few extra busy days at work coming up. But I know we'll find time to be together."

She took a deep breath. Perhaps showing Ethan her painting wasn't such a major life decision after all. Why should it be?

The next morning, she sat on the bench in front of *Portrait of a Mother*. She had unrealistically hoped Morgan would be sitting here for this final sketching session, but of course he wasn't.

She pulled out her charcoal and examined the painting in front of her. *I will do this. If it's meant to be, it's up to me.*

Under her examining eye, Amanda was certain she could replicate the mother. Her charcoal had defined the rounded cheeks, the heart-shaped chin, the long eyelashes that turned outward, and the thin lines by the mother's temples.

But it wasn't quite right.

As much as she hated to admit it, Michael was correct. It didn't look like *her*. Amanda pulled out her kneaded eraser and started from scratch once again. She poured forth more effort, examining every quality and facet of the mother's face.

I will sketch you! Yet Amanda's second sketch was just as erroneous as the first. She had drawn a lovely face, but it wasn't the mother's face. The singular characteristic that defined the mother was missing. She erased her work. The morning turned into afternoon, and the hours flashed by. Try as she might, nothing she did improved the image in her sketchbook.

Her eyes narrowed. *Why can't I sketch you?* She sat, at a loss for the next step. What was she doing wrong?

Her mind drew a blank, but in that stillness, Morgan's words echoed: *"That's my favorite painting! ... If I tell you what the painting means to me, it will prevent you from seeing it with fresh eyes. You have to discover its beauty for yourself."*

Morgan would know what was missing in her sketch. Plus, she admitted, she missed him.

~ ~ ~

She strode into Ethan's office, not bothering to knock. Of course *he* had an office. Daddy must have arranged it for him. Meanwhile, she was stuffed in a cubicle on the fourth floor, along with twenty other employees. But one day ...

Ethan didn't look away from his computer monitors but kept typing, his fingers flying along the keyboard. She flopped into one of the crimson armchairs, propped her feet on his mahogany desk, and helped herself to one of the mints in the crystal candy dish. She made sure to crumple the wrapper as loudly as possible and then tried to shoot a basket into the garbage can across the room.

Ethan at last sat back in his leather chair. "Nikki. What brings you off the fourth floor?"

"It's reckoning time. I've kept my part of the bargain. Said my lines, acted my part." She put her feet down and leaned her elbows on the desk's shiny surface. "What dirt did you dredge up on Amanda? When are you turning her in?"

"I think you forgot my assignment. Maybe because it's not *your* assignment at all. It's mine, and I'm taking care of it. My job was never to apprehend Amanda; it was to keep an eye on her."

"Okay, sure, whatever. What'd you see?"

He stood up and walked over to the tall window overlooking Park Avenue below. "The NCP asked me to investigate her, but I'm not stopping at that. You see, I'm going one step further: I'm converting her."

"You can't possibly be serious right now."

"I know her far better than you do: she let me in, but you shut yourself out. She's no enemy ... she's one of us. One day, she'll be working here—not against the NCP, but for it."

Nikki stared at him, dumbfounded. He was clearly an idiot, but this ... this was a whole new level of stupidity. "Look at her family! The Academy she went to!"

"She rejects her family. She left them to move here, to start a new life. She doesn't have the same values as they do.

As for the Academy, she wasn't involved in the opposition activity there."

"And you believe those lies?"

"She's not lying. I'm good at detecting lies. She's genuine … refreshingly genuine, actually."

She jumped up from her chair and whipped a piece of paper from out of her pocket, shoving it into his face. "Explain this then!"

He held up the paper and examined the photograph on it: a man with brown hair combed to the side, a gentle smile, and light blue eyes. "I've seen this face before. Who is it?"

"If you were doing your job right, you'd already know. That's Amanda's new BFF. They were spotted together at the Met and outside St. Patrick's. His name is Morgan. I'm surprised you didn't recognize the image: it's on the wall of suspected offenders in the conference room."

Ethan stared at the picture for another few seconds, then handed it back. "I don't need your help, Nikki. I should say, I don't need your interference." He stopped, his face darkening. "How did you know Amanda's whereabouts?"

She smiled back at him. "I had her tracked by the JPD."

He stepped forward, his eyes slit, his jaw clenched. "Leave us alone. Amanda is with me."

"Oooo … now we're getting to the real heart of the matter, aren't we? Amanda isn't with the NCP. She's with *you*. And isn't she just what you need? Someone who will stroke your ego at every turn. Someone who will sing your praises on end. You need to be adored and worshipped, don't you? She knows exactly how you tick, and that little bitch has you completely blind. That's why I'm having her tracked. I'm not letting her damage the NCP. *You* might not get her detained, but the hell if I won't!"

He grabbed her arm, his fingers clenching and twisting her skin. "If you harm her in any way …"

Despite the pain, she burst out laughing and bowled over in amusement. "I can't believe it! That's what this is about? You *like* her? … You do! You actually like that worthless piece of trash!"

He shoved her away, and she stumbled backward a few paces. His eyes blazed with fury. "Get out of my office! But I swear: you do one thing against Amanda and I'll end any chances you have at moving up in the NCP. I'll have you kicked right out of here onto the street. You're completely expendable."

Nikki smoothed her shirt and ran her fingers through her hair. She walked toward the doorway and then turned around, glaring at Ethan. "You know what? Amanda's going to destroy you before you can even raise one finger against me."

Chapter Twelve

The Living Dead

Amanda stood before St. Patrick's. The massive bronze doors, several steps above her, bore the sculpted images of famous religious figures. Her eyes roved up the cathedral's façade to the famous rose window, the finials running along the roof, and—even higher—the towering double spires. She kept her sneakers planted on the sidewalk, not quite ready to commit to the bottom step—one step closer to inside. From her close proximity, the organ's swelling hymn rivaled the shouts and sirens of the street behind her, and the sweet scent of incense lingered in the air alongside the exhaust of the cars and taxis.

Still, she remained, hands stuffed in her pockets and her glance wavering between the cathedral and crowded avenue. Maybe this was a complete waste of time. Weeks had passed since her last conversation with Morgan. For all she knew, he resented her never coming to find him. He could have moved on. He also could have simply moved: Hadn't he said he would only be in the city for a short time with his temporary work? What if he had already left?

"Amanda!"

Then, as if on cue, he appeared, waving from the other side of the street. With fast strides and a beaming, unabashed smile, he approached. His almost transparent blue eyes, his predictable attire, his joy—nothing had changed.

"You're here! You came back!"

She had rehearsed this conversation multiple times on her way to St. Patrick's. She was ready to confront his anger or bitterness. She had rebuttals prepared for any sarcastic, stinging comments. In other words, she had prepared for the reaction *she* would have given. She exhaled, relaxed her shoulders, and smiled in response to his warm, genuine welcome. She had missed this ... she had missed him.

"Hey, Morgan! How're things going?"

"Work is picking up. But what about you? What's new? How's art school? How's your sketch?"

"Things are okay. They'll be better as soon as I finish my assignment. I'm having some issues with *Portrait of a Mother*. That's actually why I'm here. I kind of need your help."

"You need help? That's the only reason why you came to see me?"

She glanced down. "That's not the *only* reason. I haven't seen you in a while ..."

"I understand. It's nice to have our connection back."

She nodded, grateful for his understanding. Talking with Morgan, even after some time apart, felt just as effortless as before.

"So what's the problem with your sketch?"

She sighed. "My professor said that it isn't *her* face. I'm missing something. I thought, since it's your favorite painting, you might have some insight?"

"Absolutely! I'm more than happy to help."

139

"Thanks. If we start walking now, that would still give us a chance to work on it before the Met closes."

"As lovely as that sounds, I'm afraid I can't—Mass is starting in a few minutes. But perhaps we can catch up for a bit?"

She couldn't ignore the hopeful note in his voice or his encouraging smile. What were a few more minutes, anyway? "Yeah, we can talk." She took a seat on the bottom step, gesturing for Morgan to join her. "It's okay we're sitting here, right? Are the people inside going to have a problem with this?"

"No, not at all. The cathedral belongs to everyone. That's one of the reasons why it's my favorite place."

She grimaced. "Have you always been into religion?"

His look became unfocused, and he spoke in a distant voice. "It's my purpose. It's who I am."

"I just don't get it. This God of yours doesn't answer prayers. Tragedies and suffering happen all the time. How can such a God be your purpose?"

"God is never the cause of evil."

"That doesn't explain why he allows evil. This world God created is pretty messed up. Isn't God supposed to be 'all-good'?"

"He permits evil because He so highly honors that word you hear everywhere these days: freedom. Freedom is not obtained by a repeal of laws or unleashing of passions. It is given to us by God."

"That's ironic, don't you think? The supposed giver of freedom straps people down with commandments and a list of 'don'ts' they're forced to live by. What kind of freedom is that?"

"It's true freedom! You see, it's actually the law that makes us free. When you play a sport, you need rules. How else would you know what you need to do, how to win, what makes you lose, or where the boundaries are." He counted off the points with his fingers. "The sports player achieves his glory when he's doing amazing things within the boundaries of the game. If anything goes, we aren't free; we become enslaved to our own lower desires and drives."

She rolled her eyes. "You and my dad would get along great."

"Well, freedom always means having a choice. That's the risk God took. He let us be free so we could choose good, in order to love. But that also means we can choose a lesser good … and that's where you find the origin of evil. People need the law that's inscribed on their hearts to guide their conscience to the truth. And it's the truth that sets us free."

"I'm following my own understanding of right and wrong. I don't need someone else to tell me what to do. I'd say I'm doing alright. I'm free and I'm happy."

"Happiness can be fleeting. It comes and goes, but joy … joy springs forth from the deepest recesses of your soul. No one but God can produce that."

A taxi sped by, its horn blaring. He paused a moment to let it pass and then continued, "Many movies and books feature zombies: the living dead. The reality is that 'zombies' are everywhere: people who go about day-in, day-out without knowing the purpose they were created for. They eat, they sleep, they work … but there is no life, no real freedom within them."

"Despite our connection, Morgan, you and I live two very, very different lives."

"Then, come, see my life. Just walk around the cathedral with me sometime."

A strong breeze rushed by, causing a flapping noise from behind them. Brushing a few curls from her face, Amanda turned around. Hanging from the cathedral beneath the United States flag was a large white banner. The banner bore an image—a man with a furrowed face whose piercing eyes stared back at her from behind silver glasses. Red piping lined his black cassock, and a large crucifix hung on his chest.

She stood up and walked closer, squinting at the picture. "Who's that on the banner? I could have sworn I saw his face before somewhere, but I'm drawing a blank."

The breeze brushed the banner again, unfurling it farther to reveal a heading in large Gothic typeface: *IN MEMORIAM*. Beneath the image were the words: *BISHOP STEPHEN FISHER*.

"Oh," she exhaled, as though she had been kicked in the stomach by an unforeseen enemy.

The memory came: the bishop's face as he stood on the stage, facing all of the graduates on that perfect May morning. She closed her eyes, bracing herself for the next recollection: the agonizing screams of her fellow graduates, burning to death in front of her.

She sensed a movement next to her. Morgan came to stand before the banner too. His close presence comforted her. He understood because they had shared that horror together.

She turned to him. "Do you think about that day often?"

"All the time."

"I guess you can never erase a memory like that. I know because I've tried so many times." She stuck her hands deep in her pockets. "Morgan, I've been meaning to tell you—I'm sorry. I … I never really thanked you for saving my life."

"It is a life worth saving."

She smiled for a moment, but then scowled. "And the graduates who died? What about their lives? God didn't consider them worth saving?"

"God loves every soul eternally and unconditionally. The people who died that day died because of freedom—an abuse of freedom. Didn't you listen to Bishop Fisher's speech?"

"I listened. I guess I don't remember much of it, though."

"He was assassinated because of those words."

"What are you talking about?"

He cast a furtive glance around and, stepping a little closer, lowered his voice. "The NCP lauds the uninhibited freedom of everyone … unless you inhibit the party's ends. The NCP will protect this 'freedom to do whatever you want' to the point of eliminating those who resist their agenda. The Justice and Protection Division protects the NCP, not the people of this nation."

"I don't know, Morgan. This sounds a little like a conspiracy theory."

"If only it were theory! In reality, it's too genuine. Valor Academy was one of the NCP's targets because it was a hotbed of opposition, raising up young leaders who wouldn't go along with the current popular opinion, but would rather take a stand against the NCP's philosophy and tactics. The JPD conducted the bombing. And that's why Valor is now closed—just one more religious institution shut down."

"What? Valor is closed?"

"Yes. Oppression, intimidation—it's all around you. And don't jump to the conclusion that the targets are any particular creed or religion … or any religion at all. Summer

Zünd—the councilwoman from Queens who's been publicly criticizing the NCP for months—hasn't been seen for two weeks now. The imam in the Bronx who had been encouraging his congregation to distribute anti-NCP fliers was found by his wife last week, dead in his mosque. And in the Upper West Side, the famous Buddhist leader, Do Quang Huyen, just fled to Vietnam after he appeared on television last month, voicing concerns about our current political climate."

"If people were actually missing, wouldn't we hear about it in the news?"

"The press is 'free' to cover whatever they would like, except anything that might jeopardize the NCP's freedom."

"Are you sure? How is that possible?"

"When freedom is understood as being secured through the action of man, then man sets himself up as the arbiter of freedom. And man's 'freedom' is always empty. It is just an illusion."

She stared at him. Morgan came across as a normal, well-informed individual. But this tale he was weaving now … it was a little out there. Sure, he adamantly believed it. How could she, though? Ethan and Nikki and their friends—all avid members of the NCP—were decent people. They were, in fact, her favorite people. Just because they didn't share Morgan's same religious views didn't make them bad … and certainly not murderers. Perhaps Morgan was a little more extremist than she had originally thought.

The church bells tolled the hour, interrupting her musings.

Morgan walked toward the cathedral door. "I need to be going. If you meet me here again tomorrow, I'll have time to help you with your sketch. See you then?"

"Yeah, okay, thanks." She waved goodbye and began walking to the nearest subway station.

The moment she got off the subway at the South Bronx stop, the clouds let loose a torrent of rain—a steady, drenching shower. She had no coat or umbrella, and within minutes, her saturated clothes stuck to her body like glue. She didn't care; she strangely enjoyed the rain. Maybe it was because of her favorite painting. Even now the raindrops seemed like tears, falling from the dark storm clouds above. She kept her head down, watching the puddles that she sloshed through. It was just like her painting, except these puddles didn't contain the face of the beautiful woman who gazed back at her. That treasured painting always made her feel better. It just had that kind of effect.

The rain relented in its fury, and within a block, it had slowed to a gentle sprinkle. She still had at least fifteen more minutes until reaching home—the perfect amount of time to call her dad. A call home was long overdue. She spoke "Call home" into her phone and waited. *Ring … Ring …* Perhaps her dad stayed late at work today. Sometimes he did that if his crew had a deadline to meet. *Ring …* Maybe he misplaced his phone again.

Her dad's voicemail came on—she would have to leave a message: "Hey, it's me. Sorry for not calling you back sooner. I hope things are going okay. … I'll try to call you tomorrow."

Ethan and Nikki were both at work. It seemed like they were spending more and more time there now. Without their company, the evening dragged by. Amanda put the final touches on a still life for Advanced Drawing … one assignment complete, at least.

On Tuesday, after her Visual Perspective and Advanced Drawing classes, she headed toward St. Patrick's. Rain continued to pour down, but she came armed with an umbrella this time. The bright lights inside the cathedral illuminated the stained glass windows, providing a stark contrast and colorful welcome against the grayness of the dismal sky. She wouldn't find Morgan outside today, so she climbed the steps and, after taking a deep breath, crossed the threshold.

The enormity of the building was evident from its exterior, but it still did not prepare her for the immensity within. Everything about the cathedral and its Gothic architecture was huge; standing there, she was so very, very small. She was plain too, compared to the regal, white marble splendor. The impressive cross-ribbed vaulting soared high above her head on the ceiling. The stained glass windows lined the walls, even more striking from this interior view: the brilliant shades of glass glowing in the light.

Yet perhaps equally astonishing was its emptiness. She had anticipated having to maneuver her way through a sea of tourists snapping pictures. Instead, the only signs of life were bodies lying prone on the back pews, asleep. A man rested just a few feet from her, his baseball cap covering his face, a plastic bag full of soiled clothing perched beside him. Aside from the slumbering Unfit, she was the only person standing in the far back of the church.

She began to walk up the center aisle, staring at the columns lining either side and analyzing their features. They had foliated capitals, another Gothic characteristic. Back at Valor, she had taken a Greek civilization class. She wrote a term paper about their architecture styles ... and now recalled that their columns had three kinds of capitals. What was the name of the one most like these? *It must be Corinthian.* The block capitals of the Romans later on had an even relief in line with the walls; these capitals moved diagonally in space, toward the interior. The labor involved in producing the individual leaves and vines must have been outstanding. The foliated capitals served no architectural purpose, but, as ornamentation, they were finely produced.

Amanda spied Morgan in his crisp white dress shirt kneeling in a pew toward the front and went to stand next to him.

He lifted his head after a moment, made the Sign of the Cross, and then turned toward her. "Very good timing. I just finished praying for you."

"Well, if praying actually accomplished something, then I guess I would say thanks."

"Pray with me sometime. Then maybe you'll understand."

"I know about praying. I could say the 'Our Father.' I went to Sunday school growing up. You don't need to teach me anything. Life has already taught me enough. Life has shown me that praying is nothing beyond empty, habitual words. I don't pray to anyone; if I need something, I'll pray to myself. So you keep on doing what you do, and I'll keep my safe distance away."

"If you should ever change your mind, I would like to ask you the favor of saying a prayer for my work."

She raised her eyebrows. "You want *me* to pray for *you?* What could possibly be so bad that you're desperate enough to ask me for prayers?"

"It's about my job. It has become increasingly difficult."

"Well, what kind of work are you doing? Maybe I can help you with something?"

"Yes, you can help: your prayers are the best help you can give me. But you are free to do as you will. Anyhow, I think we've spoken enough. Shall we?" Morgan rose and motioned toward the doors. "I believe you have a sketch to complete."

She returned his smile—it was hard not to.

They traveled toward the Met, walking together under the umbrella. Morgan held it, but to his own disadvantage.

She glanced at his shirtsleeve, exposed to the steady rainfall. "You should move the umbrella more toward your side. You're getting wet!"

He laughed. "The rain doesn't bother me. It's fine."

"If you're sure." She shrugged. "This better be my last trip to the Met. I've never struggled with an assignment this much. But it ends today. I'm getting it over with, come hell or high water. Then everything can go back to normal."

"What do you mean? What is going back to normal?"

"Well, there's this boy I know …"

"A boyfriend?" His voice remained neutral, but he flattened his lips into a thin line.

"Yeah. You could call him that. It's time he and I get closer. And once I have this sketch behind me and no longer consuming my time and energy, we can take our relationship to the next level."

"Hmm."

"Well, what about you? Any special woman in your life?"

"Yes … I suppose you could say that."

"Really? What's her name?"

Morgan stopped walking, and Amanda, huddled under the umbrella, came to a halt beside him. He studied her for a moment—a penetrating, searching gaze that seemed to probe deep inside her. She stood, holding her breath. The moment of silence lengthened, and her expectations mounted.

He turned away. "This might be a conversation better suited for another time."

Amanda's cheeks burned, and her stomach knotted. Her words came out a little too quickly, her voice a little higher than normal. "Yeah, sure—absolutely. No problem."

She began walking, staring at the laces of her sneakers. Had she missed something? She couldn't deny that her connection with Morgan was something special. But it was strictly platonic. At least, that's how she'd always understood it. Was it possible that he felt differently?

They entered the Met. Morgan didn't pay for her admission—a reassuring sign. There was no conceivable way this could be misconstrued as a date, then. No, this was strictly business: a friend helping a friend. He *must* see it that way too. She cast a glance at him. He walked with a smile, swinging his arms by his sides. His face seemed composed, and his eyes darted back and forth between different art pieces. Maybe she had misinterpreted his statement. She started chewing on a fingernail.

They came to their destination, and he bounded forward to sit on the bench before *Portrait of a Mother*. "What a marvelous piece of work! I wish I could stare at her all day."

She plopped down beside him, flinging her book bag onto the floor and bending over to rummage for her sketchbook. "Better you than me." She flipped to her unfinished sketch, displaying her work for him to see. "Okay, what am I doing wrong?"

He took the pad into his hands, examining it. "Let me ask you a question first: Why do you want to do this sketch?"

Amanda stopped herself from rolling her eyes and laughing. "Isn't it obvious? I don't want to flunk my Studio Painting course. But even more than that, I want to show everyone, especially myself, that I can finish this. I have the skills to sketch her: it's up to me to do it."

"There's your problem."

"My problem is that I want to do the assignment?"

"Your problem is *why* you want to do the assignment." He shook his head and handed back the sketchbook. "It's all about you. It's pride; it has nothing to do with *Portrait of a Mother*. You just want to conquer."

"And how else am I supposed to approach it?"

"The greatest works of art are an *emotional* response to something. There is something powerful about a work of art. It's more than lines, colors, and texture. Art speaks to us ... sometimes in a mysterious way that the artist does not even realize. There is meaning behind the image, just as there is meaning behind our words. You are missing something in your sketch. You are missing *who* this mother is—her inner spark, so to speak. That is making your sketch one-dimensional—lines and shadows without feeling or life."

"How am I supposed to know a mother's 'inner spark'? I'm not a mother—and I don't even have one anymore."

"But you do. You have always had a mother. And you still have a mother." He stood up.

"Wait a minute! Where are you going?"

"I gave the help I have to offer. You have what you need to complete the sketch."

"Really? That's all you've got?"

"Spend time with her." Morgan gestured to the painting. "Put your proud ambitions aside for a moment and be with her. Become acquainted. Learn who she is. When

150

you have done that, begin sketching again." Waving, he turned and walked away.

Amanda stared at the painting, furrowing her eyebrows. *I have to finish this assignment. And somehow I need to know you to do it. … So here I am. Teach me who you are.*

She sat—for ten minutes, for forty minutes, for an hour. She was still, silent … directing her thoughts away from deadlines or acclaim. Instead, she put forth all her effort to enter into the mystery of the painting before her—something she was skilled at with her own work. She had become an expert at tapping into that internal wellspring of inspiration that guided her personal work. It was not a skill; in truth, it was a kind of gift, one she did not wholly understand, one she maybe didn't even fully appreciate. *Portrait of a Mother* was a bit of an enigma, but so, too, were her own creations. Was there a key to understanding? Something that originated in the quiet recesses of her soul that drove her brushstrokes?

The longer she stared and contemplated, the more she began to see. She had tried to sketch those honey-brown eyes, but her initial attempts missed something. Those windows of the soul revealed humble wisdom: the mother did not look arrogant or haughty, but she was intelligent, brilliant in her own way. Amanda had also attempted that smile. It seemed, at first glance, a bemused smile, perhaps in response to the baby's movement. But, no … that wasn't quite it. The mother directed her smile to the viewer, not the child. It was as though she was encouraging the viewer, inviting him or her to stay. Maybe it was even a smile of recognition. Soft, rosy patches graced her cheeks, granting her a sign of joyful vitality and life.

Not wanting to lose the revelations opening in her mind, Amanda reached for her pencil and began again. Her strokes and shadings became faster: she felt driven by the impulse that she'd at last began to understand.

A long time later, she sat up straight and examined her work. It wasn't a perfect likeness. No, not quite—she hadn't fully acquainted herself with the mother. But it would have to do for now. She packed her bag, stood, and started to leave. Where the hallway turned, she paused and took a final glance over her shoulder at *Portrait of a Mother*. It had been an obstacle that she'd wanted to rid herself of. Now she was free at last, this part of the assignment done and finished. Why, then, did she feel like she had just met someone she would have liked to have known better, but had missed her chance?

It still rained, so she scurried down the steps of the Met, huddled under her umbrella. She glanced at the parked cars nearby, wishing to spot Ethan's red Anaconda, just as it had been waiting for her another time. If only he were there now. She longed to see him, to feel him. Now, with the sketch actually done, she wouldn't be pulled away from him any longer. Ethan had promised they would talk later that day, but she couldn't wait that long. As soon as she got home, she would call him. With that driving motivation, she hurried her steps along.

～～～

Nikki stood sentry by the window, her breathing rapid and shallow. She glanced at the tracking app on her phone: Amanda came closer, a flashing dot of red making its way down the block … red like the fiery rage burning inside of Nikki. She clenched her free hand into a fist, her manicured nails digging into her palm. She pushed them deeper into her flesh, welcoming the sharp pain: a concrete way to release the pressure building in her chest.

Maybe ten more minutes and then the flashing dot would reach this location. Ten more minutes until Amanda would step into the apartment. The rain was probably making her curls even more frazzled. Nikki would give anything to be able to yank each strand out of that freakin' creep's head.

Amanda had spent her morning—again—at St. Patrick's, fraternizing and consulting with a classified perpetrator, known only as "Morgan." They still didn't know his last name, but Nikki would have recognized his face anywhere: his picture was plastered all over the NCP monitoring systems. *He* would not be a threat for long. Morgan would be taken care of tomorrow night. The problem was Amanda.

Just the thought of her name made Nikki's head pound like the jackhammer tearing up the street below. Amanda dared to spend even more time at St. Patrick's—that accursed place—and then had the nerve to show up now at their apartment, acting like they were the best of friends. To think that the miserable traitor slept in the bed next to her … Nikki's stomach churned. The girl was a complete fake. She had sensed it from day one, and she had been exactly right. The cheap, beat-up sneakers, playing tagalong like a needy puppy, the constant awkwardness: it was all part of the persona Amanda had adopted. Nikki ground her teeth.

And, of course, Ethan had played right into Amanda's ploy. He had fallen for it—and for her—completely. He was so blinded by his pride and desire, he couldn't see it. How much info had Amanda sucked from him? What classified details had she then passed along?

Nikki's pulse raced. She swallowed and forced herself to inhale. She had this. Ethan was worthless: she couldn't give a crap what happened to him. But Amanda … Amanda was dangerous. She had completely infiltrated their inner group. That little twit was so confident of her plans that she was associating with defectors in broad daylight!

That wasn't all, though. Amanda could destroy Ethan. ... She could destroy Nikki too. If the top leaders of the NCP found out what was happening, then Nikki would be implicated. How could she not be? They were living together! Sure, she never really trusted Amanda and had been tracking her. That wasn't going to get her off the hook, though: she should have turned in the imposter a long time ago.

She caught sight of the portrait Amanda had done of her. The bold rebelliousness in the painted face was her favorite part of it. Amanda had seen that in her. ... She had seen too much. Well, fine: now Nikki would use that violence against her. She'd be damned if she would let that phony take her down. No, she would make the next move. It would be easy enough. The gun was under her bed. She could frame it as a suicide—coerce Amanda to write a letter to her family, stuff a bunch of pills down her throat.

Nikki's phone buzzed. She looked down: the red dot had reached its destination. She glanced out the window at the street below. No sign of Amanda. She was probably already on her way upstairs. *Click!* There was the key in the lock, then the doorknob turning. If only she had the gun in her hands right now, she could blow Amanda's brains out before she could utter one more cursed lie ...

She stood there, staring at the front door. Amanda scuffled into the apartment and, upon seeing Nikki, jumped. Could Amanda read the sheer hatred written on her face? Amanda dropped her umbrella, and little streams of runoff trailed across the linoleum floor.

"Umm ... hey. Are you ... Were you waiting for me?"

Of course she would play the part of the fool. "Yes."

"Oh. Sorry. What is it?"

"Cut the crap, Amanda. I know exactly what game you've been playing."

"Wh-What are you talking about?"

"You think you're clever, right? You play your role well. Say all the right lines. I mean, you do it so well that you've even convinced Ethan."

"Nikki, please. I don't know—"

She couldn't take it—she couldn't stand still a second longer. Springing toward the kitchen counter, Nikki grabbed the nearest object—a cup—and hurled it against the wall, where it burst into dozens of pieces. Amanda jumped back, flinching from the sound of the impact.

Nikki's voice rose to a scream. "Stop! Stop pretending that you don't know what I'm talking about! I *know* where you were today."

"I was at the Met. Finishing my sketch. But how did you—"

"Yeah right ... at the Met ... sure. That's been a real convenient pretense. I warned Ethan over and over about you. I've told him you've been visiting St. Patrick's. I told him who you've been with."

Amanda's face relaxed. "Oh, you mean Morgan! There's nothing to worry about. Honestly, he's just been helping me with my art assignment. He's an old friend from back home."

"'An old friend?' ... Of course you've been friends for a while. You and all your buddies at Valor. You must be great friends with lots of benefits. I can only imagine the kind of 'projects' you're working on together."

"What! I would never cheat on Ethan!"

"Lies. You've been lying to me from the very beginning." Nikki positioned herself in front of Amanda, letting her rapid breaths push Amanda's dangling curls back and forth. Nikki dropped her voice to an icy whisper. "I've been watching you. And I won't stop until I've crushed you."

Amanda swallowed. Then, cowering away with her head lowered, she hurried into their shared bedroom.

Nikki smirked. What a wimp. That should shut Amanda up for a little while.

For now, she would need to focus on tomorrow's work, but then, as soon as possible after that victory, she would be free to take care of Amanda for good … a permanent solution. Then *she* would be the one praised by NCP leadership, not Ethan. *She* would be the one who took down, single-handedly, that filthy spy.

She yelled out one final time, "Don't go to Ethan with your sob story! He's at work and won't talk to you."

~ ~ ~

Amanda returned the phone to her pocket and sat on the edge of her bed, her eyes not straying from the door. Her teeth were chattering, even though she didn't feel cold, but she still pulled a blanket around her shoulders. She tried to process what had just happened. Was Nikki crazy? Did she have a psychiatric condition? Had she taken too many pills?

Whatever the case, Nikki had wrongly accused and threatened Amanda. So much for any friendship they'd shared. There was no point to argue and debate with someone who already had her mind made up.

She glanced at Nikki's bed, just a few feet away, and squirmed at the thought of sharing the same bedroom tonight. She probably wouldn't sleep at all. Maybe she could stay the night somewhere else? Ethan wasn't an option: as Nikki had said, he was working. Obviously, spending the night with Morgan wasn't a wise idea—no sense giving credence to Nikki's false claims. She didn't know the others in Ethan and Nikki's social circle well enough to impose upon them. Besides, they were Nikki's friends anyway.

So she had nowhere to go for now. Tomorrow couldn't come fast enough. Then she would see Ethan, and she could ask him about Nikki's episode. He would have some advice or even offer her a place to stay for the time being until this blew over.

But maybe this wasn't just a passing thing with Nikki. Maybe Amanda would never be safe here again.

CHAPTER THIRTEEN

UNVEILING THE PAINTING

Amanda arrived at 5th Avenue, between 50th and 51st, the next morning and found St. Patrick's even more stunning in the early-morning radiance. She paused on the sidewalk, admiring the cathedral, awash in sunshine.

Inside, she paused for a moment in front of the *Pieta*, one of the cathedral's prized works of art. The Virgin held the dead body of her Son in her arms. They were two figures, but the sculptor had fashioned them as a unified composition: so interconnected that they were almost one. She could understand that. She knew well the bond between a mother and child ... and the pain that came when death severed that bond. The anguish and devastation Amanda carried inside, she saw reflected back on the Virgin's face. But something else was there too, evident beneath her veil. The Virgin wore a look of peace, of resignation. Amanda shook her head and backed away. How could anyone find peace when she literally looked death in the face?

She found Morgan in a front pew, praying. She sat in the pew behind him, taking in the beautiful resplendence of the building.

He then made the Sign of the Cross and turned around, facing her. "Good morning, Amanda."

His greeting was a bit more subdued than usual, his smile not quite so wide. She sat up a little straighter in the pew and peered at him. "Hey, Morgan. Everything okay?"

"I just have a lot on my mind today."

"Work stuff? Still hard?"

"Something like that. But how are you? What brings you here today?"

"I don't know actually. I just needed somewhere to go and think. Somewhere peaceful … My apartment isn't the most welcoming place right now." She shuddered a little. "You know, as I'm sitting here, looking around, I can see why it's your favorite place. From an entirely aesthetic standpoint, the cathedral is very impressive."

"I'm grateful that you've had the opportunity to experience it."

"I might stop in here again. Not to pray, but just to be here."

They began to walk down the aisle together.

"It's kind of an oasis in the center of New York," she said.

"I spend hours just being present here. Words aren't even needed."

Outside, they lingered on the sidewalk.

Morgan faced her. "How did things go at the Met yesterday?"

"Yeah, I wanted to tell you about that."

"How about we take a walk to Central Park? There won't be many more beautiful mornings like this."

"Okay."

The trees lining the park revealed hints of autumn colors: auburn, gold, and crimson. It seemed odd that there could be such beauty in something that was dying. The air felt cooler today, and she wrapped her corduroy jacket closer around her.

Morgan glanced at her. "So tell me about *Portrait of a Mother.*"

"The experience wasn't what I expected. I kind of enjoyed it—I just sat and thought about her."

"What did you learn?"

"I'm not certain I learned anything about her, *per se.* I suppose it's more of a feeling. You were right: I could understand the painting better once I stopped trying to conquer it. The mother is paradoxical. On the surface, she's like any other mother, just sitting there and holding her child. Yet there's this unspoken majesty and power about her that draws you in and holds you there. I can't express it fully."

"I think it would require a lifetime, gazing upon that painting, to understand her." He paused by a park bench. "Do you mind if we sit?"

She looked around. In front of them, the pond water rippled in the slight breeze, shimmering crystals sparkling in the light. She had been here before: this was the precise spot where she and Ethan had sat on their first date. It made her miss him even more.

They took a seat, neither one speaking. She didn't need to cover the space between them with words: their connection filled any emptiness. Meanwhile, the haunting, andante strumming of a nearby street guitarist provided a musical backdrop. The acoustic melody seemed to come from some other time and place. She leaned back on the bench, tilting her head toward the sun. The song transported her away from her worries and cares.

The final note trembled in the air, and she kept her eyes closed, not wanting to leave the brief moment of tranquility just yet. "Thanks for suggesting that we come here, Morgan. It's nice just to sit in the sunshine."

"I wish it would rain."

He spoke with heavy sorrow. Rattled by his unexpected reply, she opened her eyes and studied him. A frown creased his normally bright and jovial countenance, his blue eyes troubled. She had never seen him like this before, and it jarred her. All she wanted in that moment was to erase the pain that marked her friend's face and to return the beaming smile that was so inherently Morgan. Impulsively, she leaned over and hugged him. His pain had become her pain too.

Footsteps approached and stopped just behind them. She sensed someone's presence looming behind her. She pulled away from Morgan and turned around.

Ethan's face was dark in the shadows where he stood beneath a leafy maple. Yet his eyes, furious and accusatory, couldn't be more obvious. She bolted from the park bench as if it had been on fire and stared at him.

"Amanda?" His voice was icy with disgust and accusation. "*This* is how you work on your sketch?"

Her chest tightened. This had to look so terrible to him … "Ethan, this is my friend, Morgan. He and I went to Valor Academy together. He's just an *old friend.*"

Ethan's gaze shifted to Morgan, who had risen and now stood beside her. "I'm Ethan, Amanda's boyfriend." His words hung in the air like a swarm of bees. Ethan confronted her again. "I went to your classroom today to see you. You weren't there."

"I wanted to show Morgan my sketch. … I finished it yesterday and he's been helping me with it, so I thought—"

"Wait a minute. Let me make sure I understand you: I offered to help you with that sketch weeks ago. You rejected my offer but let this guy help you? You told me you were going to finish the assignment as soon as possible so we could get closer. And now that it's done, the first person you seek out is *him*? Have you been lying to me this whole time?"

"This isn't what it seems! You know you're everything to me. Morgan is just helping me with my assignment. I've known him for a while now. He … He saved my life once."

"I thought I was doing that for you. But I must have been wrong all along. I assured you awhile ago that I would always tell you the truth. I won't be strung along with lies and false promises. I have a good solution for you, Amanda." He clenched his jaw. "We're through."

Ethan turned around and stormed off. She watched, stupefied. She should be beside him, holding his hand. Now he walked away from her, a permanent goodbye. She should call out to him, stall his exit from her life. At least she could run after him and clamor for some fleeting shred of reconciliation. But her throat constricted, and her feet froze to the pavement. Soon he disappeared into the distant crowd. Her whole being focused on those two acerbic words, words now burned into her consciousness: *"We're through."*

How could they be through? They were just beginning. Astonishment and regret at what just transpired, so unexpected and spiraling out of control, overpowered her.

"Amanda?" Morgan touched her arm.

She spun around and glared at him. "Leave me alone!"

"What do you mean?"

"How can you be so stupid?" she screamed.

A passerby stopped and stared at her, but she didn't care.

"I've let our friendship destroy what I had with Ethan. You've been so nice to me, but look at the cost! Don't you know how much Ethan means to me?" She was dizzy, the shock ebbing away to be replaced by a deep agony.

"He's dangerous for you."

"What? Here you are, Mr. Holier-than-thou, and you judge him before even talking to him? You hypocrite! If our friendship means anything to you, I'd think you would at least care enough about me to be considerate to my boyfriend."

"Why does he mean so much to you? If he were committed to you, how could he walk away from you so easily?"

"Maybe because I wasn't committed enough to him. Or rather, I didn't show it. But you know what, Morgan? You know nothing about it. In fact, you know very little about me. Ethan was the only one who truly knew me. Not the person I portray to others, but who I really am—the person I try to hide."

"Does he really know you? Or did he just convince you that he does? It seems to me, if he knew you, he would be the one consoling you now. But where is he?"

"If you really knew me, you would know that the man who just left means more to me than anything else. You would know that I love him, and now I've lost him." A stinging pricked her eyes and she startled. Tears? She hadn't cried since her mother died. But of course she would cry now: she had let someone else into her heart and gotten hurt, just as she'd worried she would.

"Do you know what love is?"

She ignored Morgan, her thoughts wild with plans. She had to win Ethan back ... she had to show him how much she cared ... how much she loved him. She snubbed Morgan and strode away.

"Amanda!" He dashed after her. "Where are you going? What about us? What about the sketch?"

"The sketch is done. And so are we."

"Where are you going?"

"That's none of your business. I think you've caused enough damage already."

"It is my business. I care about you. We have a connection."

"No. We *had* a connection." She stopped then, turning to face him. "I don't want to see you ever again."

"Please don't do it."

"Don't do *what?*"

"What you're planning to do. You'll regret it, Amanda. Please, listen to me!"

"You have no idea what I'm going to do. And besides, I'm free to make my own decisions. Why don't you go back to St. Patrick's and pray?"

At the crosswalk, she cast a glance behind her. Morgan stood motionless in the spot where she had left him, his eyes still begging her to come back. She glared and then joined the other pedestrians making their way across the avenue. She checked the time on her watch. If she ran, she would have barely enough time. Amanda began a frantic sprint, weaving her way through the crowded sidewalk, ignoring the curses and exclamations of people that she bumped into during her mad dash.

Winded and hoarse, she reached the Masters Academy, forcing herself to keep going, running up the steps and through the hallways to the classroom. Skidding to a halt, she watched students file out of the room.

"Leila!" Amanda's shout prompted a dozen people to turn and stare, but she saw only one.

Leila looked at Amanda like she was a raving lunatic. Maybe she was. Leila half turned—as though to ignore her—but Amanda rushed in front of her and said, "I need your help!"

"What is your problem? You're a complete psycho, do you know that?"

"Forget that for a sec." Amanda pulled her to a corner of the hallway, out of earshot. "Do you have the pills with you?"

"Maybe. What's it to you?"

"I need one. No, wait …" Amanda weighed how hard her task would be. "Make that two. Look, I know you have them. You always bring the box to Little Pete's. Please, Leila."

"Well, where's your cocky attitude now? I might be able to help. But it depends on how much you got."

"I have enough."

Leila gave a smug smile and told her the price of two pills.

Amanda raised her hand to her forehead, rubbing it as though to produce some idea of what to do. The pills would bankrupt her account. "Are you serious? It's that much?"

"Of course I'm serious. In case you never picked up on it, I don't like you."

"Okay, fine."

"What was that?"

"I said, 'Fine!'" Amanda shouted, her emotions spiraling out of control. "Let's just do it fast. I don't have all day."

Each minute meant sixty seconds further from fixing things with Ethan. She feared she had only a small window of opportunity in which he would reconsider his decision. Then, she was certain, he would forever lock the door of forgiveness.

She and Leila walked together to the nearest ATM. Amanda bypassed the warnings informing her that this would close the account and then removed the bills from the machine—the hard-earned cash from years of scanning groceries at Supermarket Saver. In a simple exchange for two pills, it was all gone. Leila walked away jubilant, already yakking on her phone, likely bragging about her ridiculous profit, reaped from desperation. Amanda raced the other way, the pills tucked in her pocket and the next step forming in her mind.

She reached her apartment. Thankfully, Nikki was absent. Amanda only needed one thing. She grabbed it and then popped the pills into her mouth. In less than five minutes, she hurried back outside and paused, about to hail a cab. But what about money? She dug into her pocket and pulled out a ten-dollar bill: the last cash left to her name. It would be sufficient for one ride on the subway into Manhattan. She sprinted toward the station, hoping that the two pills wouldn't kick in until she reached Ethan's apartment.

Waiting for the subway, her mind flooded with the mental bombardment that had been flung at her, not just today but for weeks. She could hardly think straight anymore. What was up or down, right or wrong? Did such dichotomies even exist? In a way, ever since she stepped into that lounge on her first day at the Masters Academy, she was powerless. Ethan had captivated her. He was larger than life, the man she admired more than anyone. He enthralled her.

So how could she help what she was about to do? He was worth it. Besides, she had the pills. They would make everything safe. Once she entered that confident, wondrous bliss of euphoric existentialism, consequences wouldn't worry her anymore. As she hurried onto the subway and then sat down, she could already feel the pills manipulating her body, pulsating within her, intermingling within her bloodstream.

She never created a Plan B. She fidgeted in her seat, her anxiousness fluttering like the subway car. Ethan could be working right now. What were his hours anyway? Where exactly was his office? She still didn't know many things about him. But she couldn't blame him for not disclosing everything to her. Goodness knows that she kept enough from him. She'd kept too much from him: her aloofness had contributed to this seismic schism between them.

Amanda left the subway, her heart racing. She ran, frantic that she might be too late, and turned onto his block. What possible reactions might she face? She spotted his apartment, five buildings down. A lump formed in her throat. ... He might not even invite her inside. Maybe this time—this brief, impersonal encounter at his front door—would be the last time that she would ever see him. No more soothing voice, no more placing her hand in his, no more evenings spent with familiar faces at Little Pete's. This wonderful world she had built around him would crumble in an instant.

If it were even possible, her heart began pounding faster: she saw his car parked outside. He was here. It was now or never. She hoped against hope that a closed heart would not similarly close the door on her.

She rang the doorbell, the cheerful chime mocking her somberness. The chimes rang in her head, reverberating over and over again. The front door seemed to spin in front of her, almost like a revolving door to an old-time department store. Good: the drugs were beginning to work.

The door stopped spinning, and Ethan opened it. He leaned on the doorframe, blocking her entrance. "Can I help you?"

Amanda hated the coldness, as though she were a stranger coming to sell him pet insurance. "Can ... Can I come in for a minute, please?"

"You better give me a good reason." His face was a blank mask. Didn't he care at all?

"I want to show you something."

"What?"

"I want to show you myself. I want to show you my painting."

He stared at her, wide-eyed. "Come on in."

His apartment was dark. The large living room curtains, blocking the sunshine, gave the illusion of night. He took a seat on the edge of the couch, waiting for her.

In some ways, she had waited for this moment her entire life. To be close with someone, to let him into her heart and to feel secure enough with him to share this intimate piece of herself, was a tremendous gift. She had assumed it would never come. She pressed the canvas close: it was wrapped modestly in brown paper, shielding it from unwanted viewers. She looked at Ethan, his lustful stare not straying from the covered painting. Why wouldn't he meet her gaze? This wasn't just about what the painting looked like … it was deeper than that … it was sharing her very self, her "inner spark" with him. She hadn't imagined the first time being like this: removed, impersonal, a desperate attempt to salvage a failing nascent relationship.

She shook her head, dismissing these flighty doubts. Now was the right time. He was the right man.

Amanda tugged at the brown paper, beginning with the upper corners. Once given, it could never be taken back. But she loved him. That made everything right. She justified it. Everything undone, she deliberately removed the paper, the painting laid bare before him. There were the drops of tears flowing from the stormy sky. There was the umbrella composed of the three interlocking hands. There was her image, standing and looking at the puddle formed at her feet. And there was the lady ... the beautiful, mystifying lady whose reflection shone from the puddle.

For a split second, it seemed as though everything stopped. She waited, holding her breath, for his reaction. Then, without any warning, the entire room jolted, tilting onto an angle. Gasping, she caught herself, just preventing herself from tumbling to the floor. Just as quickly, the room jerked the other way, like a ship tossed by angry waves, trying to right itself. Meanwhile, the floorboards began to rattle and shake. The wood panels began to burn, the heat reaching her feet even through the soles of her shoes. She coughed, as though smoke filled her lungs, and her heart pounded. She cast a furtive glance around the room. The paint on the walls begin to ripple, their surfaces becoming an effluent stream of dark, liquid red: blood. She started to shake, an overriding sense of darkness and doom spreading through the room. Paranoia consumed her.

Shadows inexplicably appeared on the walls. But how was that possible? The curtains were closed—no light existed to cast such projections. Enlivened, the shadows emerged from dormant positions, transforming into prowling, terrifying creatures of the night. Thick, black pus oozed from their disfigured limbs, the stench of rotting flesh wafting toward Amanda, her stomach struggling to blockade its vomit.

She wanted to scream in horror, but no sound escaped from her open mouth. The shadowy, fallen creatures continued to grow, unfurling their scarred, mangled bodies, disproportionate in height and figure. Then they spoke, each in a strange, unearthly language. It was a jarring, disillusioned jumble of consonants and guttural expectorations that— though unintelligible to human ears—somehow cut to her core.

Panicking, she sought out Ethan's eyes, but he stared at the painting in her hands, his smile a bizarre and twisted aping of true joy. She looked at him, not sure whether to be more terrified of him—and what was about to transpire—or these peripheral puppets of some even more nightmarish fiend.

Ethan rose from the sofa and approached her, his gaze ravenous as he said, "This is finally ... mine." He seemed to relish his own words and prowled ever closer.

The hideous sounds surrounding them heightened, a frantic chorus approaching its climax as Ethan's hands stretched forth upon the object of his desire.

In an instant, it was gone.

Amanda had relinquished it, and it was never to return.

Blackness followed, and she welcomed this darkness: a numb and obfuscated escape.

CHAPTER FOURTEEN

UP IN FLAMES

Amanda reopened her eyes—perhaps minutes or hours later, maybe even days. Her mind was cloudy, as though a thick fog had descended upon her. Her cheek rested against something smooth and hard. Everything was quiet and still. She lifted her head.

She lay prone on the wood floor in Ethan's living room. Nearby, she spied her book bag, unzipped and its contents spilled out. Searching her hazy memory for what had brought her here and then transpired, fleeting images flashed across her consciousness, snapshots of a living horror. A long, whimpered moan escaped her. Hurried footsteps came in response.

"Amanda?" Ethan crouched beside her, his voice full of concern. "Are you awake?"

Instinctual fear gripped her, and she shrank from his outstretched hands. She considered him. He appeared perfectly normal, save the worry that creased his brow. She scanned the living room. Everything seemed impeccable: nothing out of place. The only difference was that now the curtains were open, revealing a night sky.

Ethan watched her, frowning. "How are you feeling?"

"What happened?" Her voice sounded hoarse, and her words trembled.

"Do you remember what I told you the first night you found out about the pill?"

She closed her eyes, wishing the panic would ebb and her racing heart would stop pounding. "N-No ..."

"I told you that when I take the pill, I make sure I'm always in control. I don't exceed my tolerance level. How many pills did you take before coming here?"

"Two."

"That's what I thought. One too many."

"So ... everything that happened ...?"

"When you take a small dosage, you have pleasant hallucinations. Take one too many and you end up ... well, you've experienced what you end up with." He took her hand. "I'm sorry it was so bad for you. I couldn't even help: you wouldn't let me touch you. Here, let's move to the couch. That'll be more comfortable."

Amanda swayed, light-headed, and clung to his arm. She moved her body, but it felt like it belonged to someone else.

"See?" he said. "Everything is fine now. You're safe here."

She began to nod but gasped instead: her left arm was streaked with dried red liquid. "I'm bleeding!"

"Oh, that?" He chuckled. "Relax, Amanda. It's just paint."

"Why do I have this on me?"

"I tried to stop you, but you were determined to paint, and it's hard to reason with someone who has taken too many pills. I guess you had a fit of creativity that couldn't be contained. You said you wanted to work on your sketch."

He pointed to the coffee table in front of them, where her sketchbook sat. It lay open, though her angle prevented her from seeing the image. Gripping the table for support, she reached over and held up the sketchbook.

Her knees buckled and she collapsed back onto the sofa, the fear that had never fully subsided now coming back in full force. She stared, transfixed, not being able to turn away from the revulsion in front of her.

Her sketch of *Portrait of a Mother* was there, all as before ... except for the mother's face. A strange image stared back at her, not with maternal affection, but with a monstrous beckoning to torment. Dry, caked lips, though ghastly thin, opened in a sneer; the structure of her nose was corrupted, bones jetting out in an abnormal monstrosity; her cheeks were sallow, the grayish skin dangling as though dead.

The mother's eyes revealed the necessity of the red paint. Small, snake-like slits encased two fiery red pupils, themselves enshrined in a cloak of bloodshot chaos. It resembled the face of a corpse, yet somehow still looked alive. It was more than a sketch made by flesh and blood. It was here—with her ... and she couldn't take it anymore.

Casting the sketchbook away from her, Amanda attempted to liberate herself from this inexplicable force, now prowling there against her.

"What's wrong? What is it?" Ethan picked up the sketchbook. He looked at it for a moment, then shrugged his shoulders, unperturbed.

"Can't you see? Can't you feel it here with us?"

"Trust me: it's just the pills. Actually, if you ask me, I think your sketch looks much better. It's a huge improvement over the original. What you've done is provoking and bold—very avant-garde. I don't know why you don't like it now; when you finished, you told me it was your greatest work."

She hid her face in her hands, despair overcoming her. What if the most frightening thing was inside, *in* herself? "What's happening to me?"

He put his arm around her, but Amanda felt nothing. "Just give it a few more hours. The drug will wear off and you'll be back to normal."

"I think I've reached the point where I can't return to who I was. I don't know who I am."

"Everything is out of proportion when you're in this state. Why don't you try to rest for a while?"

He helped her lie down and tucked a soft throw around her. Then he stood up and began to pull on his jacket.

"Wait! What are you doing? You're leaving? Where are you going?"

"I'm sorry; the timing is terrible. I've got to go to work."

"What time is it?"

Ethan glanced at his phone. "It's ten o'clock at night."

"You work nights now?"

"They called me in. We have a special assignment. Everyone is required to be there."

"But what about us? What about everything that happened? I showed you my painting and ... and you're just leaving me?"

"Everything is going to be fine, Amanda. *We're* going to be fine. I'll be back as soon as possible, and we can talk more. You can stay the night. Just promise me that you won't leave the apartment. You're liable to do anything in this condition, and I don't want something to happen to you."

In spite of everything, she smiled faintly: he still wanted her. Her eyelids grew heavy. "Just don't be too long."

He stroked her hair and kissed her on the forehead. He walked out the door, and shortly after, she heard his car roar to life. He sped away, the wheels squealing.

Sleep seemed like a welcome reprieve. She began to slip into a still oblivion …

"I showed you my painting." Her words to Ethan echoed in her mind. She sprang from the couch, every nerve in her body alert.

Where was her painting?

She didn't see it anywhere. The stillness of the apartment felt eerie, as though some unseen stranger watched her every move. Unnerved, she crept toward the front door, ensuring that it was locked, and then closed the curtains.

She performed a meticulous search of the living room, even looking underneath the couch on the off chance that her painting had ended up there.

Amanda stood still, suspicion rising within her. Ethan hadn't said when he planned to return. He wouldn't be back soon, but how much time did she have?

She made her way down the hallway, trying to control her fright. The pills were causing this paranoia, nothing more. She peeked into the first room on the right: his bedroom. There didn't seem to be anything out of the ordinary. His open closet revealed a row of designer shirts hanging alongside his dress pants. A single picture sat on his dresser, and she picked it up to take a closer look: a man and a woman standing together, with the United States flag waving behind them on a large flagpole. The man had dark black hair, the woman a dazzling smile—Ethan's parents, she guessed. She replaced the picture, doing her best to return it to the exact same spot.

She checked the bathroom and then came to a closed door at the end of the hallway—the final room. She stood in the dark hallway, debating. Ethan had never shown her inside here. Footsteps sounded nearby and she jumped, gasping. But there was no one; the footsteps belonged to the tenants upstairs.

Amanda needed to do this and do it quickly. She had no idea when Ethan would return. She grasped the doorknob and turned. The door opened, emitting a loud, high-pitched creak. In the dark, the vague outline of a large desk hovered against the opposite wall. She fumbled along the wall for the light switch, flicking the power on to reveal what lay hidden.

What was presumably Ethan's office sat before her. Breathing a small sigh of relief, she walked in. But what did she expect anyway? It's not like he would have dead bodies piled in here.

And there was her painting, lying face down atop his massive desk.

But her relief plunged right into despair: a carving knife lay discarded next to her painting, and tiny shreds of canvas lay strewn about the desktop like confetti. Trembling, she picked up the canvas and turned it around. The beautiful woman's face in the puddle was utterly destroyed. He had used the knife to rip and shred it, leaving a gaping hole in her beloved painting.

Tears streamed down her cheeks unchecked, and her mind grappled for some kind of rational explanation. It escaped her, though, leaving her reeling from what had been stolen from her. She gathered the tiny shavings of what had once been the beautiful lady's face, like the ashes of a beloved kin, now cut and severed. She let them fall from her hand, still in disbelief. *Why? ... WHY?*

The pain, overwhelming in its intensity, engulfed her. Never had she felt a sensation like this before: to have been hurt so deliberately and profoundly by the one she had loved like no other.

The realization stifled her, yet the pill's lingering influence fanned the flames of a growing fury, unmatched by any she had previously known. The suffering within her spewed forth into a fury so potent, so encompassing that all her desires fueled into one: revenge. She wanted to wound Ethan as much as she could … to make him experience all of her excruciating pain and a million times more.

Like a chainless lion, she raged upon everything that was his. Stacks of neatly piled papers, thousands of dollars of audio equipment, a priceless lamp of exquisite Italian glass, brand-new commercial-grade computer monitors, Swiss-made leather chairs—these she pounced upon, ravaged, and destroyed.

Then her eyes fell upon his laptop. It was his work computer. Three simple, yet haughty letters were etched upon the casing: *NCP*. She raised the marble paperweight, about to smash the laptop with it. But … no. His career at the NCP meant everything to him. It was more than just a job; it was his livelihood, his frame of reference, his system of belief. She wouldn't destroy the computer. She would *steal* it. It would inflict more pain on him to know that his work … his precious projects that should bring him power and fame … all of it was in the hands of someone else. She didn't give her actions a second thought; after all, Ethan himself had taught her that stealing was subjective and could be justified. And so, taking the laptop and her painting, she dashed from the carnage of the room.

Arriving in the living room, she threw her sketchbook and the laptop into her book bag and then, clutching the ruined painting close to her chest, rushed out of the apartment. She barreled down the steps, never looking back. She had come here mere hours ago, gripped with a despairing fear that she would never be welcomed back inside. Now she left, fleeing, with every desire never to return.

She had no money for a cab or even the subway. Walking was her only option. Her most pressing concern at that moment was Ethan's Anaconda rearing its arrogant head, the unforgiving headlights pinpointing her escape. But, in her fury, she almost felt ready to confront him.

She couldn't return to her own apartment. Nikki would be there, and she was just as much a part of this as Ethan. Everybody Amanda knew, in fact, was part of it. Everybody but one person. And now she ran to find him.

Amanda raced beneath clear black skies. There were no stars out, but a full moon cast an ominous glow about the vacant Upper West Side. Why were the streets so empty? Wasn't this the city that never sleeps? She hurried, knowing it must be close to midnight. Morgan would not be in the cathedral at this time, but he would return tomorrow, as he did every day. She could safely pass the final hours of the night in the sanctuary of St. Patrick's. This horrible night would give way to day, and with morning would come Morgan. The stinging, caustic words she had flung upon him earlier in the day returned to haunt her.

He'll forgive me … he has to forgive me … why wouldn't he forgive me? She chanted the phrases in rhythm with her feet as they pounded the concrete.

She reached the Midtown section and reassured herself that it wouldn't be far now until St. Patrick's. Panting from the fast-paced run, she slowed to a walk. Just a few more blocks and she would be safe. Moving down the sidewalk, the night air around her became warmer. She slowed her pace even more, pressing her hand to her forehead. Was she feverish? Another block later and the waves of heat increased, but she still couldn't place their origin. She turned the corner, and the heat became even more intense—and, along with it, the unmistakable sound of crackling, hissing, and burning. She resumed her fast pace, unease growing within her.

The skyscrapers obstructed any clear view of what lay ahead, but now—amidst the tall rooftops of office buildings and high-rise apartments—she could distinguish bright orange flames climbing high into the dark October sky. The heat and noise escalated with each step that brought her closer to St. Patrick's. Now dread drove her forward.

She stopped across the street, gazing from the curb. St. Patrick's stood before her, engulfed in flames. One half of the cathedral was missing. A massive hole filled the space where one steeple used to stand. Its twin now crumbled with a deafening roar, clouds of smoke and dust billowing forth. The intense heat made beads of sweat trickle down her forehead. The smoke suffocated her, but she couldn't move. The few remaining stained glass windows burst, and broken shards of glass showered down to the sidewalk, her right arm rising to shield her face from the sharp fragments.

Amanda sensed movement on the other side of the street and looked through the dust and smoke. A small crowd of people—the Unfit—stood gathered there, watching. And there, in the back of them …

"Morgan!" She ran toward him. "Morgan, what happened?"

He looked at her, apparently not at all surprised to see her there. "Can't you recognize evil when you see it?"

"How did this happen?"

"There was a meeting at the cathedral tonight. A large group of people gather here regularly to organize opposition to the NCP. This bombing is the NCP's way of sending a message to us and to anyone who dares to stand in their way of radical liberty."

"How can you be sure? Where are the firefighters? Where's the JPD?"

"The JPD won't help us! This was done *by* the JPD."

He and the others held a silent vigil, beholding the destruction. She stared blankly ahead, the story at last coming together. Nikki and Ethan both spoke of a large upcoming project for the NCP ... Amanda had spotted Chloe scouting out St. Patrick's ... Ethan had left mere hours ago for some urgent task ...

"Morgan!" Amanda wrung her hands, wild panic in her voice. "I know who did this. I was so wrong about you! I was so wrong about everything. Please!" She grabbed his arm. "Please help me. I want to fix things. I want to join you. I know I've messed up ... more than you realize. But I can give you information, tell you all about them. Please!"

"There is one thing you can do. But you have to promise me that you will do it."

"Anything. Just tell me."

"Leave." He stared at her, his blue eyes cold. "I want you to leave the city."

"Leave? Look, I know I made mistakes. I can imagine why you want nothing to do with me anymore. But please don't send me away!"

"You promised! You have to go! Now!"

"In the middle of the night?"

"Go back home. Take the 1:00 a.m. train from Grand Central. You can make it if you leave immediately. You'll transfer at Poughkeepsie and then, after the train, take a taxi the rest of the way."

"I—I can't."

"Why?"

"I don't have any money left."

"Here." He pulled a wad of bills from his pocket and thrust them into her hands. "That will cover the expense. Now go!"

"You don't even want to say goodbye?"

"We have no time. Go!"

She turned, tears flowing, and ran toward Grand Central, the hellish flames of St. Patrick's bidding her a permanent farewell.

CHAPTER FIFTEEN

GOING HOME

Amanda sat alone by the window, the train hurtling northward and the city growing more and more distant. Soot peppered her hair, and the stench of smoke permeated her clothing. Everything had changed so drastically and so jarringly: she existed in a numbing state of shock. She felt like she had stepped outside the present time and place and witnessed the fallout of her actions as though all of them belonged to someone else. She found it easier to pretend that she was a mere actress, and that sometime very soon, the play would end, the curtain would fall, and she would remove herself from this horror.

Was it possible that just this morning she had strolled through the beautiful autumn air, walking to St. Patrick's, and had stood admiring the building, desiring to snap a picture of it? If only she could return to that moment. If only she could remove herself from her perdition. But she had done this, and in many ways, she had set into motion the events that snowballed into this tragedy.

She replayed that final encounter with Morgan over and over again. The train was empty, discarded soda bottles and gum wrappers the sole artifacts of travelers gone by. So she let her tears flow unchecked. She wished Morgan's reaction had been different, but she didn't blame him for what he did. Everything had changed. In that desperate ploy to convince Ethan not to leave her, she had given herself to him in a way that could not be undone.

One day, a few months ago, she'd rode on a crowded bus to the city to begin a new life. Now she rode away on a deserted train, away from broken hopes and dreams. Popping pills, skipping classes, emptying her bank account, ending her friendship with Morgan, sketching that horrific face on her *Portrait of a Mother* ... she had done these things of her own choosing. No wonder Morgan wanted her out of his life. Many times he had tried to encourage and convince her to choose the better path. In return, she had insulted and rejected him. Now it seemed only fair that he would sever their friendship.

In her self-absorption, she had failed to ever gain even basic details about Morgan. Despite their connection, she had no way of reaching him. Where did he live? What was his number? Not that it mattered much now: in her frenzy, she had left her phone behind in Ethan's apartment.

Following Morgan's final instructions, she prepared to transfer at Poughkeepsie to the Adirondack train. She faced a long layover, however; her next train wouldn't depart until 5:30 a.m. She passed the early-morning hours in the drafty, desolate train station, similarly cold and empty inside. Morgan had described zombies: the living dead. Had she become that? Had she chosen that life?

Daylight broke, and she began to watch commuters lining up to enter the morning train headed into the city. She joined the smaller crowd on the opposite track. The plush seats aboard the northbound train were a welcome change compared to the wooden benches in the station, and she appreciated this fleeting comfort, leaning back and curling her legs underneath her on the seat. The train departed, and she turned her painful thoughts toward Ethan.

Even here, miles outside the city, the littlest remembrance of him plunged her heart into boiling torment. He had betrayed her, destroyed her, and no matter how far she fled, she could never run far enough. She looked at the ruined painting beside her. ... She couldn't come up with a single motive for his cruel deed. Why would he hurt her so purposely and deeply? Amanda looked at the empty spot on the canvas where the lady's face should be, and her vision blurred once again with tears. Ethan had used her, like this canvas—and then discarded them both. She had the sudden urge to drench her mouth with disinfectant, to somehow erase the feel of his corrupting kisses on her lips. He was not confident; he was self-centered and cocky. He was not brilliant; he was cunningly deceptive. He did not love her; he loved to use her.

Was any of it ever real or genuine? Did she even truly know this man she thought she loved? She couldn't have. How could she ever fall in love with a man who orchestrated bombings and presided over murders and persecutions? Maybe the Ethan she knew never even existed. All those moments of happiness, of belonging, of feeling loved … they had been a mask, a grand ruse. Those pleasant feelings lacked any substance: they had all been manufactured, illusory sentiments that had now vanished like the ephemeral effects of the pill, leaving her even more empty and alone. It was just the shadow of love.

She couldn't sleep, so she stared out the train window, recognizing the familiar territory of the majestic Adirondacks—home. It had changed since late summer, when she had left for the city. The grass had turned brown, burnt from the heat and dying in the cooler autumn weather, the threat of frost looming closer each night. The trees provided a stunning display in the early-morning light: bright oranges, blazing reds, and golden yellows, but she turned her eyes away. The reds and oranges reminded her of the flames that had consumed St. Patrick's.

The train approached the station at Westport. Good old Westport: "A gateway to the Adirondacks," as the town motto boasted. It was her gateway to home. That was her sole comforting thought. She hadn't seen her dad and Chiara in months, and at this moment, she desperately wanted to be with them. Their unconditional acceptance would be a healing balm for her waywardness and their house an ideal refuge from the trauma of the city. She didn't know what explanation she would provide or what details she would relay to them. But, ultimately, it didn't matter: their love was greater than her errors.

The pull of home motivated her to hurry off the train. Unexpectedly, she found a taxi waiting outside the station and entered it, sighing with relief to be on the final leg of the arduous journey. She glanced at the driver. He wore a Yankees cap, which shadowed his thick black eyebrows.

"Where to, miss?" he called over the country song playing on the stereo.

She pulled the remaining bills from Morgan out of her pocket, counting them. It wouldn't be enough to get her all the way home, but it would at least get her mostly there. She could walk the rest of the way.

"Fort Christopher, please."

"The real boonies, huh?" He took a swig of coffee, placed the Styrofoam cup back in the holder, and put the car into drive. "So where you coming from?"

"South." She looked out the window, hoping to give him the pointed hint that she didn't wish to speak with him.

"You from around here?"

"Yeah."

"Nice, quiet area. Great place for fishing and you can't beat the views. I like it. ... Been here about eight years now."

The twangy song came to its close, and the DJ came back on: "It's a pristine fall day out there, folks. Really couldn't ask for better weather. High's going to reach 63 by the afternoon; slight chance of rain this evening. We've got a short commercial break, but stay with us for another forty-minute block of today's best country! Right here on *your* WP 104.7!"

The driver removed his gaze from the road and studied her in the rearview mirror. "You know, your face looks awfully familiar. What's your name?"

"Amanda."

"Last name Burrow?"

The little hairs on the back of her neck rose, and her glance shot upward, meeting the man's scrutinizing stare. Her gut instinct told her to lie, and so she shook her head no. "Amanda Johnson."

"Huh." He scratched the stubble on his chin. "I could've sworn you were Kevin Burrow's girl."

"No ... the name doesn't ring a bell." But her response was a little too delayed.

The taxi driver fell silent, his face now bearing a pensive frown.

Amanda's pulse began pounding, and she commanded herself to calm down. Her dad met all kinds of people through his construction work. Unlike her, he was an extrovert who made friends effortlessly. This taxi driver was very likely one such friend.

186

Outside the window, familiar sights greeted her: Scoops, where they would get ice cream in the summer ... the single-pump gas station ... Supermarket Saver, bedecked with pots of mums and grinning scarecrows ... all of Fort Christopher's meek array of services and amusements. And in every direction, like silent giants overlooking the sleepy town and its dwindling population: mountains. Everywhere mountains. They were the skyscrapers of Fort Christopher.

"So, uh, where you headed to, exactly?" The driver kept shifting his hand position on the steering wheel.

"I'm just visiting a friend a few miles down the road." She pointed in the opposite direction from her house. "You can just drop me off here at the corner of Follen and Larch."

"Nah, I'll drive you. Just give me the address."

"Thanks, but it's such a nice day that I prefer to walk."

Once parked, she gave him the money (all that was left of the cash from Morgan) and hurried out of the car. She struggled to keep a relaxed, normal pace. About thirty yards away, approaching Upland Avenue, she dared to peek behind her, just to reassure herself that everything was fine. But the taxi was idling, and its driver stared at her.

Her unease grew with each step. What was the driver's problem? She couldn't do anything, however, except walk. At last, ten paces later, the car engine roared to life, gradually fading into the distance. She waited a solid fifteen minutes— just to be extra careful—then swiftly retraced her steps, crossing the street past the old barber shop and then beginning her trek on Tillinghast Avenue, which would lead her home. She tried to shake off the unsettled feeling that had come over her. Soon she would be on *terra firma* and could tell her dad about the weird episode. He would likely get a good laugh out of it, reassuring her that the taxi driver was an old buddy of his.

Each time a car passed, she looked up to see if it was the taxi back again, but each time she was wrong, and as the minutes ticked by, her panic subsided. The farther she walked, the greater the distance between the houses ... and the larger the plots of land. The sidewalk had long ago ended, and gone were any streetlights. Now she treaded on familiar territory: backcountry roads that winded and curved, lined with old oaks and maples. Shadows filled the potholes dotting the surface of the road, moving snatches of light. The branches above shuddered in the silent breeze. The dead leaves crunched beneath her feet. She had missed this.

At long last, she spotted her family's mailbox standing at the end of their driveway. The nearest house was about a five-minute walk away. Gazing across the lane, she saw endless mountain peaks. She turned to begin the ascent: their house sat far off the road, on top of a hill, making the driveway always a tiresome hike. She trudged up the gravel path. Large piles of leaves and pine needles had accumulated, so much so that they filled the tire ruts. Why hadn't her dad raked yet? It was now the first day of November.

Winded from the steep incline, she passed the crest of the hill and entered their secluded refuge. Here she always enjoyed complete isolation: from the front yard, someone could see no other home or sign of human life. Chiara was likely at the apprenticeship she had at the horse farm a few miles away, but her dad's pickup truck was parked in its usual spot on the side of the house. It struck Amanda as odd that he hadn't left for work yet, but she hurried to the porch: she had an incredible urge to see his face and hear his voice. Here she stood, the prodigal daughter, but her dad would run over to greet her with open arms.

Of course her house key was back in Nikki's apartment, so she gave a loud knock on the front door. She waited. No response. Perhaps her dad was upstairs and couldn't hear her? She pounded a bit more forcefully—they really should get a doorbell. She bent down and pulled the spare key from underneath the welcome mat at her feet.

"Dad?" She walked inside the front hallway and heard the sound of canned laughter. The television must be on in the living room. "Dad?" She peered inside the room.

A talk show played to an empty room. She went over to her dad's chair, an overstuffed recliner, worn and threadbare from overuse. His favorite mug, which her mom had given him on his birthday years ago, sat on the end table, half-filled with coffee. Commanding the television to turn off, she listened for sounds of movement. Silence.

She moved into the kitchen and reeled from a horrid stench. An open gallon of milk sat on the counter, its spoiled, sour fumes wafting throughout the room. Chiara's chair was pulled out from the kitchen table, a bowl of cereal at her place. A spoon sat in the bowl, the cereal bloated from the moisture of the milk, soggy and entirely unappetizing. Her dad might have let the dishes go, but Chiara was almost compulsive about cleaning.

Amanda walked toward the reeking milk container with the intention of throwing it out, but the daily calendar perched nearby caught her eye. It belonged to her dad. Tearing the page to the new date was part of his morning ritual—as much a habit as pouring his morning cup of coffee. She picked up the calendar, puzzled … October 18. That was two whole weeks ago. Swallowing uneasily, she picked up the milk jug and walked toward the garbage can on the other side of the kitchen. But there, lying on the floor, was her dad's cell phone.

Had he dropped it? Why would he just leave it there? She snatched it up, swiped in his passcode, and saw that he had a message. She played it back and heard her own voice: "Hey, it's me. Sorry for not calling you back sooner. I hope things are going okay. … I'll try to call you tomorrow."

She had called her family on Monday. Today was Thursday. She tried to trace the days back in her mind. When had her dad called her last? She had no idea: thanks to the pill, a whole swath of her time in the city was a formless void in which she couldn't remember what she said or did and when.

Regardless of that, the dated calendar page, the playing television, the bowl of cereal, the phone inexplicably lying on the floor—these all pointed to one conclusion: something was wrong. For some reason, her dad and Chiara had left very abruptly. Had they gone somewhere, not expecting her return, and were waiting to call her? Yet why would they leave no information? And her dad's truck … they couldn't have gone far without the family's sole vehicle. No, they couldn't have left, at least not voluntarily.

No, not voluntarily … but *forcibly?* She laid a trembling hand on the counter to steady herself. Waves of icy fear poured over her. Twenty-four hours ago, she never would have considered this explanation realistic, but in light of what she had just witnessed and experienced—that the NCP was willing to resort to anything to protect itself—Morgan's claim about people being abducted now seemed terrifyingly credible.

No, it was more than credible. It explained everything. Of course the NCP would be concerned about her dad. He was far from being politically correct and made a concerted effort to blast the reigning party, a trait that solidified him as one of the most active members of the local opposition group.

The government prosecuted only one crime: treason. In the eyes of the NCP, her dad was a criminal.

Had Ethan known? Did he realize her dad was a target? Did he … help arrange her family's disappearance?

No … no, she wouldn't think about that. … Ethan didn't matter right now. She only needed her family. She wanted to be with them more than she wanted anything else now. Everything else faded into distant shadows in her mind: Chiara and her dad instantly consumed her thoughts, desires, memories, and feelings. She had always assumed they would be here: she had taken their presence and love for granted. And now they were gone. She couldn't lose them … she couldn't lose her dad and Chiara, not like she had already lost her mom. Overwhelming panic began to cloud any rational thinking she had left.

"Dad!" Her petrified screaming, sputtered with half sobs heaving from her tightened chest, reverberated through the vacant house. She sprinted from the kitchen, up the stairs. "Dad!"

Chapter Sixteen

The Hound of Hell

Each step up the stairs raised more desperate questions: Where could her dad and Chiara be? Were they hurt? Were they even alive? At the top of the landing, Amanda's eyes darted about, even as her heart jackhammered in her chest. No sign of anyone, not a sound or movement anywhere. Amanda sank to the floor, her body shaking from head to foot, violent sobs racking her body. Her family was gone and she, too, was now lost.

She inhaled between cries, trying to catch her breath, and in that pause, a quiet moment of clarity struck her. Her dad wasn't the only person speaking out against the NCP; he led an organized group that met regularly. She had never given them a second's thought. It had always been her dad's thing, just like painting was hers. But now she clung like a life preserver to the hope of that opposition group: they could help her. Maybe someone even knew information about her family and what had happened.

She would have to look up some of her dad's contacts and call them. But first she should make a reconnaissance of the upstairs. Maybe she could find something, some sign or evidence as to what had happened.

Peering into Chiara's bright pink room, Amanda felt a lump growing in her throat. Chiara's bed was unmade, the blankets tossed onto the floor as though she had jumped up and sprang downstairs for breakfast. Amanda rifled through the items on Chiara's desk and found a blue ribbon hidden under a library book: Chiara had won first place at her horse show a couple of months ago. Amanda covered her mouth and closed her eyes: she never even bothered asking Chiara about the horse show. She had been too busy taking pills and being with … No, she couldn't think about this now. Time to go to the next room.

She entered her dad's bedroom. At first glance, nothing seemed out of the ordinary. The usual mess filled the top of his dresser: a measuring tape, a box of matches, coins pulled from his pocket at the end of the day, crumpled receipts. She rifled through his top drawer and found the pile of cash he liked to keep on hand. Putting the money and matches into her book bag, she moved on to the final room upstairs.

At any other time, entering her bedroom would have been such a comfort, but not now. Her room looked unchanged, just as she had left it months ago. Ignoring the covered paintings all around the room, she flung off her smoke-filled clothes and replaced them with an old, paint-stained pair of jeans and a black sweatshirt.

Amanda returned to the kitchen. She picked up her dad's phone with the intention of looking up his contacts, but her stomach growled: she was ravenous. It had been so long since she last ate. So she raided the fridge and cabinets, checking to see what she could find: raisins, granola bars, peanut butter, yogurt, a few pretzels and chips. She assembled some semblance of a breakfast and stuffed the balance of the food into her book bag. She didn't know where the search for her family would take her, but she wanted to be prepared. Then she wolfed down her breakfast, not caring how it tasted, as she flipped through her dad's contacts, wondering where to start.

She stuffed the last bite into her mouth and froze: a distant yet very distinct noise invaded her ears.

The house was silent save the ticking of the grandfather clock in the hallway. But she distinguished the faint sound of tires crunching on gravel in the near distance outside. Then it hit her: If they apprehended Chiara, why wouldn't they be searching for Kevin Burrow's other daughter too? Maybe that was why the taxi driver seemed so uneasy when he recognized her?

Seized with fear, she hurried to zipper her bag, then flung it on her back and crept down the dark hallway. She peeked out the corner of the living room window, which overlooked the driveway. Seconds later, bright headlights appeared, and a black sedan jerked to a stop in front of the house.

No marking could be found on the car, nor uniforms on the two men who emerged from the vehicle. But identification was superfluous: the fierce faces and pistols made it crystal clear that the men belonged to the JPD.

Heart again racing, she edged behind the curtains, not wanting the men to detect any movement, and then crept back to the front door, bolting it closed with her trembling fingers. She froze at the sound of their footsteps coming up the stone pathway to the porch. Two large, black shadows appeared on the hallway rug before her, cast from the small window on the front door.

She remained motionless, her breath suspended and her body overcome with fear. She clung to the wall, keeping flat and tight against it as their loud knocking pounded the door.

The knob jiggled as one of the officers shoved against the door, trying to open it. This was her chance. ... She had to leave, *now*, while they were still in the front of the house.

Amanda flew through the living room and kitchen to the back door, running as fast as her legs would carry her. She undid the lock just as the JPD officers barged their way into her home. They entered; she fled.

The backyard was large, and like the front of the house, it was marked by a prominent hill. The hill, for now, provided her cover. She worked her way down the slope and climbed the wooden fence at the bottom that enclosed the large paddock. Rushing into the barn, she found herself desperately pleading: *Please, please if You hear me ... let the horse be here ...*

Boots, Chiara's horse, stood in the back of his stall, his glossy black coat stained with manure. He looked at her with dull eyes, his leg pawing the ground. She unlocked the door and stepped inside the stall. She could hardly find a place to walk—there were piles of manure everywhere. She peered into the water bucket: empty. The horse was probably dehydrated, but she had no time to deal with that right now.

She raced to gather all the riding equipment she would need. It could take up to an hour to tack up a horse; she only had a precious few minutes. No time to groom, although the horse needed it. She threw on the saddle blanket followed by the saddle and then tightened the girth. She put on the reins and placed the bit into Boots's mouth. Even his gums were dry.

There, she finished. ... Shoot, she forgot to do up the throat latch on the bridle. She fumbled with the straps, sweat trickling down her back. She checked to make sure she had everything right and then hurried Boots outside into the paddock. He came eagerly, grateful to leave his prison cell.

She found the mounting block and, grabbing the reins, swung herself into the saddle. Boots picked up his head, turning toward the house, and pointed his ears forward. Then she heard it: the vicious barking of a dog, growing ever louder and closer.

"He's picked up her scent. She left the house!"

A monstrous German shepherd, barely contained by his leash, and the two JPD officers appeared at the crest of the hill.

She tugged at Boots's reins, giving him a sharp kick. "Go!"

Boots sprang forward, his flight response strong. At that moment, the dog broke free from his master's grasp. Deftly jumping between the top and bottom fence rails, he began sprinting after her, his throat filled with hateful growls.

The wind whipped into Amanda's eyes, stinging them as they galloped across the paddock, but she kept urging Boots to go ever faster. His hooves pounded the ground in a strong, steady rhythm. The deafening sound of gunfire filled the air and she gasped, flattening herself against her steed, powerless to do anything besides cling and pray. Close behind them raced the dog, not allowing any ground.

They flew across the field, and the distant fence came into view. They would soon be trapped. Boots led for now, but in these restricted confines, he—and she—would inevitably be painted into a corner.

The fence came ever nearer, and the horse flicked his ears. *That's right!* … Chiara had been working with him, setting up sizable jumps in the paddock to practice. But how high could he jump? Would he be able to clear the fence? Boots's pace didn't slacken, so she raised herself in the saddle and moved her hands up the horse's neck, muscle memory helping the old positions come back to her.

"Come on!" She held her breath.

His muscles tensed beneath her, and then he sprang upward in a mighty leap. For a moment, they were suspended midair. In a second or two, Boots carried both of them over the fence, just clearing the top rail and landing on the other side. Shortly behind them, the dog jumped the lower plank of the fence, hot in pursuit.

They plunged into the forest that lay beyond her family's property, Boots making his way through the wooded expanse, Amanda dodging low-hanging branches. Yet Boots couldn't maintain this grueling pace for very long. Already she could sense his stride slowing.

She managed a glance behind, only to see the thundering shepherd, still following them. Were police dogs always so relentless in their chase? And, more frightening, how could he match a fully grown horse's gallop for so long?

Boots, huffing and his coat wet with sweat, began to slow even more. Petrified, Amanda watched the menacing dog thrashing through the forest path, his energy apparently unspent.

"Faster!"

But her shout was futile: Boots had given all that he had. The persistent dog had now nearly overtaken them. With his target in such close range, he accelerated his pace and leapt toward her, sharp teeth seeking to bury themselves in her calf. She screamed and jerked her leg away, victorious in her attempt. Yet he surged a second time. This time, he won. His vicious teeth dug into her skin, piercing through in stinging, painful horror.

At that moment, Boots reared. Their attacker must have clawed him. With one leg already out of the saddle, Amanda fell headlong, crashing onto the dirt floor. From there, she stared into the dog's wild eyes above her, her fear and pain immobilizing her.

The snarling hunter pounced, and she futilely raised her hands to her face, cringing. Yet, somehow, at the last possible moment, Boots interceded. Boots reared and struck the dog with one of his hooves, knocking the attacker aside. Like a wounded pup, the shepherd writhed in pain, rolling pitifully on the ground. Approaching the canine again, Boots issued a loud squeal and raised himself once again, this time cracking the dog's hind legs. Whimpering and howling, the shepherd dragged himself away from Boots in defeat, collapsing underneath a nearby tree.

Still petrified, Amanda observed the wounded animal. The dog's breathing sounded strained and heavy, his side rising and falling unevenly with each inhale and exhale. Boots had moved a few feet away and also watched the dog. Amanda stood and inched forward toward the now dying German shepherd.

She gasped in horror. The dog foamed all around his mouth, and his dark red eyes rolled around, unable to focus on anything. Meanwhile, a strange gurgling sound came bubbling forth from his mouth. The dog began to jerk and thrash himself about uncontrollably. Did the dog have rabies? She shuddered. ... That didn't seem to quite explain it.

She checked her calf. Thankfully, it didn't seem like the dog had bitten her very deep. She took off one of her socks and wrapped it like a bandage around her leg. Nearby, Boots pawed the ground. He was well-lathered, especially around his shoulders. She went to him and inspected him for any wounds, but just found some claw marks, which weren't bleeding too much. She picked up the reins. She would lead him for a while to give him a break.

"Come on, let's go."

There was no path here; they were blazing their own trail. They had long left anything that looked familiar to her. Thanks to their frantic flight from the German shepherd, she had no idea where they were or where they were headed. For now, though, they were alone and that was enough.

The leaves waved. A squirrel clambered up a tree a few yards away. Geese, honking to encourage one another, flew overhead and into the distance until they shrank to mere specks and disappeared. She had no plan, no destination. Certain danger behind kept her moving forward into the unknown.

They came to a small clearing with an adjacent brook nearby, and Boots pulled toward the water, lowering his head and taking a long draught. She let go of the reins and watched him. He was a beautiful animal: his coat shone dark black in contrast to the lower half of his legs, which were marked with white "stockings," giving the illusion that he wore white boots. The most beautiful thing about him in that moment, though, was that he was Chiara's horse, her beloved pet. He was the only thing Amanda had right now that belonged to her sister. Amanda stroked his velvety coat. She ran her hand up and down his neck. He looked up at her, water dripping from his mouth, and licked his lips.

They continued to walk, Boots stopping from time to time to graze. Minutes or hours passed. She replayed the events of the day over and over in her mind. She had escaped. Right now, had events been different, she might be dead or, at best, a prisoner. But she wasn't. And in that moment of greatest need, she had done the one thing she had sworn to never do again: pray.

Why? Maybe it was a crutch she turned to out of sheer desperation. Maybe she wanted a little fairy-tale magic to save her. Perhaps it was just an ingrained response from what she'd learned as a child that was never fully rooted out, despite her most concerted efforts.

The light around her grew darker. The sun began to sink, a gold disc giving way to tall, looming shadows. Boots's body felt warm beside her in contrast to the cool autumn air. She pulled the hood of her sweatshirt over her head. With the small bit of daylight that remained, she ate a meager dinner of a granola bar and raisins. She led Boots over to a group of pine trees, took off the saddle, and secured the reins to a branch so he wouldn't wander off during the night. The trees were dense, hopefully keeping them from obvious view, and the needles provided some softness.

She opened her book bag, looking for her jacket. Rummaging inside, her fingers brushed against a hard, smooth surface. She yanked her hand out, as though she had been burned. It was Ethan's laptop. She pulled it out and stared at it, fingering the *NCP* letters brazenly engraved in gold in the corner. Her dad and Chiara were missing tonight … the work of *his* political party, the result of *his* ideology. Hatred burned within her. She placed the stolen property back in the bag, taking some perverse comfort in the fact that she must have inflicted some hurt upon him. But it could never be enough.

Amanda lay down on her back, staring at the tree branches above her. *Everything is gone. I have nothing left. My mom is dead. My dad and sister are missing. All of my friends have betrayed me. Morgan has rejected me. I'm used, betrayed, and alone.*

And now hunted. The JPD is trying to find me and kill me. I have no money. I have no possessions of worth. The only thing I have of value is ruined.

She brushed the tears from her cheeks and used the cuff of her sweatshirt to wipe her nose. *Maybe I prayed today because I needed help and I thought there was Someone who could help me. Maybe it was all just coincidence or good luck or ... or maybe Someone did help me. And if so ... thank You.*

CHAPTER SEVENTEEN

A MOUNTAINTOP EXPERIENCE

For the slightest moment, lying in the warmth of the early-morning sunshine, the cheerful chatter of birds greeting her, Amanda almost forgot where she was and why.

Then she sprang to her feet, looking this way and that, listening for any strange sounds. The birdsong transformed into a warning siren, and the sun's rays became a spotlight, pinpointing her. For all she knew, in the time that had passed while she slept, her pursuers had traversed the distance between them, and so at any point, her flight could be put to an unhappy end. She would find no safety here, no matter how pleasant the current surroundings.

She rinsed her face in the icy cold water of the nearby brook, dispelling any lingering lethargy. It was time to move on. To where, she had no idea, but she couldn't stay here. She untethered Boots, climbed into the saddle, and continued her flight.

The forest was silent, save the occasional crunching of a twig beneath Boots's hooves or the chirping of a solitary finch. It differed from her empty house, though: that had

202

been the crushing silence of impending doom. Yet here she could be still in the quiet, obscured from danger by an ocean of trees. And in the stillness, she could begin to listen ...

Amanda peered upward at the light flickering through the autumn leaves. *Are You really here ... with me? Because if You are ... if You really do exist ... and if You really are who You say You are ... I need You.*

She had relied on her own intuition, reason, and desires for long enough. Now she knew, beyond a shadow of a doubt: she was absolutely fallible. *"If it's meant to be, it's up to me."* And when it was up to her, what life did she create for herself? Her very determination to shape her destiny had brought about this miserable outcome: she was wounded, broken, and abandoned. What a cruel twist of irony that she had spent so many years of her life keeping everyone distant, and now, alone in the wilderness, what she desired most was to be with someone.

She had hit bottom. From the depths of this deep pit, she looked up. She gazed upward—to see above, to something greater, someone more powerful than her own destructive failings and the treachery of those who had let her down.

Maybe she *was* with Someone.

She had known Him long ago. All those talks about religion with Morgan—he wasn't speaking a foreign language to her. What she grasped for, in this desperate loneliness and fear, wasn't something new; it was a relationship, long neglected and frequently shunned, but one that had existed many years ago.

Morgan's words of faith and acts of charity now persuaded her to seek out this Higher Power. But Ethan's atheistic outlook compelled her even more. All his scientific, rationalistic arguments were as dust to her in this moment. If Ethan said there was no God, then she would believe there was.

Still, they traveled. One day became two ... two became three ... night and day took their turns as she and Boots traversed the wooded landscape. She had no other recourse, no other plan. Lacking any map or compass, she had no sense of direction. She tried to buoy her spirits with the pathetic hope that they might emerge from these endless miles of woods and happen upon a town far enough away from home where she could inquire about her dad and Chiara without arousing suspicion.

Thankfully, the matches she had put in her book bag provided fire, which kept her somewhat warm at night. She also had her small supply of food. Even so, she had no phone, no survival kit ... just a destroyed painting, some stolen property, and a horse.

On the third evening, she and Boots came upon a large field. Without a canopy of trees overhead, she could survey the landscape. They had apparently been climbing for a while—the slope had been gradual. A dominant, majestic mountain peak loomed in front of them, rising out of the surrounding woods, indigo against the more distant azure peaks that provided a backdrop for the evening. The sun began to set past the western horizon, casting glorious pinks, oranges, and purples across the vast sky, the array of colors reminiscent of her palette of paints. She released the reins, and Boots cantered across the open land. From her current perspective, she saw no sign of civilization, but perhaps from the peak she could orient herself better. So they continued.

Amanda soon regretted that decision. She was by no means a "46er." Far from hiking all forty-six of the High Peaks of the Adirondacks, she had only ever before reached the summit of Cascade Mountain, one of the most accessible of the group. In her ignorance, she had underestimated the height and difficulty of this unknown mountain. Scaling it quickly became a daunting task. Yet she couldn't turn back now: they had gone too far.

They stopped frequently to rest, and often she dismounted, relieving Boots of her extra weight. Boots walked ahead of her now, picking his way, trying to find the surest footing. She, meanwhile, scrambled after him using her hands and feet to go up the steep incline. Her sneakers lacked a good tread, and she feared slipping on the uneven, rocky surface.

Weak from hunger, she had just about depleted her meager food supply. Sure, she had matches and could start a fire, but what would she cook? With next to no survival skills, she couldn't pretend any longer: she would not reach a town or village anytime soon and her food would run out.

She stopped to catch her breath and leaned on one of the large boulders jutting out from the side of the mountain face. She had to take a break, even if for five minutes. Her head pounded, so she rubbed her temples. She saw a small, rocky ledge projecting outward nearby. Edging her way between some birch trees, she made her way there and sat down, grimacing, her whole body sore.

Sitting upon the rock, she was perched like a wounded bird that more and more recognizes that escape is impossible and death is imminent. Though not at the summit of the mountain yet, they had already reached a high altitude. The woods spread out like a blanket below, and neighboring peaks stood like sentinels guarding the land. Many of the autumn leaves had bidden farewell to their branches, falling dead and unceremoniously to the ground. The sky loomed dark overhead, and the wind shook the empty trees. She shivered inside her corduroy jacket, which she didn't take off anymore, and rubbed her hands together, trying to keep warm.

Amanda started to stand, but movement far below caught her attention. She held her breath and squinted her eyes, watching. The foliage before her had thinned just enough to allow sight beyond these empty branches. Movement again confirmed her suspicions: she wasn't imagining things. She could just make out a group of people, weaving in and out of the brush, maybe half a mile away. She scooted back behind the tree trunks, shielding herself, and dug her nails into the bark.

They were coming for her.

She grabbed Boots's reins, taking the lead now and clambering uphill. *What do You want me to do? I'm running out of ideas. I have hardly any food left. The temperature is dropping too low. And now the JPD is trailing me? I can't keep doing this. Should I turn myself in? Is that what You want?*

The wind began to whistle, whipping her hair into her face and fighting her ascent. She tripped and fell on her hands and knees. Boots pulled back, roving his eyes and flicking his ears back and forth.

"Come on! We've got to keep going!"

But he gave a shrill whinny and wouldn't budge.

She threw the reins to the ground. "Fine. If you won't go with me, I'll go to the top myself."

Amanda had to focus completely on climbing now, scrambling with hands and feet to balance and pull herself up. The gathering clouds had become black, and cold drops of rain started to sting her from above.

She scraped and clawed her way, huffing with the exertion. Several times, her sneakers began to slip and only her death-like grip on a small niche of rock above kept her from plummeting.

After struggling for some time, she at last pulled herself up onto the final rock and stood on the summit. Dizzy from the height and her severe hunger, she gazed across the valleys and plateaus of trees stretching out for miles in all directions. No towns, no help, no rescue in sight, nothing except enemies pursuing her. She couldn't see them in the steady, pouring rain, but they were there, somewhere below.

She raised her eyes to the storm clouds above. *I need Your help. I know I doubted You, ran away from You, denied You. I'm sorry ... I'm so sorry for all of it.* Her tears commingled with the raindrops flowing down her cheeks. *Just tell me what I need to do!*

She waited, hoping to hear a booming voice or some otherworldly locution. Maybe there would be a lightning strike in reply or, better yet, a burning bush. Could this be her Mount Sinai?

But there was nothing.

Nothing but the deafening, chilling rain, now soaking through her clothes and hair.

Where are You? Can't You help me? Her legs gave out under the panic, and she crouched on the rocky surface, hugging her knees to her chest. How could she spend the night like this, in the cold and the rain, not knowing when the JPD officers would find their prey?

Then she noticed it.

There, a little lower down on the other side of the mountain opposite from where she had been climbing ...

Could that be a crevice, covered by a large slab of rock? She stumbled toward it through the storm, hoping her hunch wouldn't prove wrong. The descent was similarly treacherous, especially with a wet surface, but in a short time, she stood in front of a small covering—a sheltered space ... a rudimentary shelter from the storm.

A nicker came from behind her. Boots approached, flicking his tail: he had found his way to her. She smiled faintly, patting him. Then she walked inside the dark cave, crouching downward as she moved farther in. At the back, she sat down, resting her back against the rock wall. She brushed a cobweb from her face and dusted off her dirty hands. Boots walked into the entrance of the fissure, which was just tall enough for him to stand and stay protected from the rain.

From her bag, she pulled out half of a granola bar, the last of her food. She nibbled it, trying to make it last as long as possible. She shivered inside her wet clothes: no dry wood meant no fire tonight. She sat there, watching the dismal rain pour outside, shivering and teeth chattering. Somehow it reminded her of a moment from her childhood. It had also been a dark night and she had been alone in her bedroom. She had awoken from a nightmare and called out for her mom.

Her mother came into the room, a ghostly specter in her white nightgown, and her loving, familiar face had comforted Amanda at once. She clung to her mom, who cuddled her and stroked her hair.

A few minutes later, Amanda had calmed down enough to explain herself: "I had another nightmare. It was a real bad one this time."

Her mom pulled the blanket and quilt back over her. "Honey, you don't need to be afraid."

"But I was all alone."

"Look." Her mom walked to the window adjacent to Amanda's bed. She pulled back the curtain, revealing a stunning night sky bedecked with stars. "See those stars? They're looking down at you. The stars are like angels, sparkling and shining above you. They're always with you; you are never alone."

"But what about when it's cloudy? I can't see the stars then."

"Just because you can't see them doesn't mean they're not there. We have faith they still shine, even on the stormiest of nights."

After that, Amanda had slept with the curtains open every night.

She stared now into the pitch black. There would be no stars visible tonight and no mom to comfort her. *I miss you, Mom. I miss you so much. I'm sorry ... I'm sorry you died.* Amanda buried her face in her hands. *But it's not my fault. It's not my fault that it was my birthday when you drove to the store.* In the silence of her heart, she could feel another message: *It's not God's fault either.*

The night seemed endless. The long hours of darkness, marked by a continuous downpour of rain, dragged by. She slept intermittently, awakened by the cold, soggy chill or by Ethan's sardonic eyes staring her down in her fitful dreams. As miserable as the night was, she dreaded the morning. If her pursuers didn't kill her, then starvation would after a few days.

The first light shone, and the rain slowed to a stop. She followed Boots out of the cave into the damp and brisk morning air. Thick clouds of fog lay about the peak of the mountain, obscuring her vision. Perhaps her pursuers had continued their chase through the night, though that seemed unlikely given the massive downpour. If the rain had halted their progress, there was still some distance between them. Yet even that brought her little comfort.

Things looked differently to her in the light of day as hunger pangs commandeered her thinking. In fact, she could barely think of anything else besides her empty stomach. If her destiny on this side of the mountain meant a slow, painful starvation, then maybe the alternative wasn't so bad. Perhaps if she surrendered herself, she could beg the JPD officers to spare her life. Maybe they didn't even want her dead. Perhaps they would only take her captive, a fate not so terrible, especially if she shared her captivity with her dad and Chiara. She would rather die with her loved ones in captivity than alone in the wilderness, her passing unknown and unmourned.

So maybe she'd found the solution. Exhaustion, hunger, and a bitter cold that seemed to enter into the marrow of her bones overwhelmed her. Escape was now futile: she could not escape death anymore. She leaned against Boots for support, lacking the energy to hoist herself back into the saddle. She would just wait here … until they found her. And if they didn't find her, starvation would. She had done all that she could. She had tried her very hardest. If she were to be saved, someone else would have to do it.

Crack!

Her head shot up, and she glanced all around her, her senses on full alert. Where did that sound come from? It seemed like a twig snapping underfoot, but the question was what—or who—had stepped on it? She stood, still as a statue, waiting for her fate.

CRACK!

CHAPTER EIGHTEEN

MEN WITHOUT A COUNTRY

The pine branches to Amanda's immediate right moved. She stared, frozen in expectation. A figure emerged.

It was a girl—a very young girl, no older than five. She gasped as soon as she saw Amanda, her brown eyes wide as saucers upon her porcelain white skin. Yet she didn't run away or scream for help; instead, she tilted her head, thumb in her mouth, and studied Amanda.

Popping the thumb out, the girl waved. "Hi!"

"Hi." Amanda cleared her throat, trying to remedy her hoarse voice. She must appear frightening: her filthy clothes, tangled curls, unwashed face and body …

"I love your horse! Can I pet him?"

"Um … yeah, sure."

The child bounded forward until she stood next to Boots. Reaching on her tippy-toes, she brushed her fingertips along the horse's coat. She giggled. "He's so soft!"

Amanda nodded. Where had the girl come from? She couldn't be alone, right?

"I always wanted a horse. What's his name?"

"Boots."

"My name is Rachel Judith Stein." She clasped her hand across her mouth. "Oops! I wasn't supposed to tell you that!"

Amanda's simmering questions multiplied. Was it friend or foe who'd commanded the girl to keep quiet? Who here needed rescuing? "I won't hurt you. My name's Amanda. Are you here by yourself?"

"Oh … no. There's lots of us. Mommy brought me here when Daddy went away." The smile faded from Rachel's face. Her lips turned downward in a frown. "Do you have a daddy?"

Amanda swallowed heavily, a lump in her throat. "Yeah. But I don't know where he is right now."

"I don't know where my daddy is either. Do you live in the woods with your horse?"

"Sort of, I guess. … I don't have a home right now."

"I know! You can come live with us! Boots too!" She seized Amanda's hand, small fingers holding tight and pulling her forward.

Amanda tugged on Boots's reins and followed. "Where exactly are we going?"

"You'll see! You'll like it. Don't worry—I know the way! Follow me!"

Just then a woman's voice, fraught with anxiety, filled the air. "Rachel! Rachel!"

"Mommy!" Rachel dropped Amanda's hand and ran forward through the woods.

Uncertain how this would turn out, Amanda waited at the rear. A few yards ahead, Rachel jumped into the arms of her mother, who was probably in her early thirties. Like her daughter, she also had straight brown hair, cut to about her shoulders. Pushing her bangs away from her eyes, she put Rachel down, revealing a bulge at her belly—Rachel apparently had a sibling on the way.

"Mommy, look who I found in the woods!" Rachel tugged on her mother's dress and pointed in Amanda's direction.

Beholding Amanda, Rachel's mother turned pale and pulled the girl close.

Amanda felt her cheeks grow warm.

"She let me pet her horse." Rachel rambled on, clearly trying to placate her mother. "His name is Boots. Wanna pet him, Mommy?"

"No, not right now, Rachel. What did I tell you about talking to strangers?"

"She's not a stranger. She's Amanda!"

Amanda took the moment to try to explain herself: "I'm really sorry. I had no idea there was anyone else here. ... I just ran into your daughter. I'm not going to hurt anyone. ... I just need some help. My food supply ran out awhile ago. Would ... Would you happen to have anything to eat?"

"So you're lost?"

"Yeah. Completely."

She smiled with a sad look in her eyes. "Why don't you come with us? We have some food to spare."

"Thank you!" Relief flooded through Amanda. At this point, she didn't even care who these people were, as long as it meant she could eat something.

Rachel and her mother led Amanda farther down the mountain, Rachel bouncing up and down in excitement. "Can I ride Boots? Can I ride him? Please?"

"Maybe later, sweetheart."

Amanda followed them, their route clearly known, though she could detect no path. They walked for several minutes, traversing the wooded terrain, and then entered a large clearing. Before them stood a small, two-story cabin. It lacked any exterior shine or comeliness. Large wooden beams that interlocked to form the structure were weather-beaten, grayed, and stripped of all beauty. Single panes of glass stood cloudy and grimy in the handful of windows, preventing any intimation of what lay inside.

A tall, lean man with silver-graying hair stood facing the house, his attention toward the top of the roof. "The rain sure did a number up there." Arms crossed, he muttered to himself, shaking his head.

Rachel's mother came beside him, and without turning around, he began speaking to her. "Bethany, can you let the others know that we're going to have to patch up that roof now? The downpour last night ripped off some of the shingles and unless we want leaks, we'll have to—"

Boots snorted and the man spun around.

He did a double-take, his mouth dropping. "Who's that? And where did they come from?"

"Her name's Amanda. Rachel found her. She's lost and hungry. Look at her: you can tell she's practically starving. I couldn't just let her go …"

"No … no, of course not." The man looked past Amanda, scanning the distance with his eyes. "Are you alone?"

It seemed plain enough to Amanda that these were kind people—she didn't seem to be in any imminent danger with them. Plus, based on what Rachel said, it was possible that they, too, were in hiding … perhaps for the same reason that she was. She decided to be forthright.

"Yeah, I'm alone for now. There are people following me, though. I'm pretty sure they're JPD officers."

Bethany and the man shared a knowing look. The man then clapped Amanda on the back. "You're in good company, then. The JPD is searching for all of us. You'll be safe here, at least for a little while."

Rachel started jumping up and down. "Really, Dr. Connolly? Amanda can stay? And Boots too?"

Amanda's breath caught in her chest. "Dr. Connolly? What's your first name?"

"Pardon my manners. My name's Mark ... Mark Connolly." He smiled at Amanda, revealing two perfect rows of white teeth, and extended his hand.

Chiara's words echoed in Amanda's mind. Chiara had called a couple of months ago, that morning after Amanda's first date with Ethan. Chiara droned on and on about the missing Connolly family. Amanda had found the conversation dull and couldn't wait for it to be over. Now her heart sank: that exchange she'd resented so much was the last time she had spoken with Chiara—perhaps forever.

She seized Mark's outstretched hand, her pulse pounding and words urgent. "You know my dad! Kevin Burrow! Do you know where he is?"

"Wait a minute ... you're Kevin's daughter?"

"Yeah, I am. When I went home, I couldn't find my dad or sister. The house looked like they had left quickly ... like something was really wrong. While I was there, some JPD officials showed up and I had to escape for my life. Now I have no idea where my family is." She twisted the cuff of her sweatshirt in her hand, wringing it. "Please tell me you know something about them. Anything!"

Mark frowned and knotted his eyebrows. "I saw Kevin every Wednesday at church for our opposition meeting—he chaired it, of course. Anyway, my family fled town over two months ago, back in late August. Someone warned us that we'd been targeted by the NCP, and I had some contacts that led us here, where we could be safe for the time being. I told your father that he may be next. But I don't know what happened after that. I'm sorry, Amanda. Your dad is a good man. ... I wish I could give you more information."

Amanda's burgeoning hope faded: Mark didn't know about her family. How could she possibly learn anything out here, in the middle of nowhere? Maybe she would never even see her dad and Chiara again. ... Her lower lip began to tremble, and she tightened her lips together, trying not to cry. Meanwhile, her head became heavy and she swayed. Images and thoughts flickered through her mind as dots of light danced before her field of vision. The trees lurched, and the sun traveled across the sky, falling ... falling ...

"She's fainting!" Mark's call seemed to come from miles away, but the strong grip on her arms somewhat revived her. He supported her as she half stumbled beside him.

Bethany hurried up the rickety steps in front of them and held the cabin door open. "She needs something to eat."

"Alright, Amanda, just a few more steps, okay?"

Light-headed, she nodded and let Mark assist her. They entered the cool, dark interior of the cabin. Mark led her to a wicker chair, where she gratefully sat. The room was large and open, though sparsely furnished. A rudimentary fireplace lined one wall, a thick log positioned on the floor a few feet in front of it—presumably another seat for two. A small table stood in the back, filled with an assortment of mismatched cups, plates, and silverware.

"The cabin's not great, but it's something." Mark crossed his arms, surveying the room.

"It becomes somewhat homey in the evening, when we're all gathered together." Bethany smiled from the back table, where she was preparing some food. "Just give me another minute and I'll have something for you to eat."

"Thanks so much." Amanda leaned her head back, still dizzy.

Then she noticed the solemn figure on the opposite side of the cabin. She stood with her back to them, staring out the window, her arms hanging listlessly at her side. Their entrance hadn't broken her stillness.

Mark must have followed Amanda's gaze. "Oh, let me introduce you to my wife." He approached the woman. "Linda, we have a newcomer. This is Amanda Burrow, Kevin's oldest daughter. ... She's looking for her family, who's gone missing."

With an obvious reluctance, Linda turned from the window. She wore a cashmere sweater and pearl earrings, tokens of a former life of finery and comfort. Gray roots covered her cropped bob, once a rich mahogany brown. Her eyes stared at Amanda, dull and emotionless. Amanda knew the look well: depression.

Linda nodded a hello and then turned back to the window.

"Here you go." Bethany placed a plate in Amanda's hands, along with a glass of water. "I think some fresh clothes might be in order too. Linda, would you mind going upstairs and seeing if we have any clothes for Amanda to wear?"

Without responding, Linda robotically walked up the staircase.

Amanda devoured the peanut butter sandwich—it tasted as good as if Bethany had handed her a platter of filet mignon from the finest restaurant in Midtown Manhattan. A large thump came from upstairs, shortly followed by feet pummeling down the nearby staircase. A lanky teenager appeared, his shaggy brown hair in desperate need of a cut.

"What's going on? Who's this?"

"We have a new guest," Mark said. Looking at Amanda, he gestured to the teen. "Amanda, this is our son, Joseph."

He leaned on the staircase railing and grimaced. "It's just Joe."

"Nice to meet you, Joe." Amanda swallowed the last morsel of bread. She could already think much more clearly. She ate a second sandwich and an apple and seemed steady on her feet once again.

Mark rose from his chair and motioned for her to follow him. "Just leave your plate on the back table. Someone will take care of the dishes later. If you're feeling up to it, I'd like to introduce you to one of our other residents. We'll go upstairs and you can put any of your belongings there." Mark headed for the staircase but stopped briefly and pointed an index finger at Joe. "Don't you go too far, Joseph. I'm going to need your help on the roof in a little bit."

Joe groaned theatrically.

Mark waved his hand for Amanda to follow him. "I think Ken is up here. He arrived a couple of weeks ago. He's our most recent addition. Well, that is until you, of course."

The second story opened into a large loft. Blankets and pillows littered the floor, intermixed with personal possessions: a wedding album, a stuffed elephant, sneakers caked in mud, a copy of Edgar Allan Poe's *Complete Tales and Poems*. Linda knelt in a corner, digging through a pile of clothing. On the other side, in a chair next to the solitary window, sat a man, most likely in his mid-forties. He bent his shaved head over a book with a torn dust jacket, but he glanced up at their approach and sprang from his chair.

"Ken, you're in for a surprise. We've got one more resident." Mark put his hand on Amanda's shoulder. "This is Amanda Burrow."

"Great—as if it weren't crowded enough in here already." Ken extended his hand, and his sharp, commanding grip crushed her fingers. "Ken Cooper."

"Hi."

Mark rambled on, "Amanda's father and I worked together in the same opposition group. He's missing now, along with her sister."

Ken placed his hands on his hips, his face drawn up in disgust. "More disappearances."

Struck by a thought, Amanda asked, "The NCP targeted your family too?"

"Listen, you don't need a missing family to be stuck in this place. You just need some convictions."

"So ... you were persecuted because of your faith, then?"

Ken chuckled bitterly. "Are you asking me if God got me in this hole? Let's get one thing straight about me right away, okay? No God brought me here because, to be frank, there is no God. I'm here because, unlike the NCP, I actually care about freedom. Not the freedom crap they're always throwing at you. Real freedom."

He took a seat again. "Let me tell you something, kid. I litigated for one of the top law firms in Manhattan. A few of my colleagues mentioned something about individuals gone missing, others killed. There's always some kind of idiocy going on in this sick, twisted world, so I didn't think too much about it at the time. I was working on litigation against the NCP—for unconstitutional practices. I saw the suit as job security for myself; in a nation with no laws, what's a lawyer going to end up doing?"

Ken pulled a packet of cigarettes and a lighter from his pocket. He held the pack toward Mark and Amanda, but with no takers, he shrugged, lit a cigarette for himself, and took a long drag.

"It was a Friday night and my date and I had just come back to my apartment. I had met Tara at my favorite bar … brunette, tall, curvy in all the right places." A wistful look on his face, Ken nodded. "I'm offering her a glass of wine when the doorbell rings. So I open the door and think this is some kind of joke. There's a priest standing there. A priest! Hell, I would have been less surprised if it had been the JPD. So he tells me the NCP is after me because of my work on the litigation. Seems they were feeling threatened and couldn't have *their* freedom jeopardized. The priest offers to help me and hands me a card with his name and address on it. I laugh in his face and slam the door.

"About a week later, I'm walking toward my apartment building. It's dark out, alright, because I just worked a twelve-hour day. Well, I look up and notice the lights are on in my room. I get this unsettled feeling, you know? I never leave the lights on, and no one else has the keys—Tara and I don't know each other *that* well yet. I'm walking past the doorman toward the elevator when he grabs my arm and whispers, 'Get out of here. The JPD are upstairs waiting for you.' I guess that guy saved my life, and I have no idea what his name is."

Ken squashed the cigarette butt on the windowsill and, cracking the window, flicked it outside.

Curious to hear the rest of his story, Amanda urged him on: "How did you end up here?"

"I drove to the address the priest gave me, and he arranged everything. Can you imagine it? My whole freakin' life, flipped upside down in a second thanks to the NCP. Tell me: What was my crime? I've studied law and politics all my life. And I believe in lots of freedoms. But this isn't what our nation is about. I'm an atheist, but that doesn't make me immoral. … I can tell the difference between right and wrong.

"So now I'm on the hit list of citizens 'unwilling to comply.' Damn straight I am! I'm not complying with any of this crap. I'll take some country living for a while over that. I won't go back until those murderers are out of office."

Amanda stared outside. The forest world out there looked so peaceful in a world gone mad. "I guess my dad talked a little more boldly than he was supposed to, then. I just didn't realize that things had escalated to this point. I mean ... how did we come to this?"

"I often wonder that too." Mark sighed. "But as the saying goes, 'Evil prospers when good people do nothing.'"

"But what if good people *can't* do anything?" The cold response came from the other side of the room. Linda stood, some clothes in her hands, and walked toward them.

Mark frowned. "We could have done something, if we had acted sooner. Our opposition came too little, too late. In the beginning, the NCP's 'freedom' looked pretty appealing to most people. A lot of folks welcomed the trimming of our bloated federal budgets and the elimination of needless bureaucracy. After all, who doesn't enjoy freedom from the endless formalities of an overgrown government ... from litigious working papers ... from excessive taxes? Many jumped right on board with the NCP platform. In theory, the NCP sounded great: minimize our centralized government so that all matters are handled by the individual, the family, the group, the neighborhood, the company. That would optimize society. The right environment would allow people in society to flourish and self-select themselves for success, without undue interference."

"Yeah ... all that sounds fine." Amanda had read the NCP literature Ethan gave her. On paper, it undoubtedly was attractive.

Mark nodded. "But 'freedom from the law' is much more alarming in practice. They did away with all censorship laws, so now something as abhorrent as child pornography is licit. Then the NCP said government is getting out of the bedroom: no more laws against incest and polygamy. Most recently, they legalized all drugs and formerly controlled substances. And if you aren't considered useful, good luck getting any help or sympathy from the NCP. People are starving because there are no more food stamps or welfare programs. The elderly, seriously ill, and disabled are 'helped' by offering them euthanasia.

"For many of us, these actions crossed a line that's common to all people. The laws that the NCP repealed weren't inhibiting our freedom—they actually corresponded to a law written on the human heart, a law needed for human flourishing and true freedom. We weren't created for utility, but for love. Our worth isn't in what we can do; it's in who we are: children of the Father."

"Alright, alright, quit the preaching." Ken rolled his eyes. "She didn't want a sermon. Long story short, once people woke up to what the NCP is really about, they started to oppose it. When the opposition group became more organized and posed a real threat, the JPD began targeting people. And here we are. Men without a country ..." Ken looked Amanda up and down. "So your father was part of the opposition? I take it that makes you guilty by association? Humor me a little: What's your story?"

Her story? She appreciated their forthrightness, warm welcome, and kind generosity. But to divulge everything with all the ugly details to these people—whom she didn't even know an hour ago—that wasn't even remotely possible for her. Not yet, not so soon.

Avoiding Ken's scrutinizing look, she turned an appealing eye to Mark. "I'm sorry, but I'm just really exhausted. Would it be possible for me to clean up somewhere and then get some sleep? I won't be able to think straight until I do that."

Mark took the clothes from Linda and handed them to Amanda. "Of course, that's fine. I'm sorry to keep you. I should have realized you needed some rest first. There's a small creek nearby that we use for bathing. Unfortunately, the cabin doesn't have running water."

"That's okay. Compared with the past few days in the wilderness, this place feels like a five-star hotel."

Ken scoffed. "I see you've never been to a five-star hotel."

Mark led the way back downstairs, explaining as they went, "Just walk back around the house. The creek is a little farther through the trees. If you need anything, come find me. I'll be up on the roof fixing those shingles. Oh, and we have some extra blankets in the corner of the loft, so help yourself once you're ready."

"Thank you so much. I'm not sure what would have happened to me without all of you."

Amanda walked back outside and around the rambling cabin, trying to avoid the puddles that remained after last night's downpour. She checked on Boots: Bethany and Rachel were with him. He seemed to be enjoying the attention.

The backyard of the house contained nothing special: just more pines and maples. She continued walking until, jumping back, she found herself no longer alone. About thirty yards from her, on a tree stump, sat a man—or, more specifically, a priest.

He embodied an imposing figure in his ankle-length black cassock. He wore a silver pectoral cross, hung from a chain with intricately worked links. His fair skin contrasted with his thick black beard, tinged with gray. He sat slightly bent, his eyes closed and lips moving, but no sound came forth.

"My dad didn't mention him, huh?"

Amanda whirled around at the sound of the voice behind her. Laughter overhead led her to glance upward: Joe was perched on a tree branch above her, a mischievous grin on his face.

"Surprise ..." He chuckled.

She decided to ignore his antics. "Who is he?"

"His name is Father Voloshin. He kinda keeps to himself. Prays a lot. You know, does priestly stuff. I'm sure you'll talk to him at some point."

"Yeah, probably." That would be an interesting conversation.

She continued on her way to the creek. She found it easily: she just followed the unmistakable sound of rushing water. It seemed to beckon her. The clean, purifying waters called her forward from the filth of the past few days and weeks. She pulled back some tree branches and beheld the wide, swiftly flowing stream.

The pristine water made it possible to stand on the bank and still see through the passing ripples to the smooth pebbles lining the creek bed. She touched her hand to the surface, feeling the crisp coolness of the water, and took a deep breath. She cupped the water, letting it trickle through her hands.

Amanda pulled off her muddied clothing, the sweatshirt and jeans weighing her down with caked dirt. She brushed her messy curls out of her face, longing for the water to wash it all away. She waded into the creek, the water swirling around her ankles and legs. She closed her eyes, moving farther inward on numb feet. The cold temperature of the water made her gasp, but she didn't stop. Waist deep, she dropped to her knees, the water embracing her on all sides. She looked above her, the clear sky broad and expansive.

I have done so many things wrong—so many countless things I wish I could take back ... so many decisions I made in error, so many beginnings that ended so wrongly. What can I do now? I hate myself. ... And You—You're supposed to love me?

Taking a deep breath, she plunged downward into the underwater darkness, the icy veracity of the flowing water breaking apart the dirt and mud that covered her. A moment later, she broke through the surface of the water, emerging once again to the light that fell around her, which caused the surrounding water to glisten.

But I'm choosing to let it all go now. Everything that's clung to me, the things I can't hide anymore—I'm giving it all to You.

Leaving the creek and shivering all over, she dried off and put on the new clothes from Linda, marveling at the wonderful sensation of soft, clean fabric. For the first time in months, she felt something like peace within her. The feeling had become so foreign to her. Maybe it had actually been years since she last experienced such a—

Chuff-chuff-chuff-chuff-chuff-chuff ...

Amanda tensed, the distant, unnatural noise a startling contrast to the gurgling waters beside her. She searched the wooded area surrounding her. She waited, her heart pounding, the feeling of being on the verge of peace now broken.

Chuff-chuff-chuff-chuff-chuff-chuff...

The sound grew louder, coming closer. She retreated from the open bank and knelt by the trunk of one of the large, dense blue spruces nearby. Through the camouflage of needles, she watched for the source of the sound, ready to confirm what she already strongly suspected.

A black helicopter soon came into view, the rotor blades whirring loudly. It followed the course of the stream and traveled as low to the line of trees as possible. The branches around her swayed in the manufactured wind, and she crouched lower to the ground. The helicopter bore no markings, but it had to belong to the JPD.

She waited until the helicopter disappeared from sight and sound and then crept back to the cabin, where she found the others assembled outside.

Mark greeted her somberly upon her return. "Did you see it too?"

She nodded. "It was the JPD, right?"

Mark's look of concern spoke an affirmation. "It's probably driven by a robotic drone, doing reconnaissance work for the NCP."

Joe peered from face to face. "I wonder which one of us they're looking for?"

Ken laughed bitterly. "Well, that's obvious, isn't it? No one has seen a helicopter like that until today, coincidentally right after our newest addition arrived. And I'm not talking about the horse."

Of course—they were looking for her.

CHAPTER NINETEEN

SOMETHING TO HIDE

"Well, there's nothing we can do for now," Mark said.

The helicopter faded to a small speck in the distance, and Mark turned away. Amanda breathed easier, though not completely. The helicopter might be out of sight, but remained top of mind. She glanced at the group gathered around her. Their strained expressions suggested that they were thinking the same.

Linda sighed and shrugged. "We'll just do what we do for everything: wait for Nasir."

Amanda jumped at the chance to change the topic and deflect the attention. "Nasir? Who's that?"

Joe grabbed a branch from the ground and began to methodically tear off twigs, flinging them into the distance. "Nasir keeps us from starving out here. He's our food delivery guy."

"And much more than that." Mark turned toward Amanda. "He's a doctor who lives with his family in New York City. They vacationed here for years. When we needed a place to stay, he offered to let us use it. Nasir's due to come tomorrow. We haven't seen him now for more than a week."

Bethany rubbed her arms in the plain cotton shirt she wore—maybe to keep herself warm in the chill, or because of worry. "A lot can happen in seven days."

Rachel grabbed her mother's hand, pulling and dragging her toward the cabin's door. "Mommy! I wanna go back inside now!"

Everyone filed into the building behind the two of them, Amanda trailing last. She checked on Boots, who seemed content, and took one final glance at the woods and the sky. Who might still be pursuing her, somewhere out there or maybe quite close? A shiver ran along the back of her neck. She closed and locked the front door behind her.

The imminent danger seemingly gone, Amanda sat down to rest her weary, blistered feet and to appreciate being clean, warm, and indoors. She positioned herself as near the fire as possible and even felt grateful for the old plastic crate on which she sat—it was more comfortable than riding in a saddle for hours at a time. She stretched out her legs, yawning.

Movement grabbed her attention. Actually, it was constant movement: Mark could not sit still. First he hauled in a stack of wood. Then she watched him attack another project: a stubborn window that wouldn't open. For a brief moment, he perched himself on the edge of a chair, his hands restlessly placed on his thighs, one knee bouncing up and down. He scanned the room, his eyes searching.

"Well, the horse is staying." Though he spoke the words aloud, he seemed to be talking to himself. "Might as well build a shelter for him. We've got a boatload of wood out there." He walked to the corner of the room where an old toolbox sat, the cover rusted, and began pulling out a hammer and creating a pile of miscellaneous nails. "Joe! I need your help! We've got work to do!"

Maybe she should offer to help—it was her horse, after all—but she hadn't inherited her dad's knack for building. She would only make things harder for them. … She already had.

His pockets bulging now with a collection of tools, Mark stood and raised his voice even louder: "Joseph, you better get in here!"

His wife stared at him from her nearby seat, a glint of resentment in her dull eyes.

"What's it now?" Joe dragged himself down the stairs. His uncombed, unwashed hair stuck up at odd angles, and he slumped onto the crate next to Amanda.

"Come on, get up! You're not going to spend another day laying around doing nothing. Grab that toolbox. I've got a job for you."

"What's the point?"

"The point is that we're the lucky ones. You understand that? We're lucky. We could be captured right now. We could be at the JPD's mercy. So quit your complaining! Come help me. Be useful for once!"

"Sometimes I wish they'd just find us!"

"Joseph!" Mark glared, his index finger wagging at Joe. "You say that one more time and I'll—"

"What? Put me in timeout? Take away my computer? This whole thing's a punishment. You think so too. I know you do. Why'd *we* end up here? What makes us so special that we're safe while other people are getting killed?" Joe's voice rose in a growing crescendo of fury. "Build whatever you want, but leave me alone!" He stormed out the door, slamming it behind him with such force that the adjacent wooden beams trembled under the pressure.

Amanda stared down at her shoes. She didn't want to be a spectator of a family argument, but what else could she do? There was no privacy here.

"I'm going to have a talk with him." Mark turned around to face his wife. "Feel free to chime in anytime. Need I remind you, I'm not the only parent here."

"I *did* chime in. I chimed in when I said coming here was a stupid decision. Joe is right. You should listen to your son, even if you won't listen to me."

"And what would you have done? Sit at home in our reclining chairs like easy targets? Enjoy your specialty lattes and trips to the spa while the JPD stands knocking at our door?"

"We have been here *two months!* Two months, Mark! It never gets better, only harder. I miss home. I miss everything we worked so hard to create and build, over so many years. We had other choices; you just didn't want to take them."

"What are you suggesting? That we should have recanted? Denied our beliefs, our values, everything we live for?"

"It was an option. God would have forgiven us."

Mark took a step back, as though reeling from Linda's suggestion. He shook his head, deep frown lines furrowing his face. "Shouldn't adversity bring people together? Lately, Linda, I feel like I don't even know you." Grabbing his tools, he walked outside alone.

Tears streamed down Linda's cheeks, but she wore no makeup to smudge. Linda rose and left the room without bothering to make a remark to anyone.

Amanda rubbed her tired eyes. Emotions ricocheted across the tiny room, and trapped in the crossfire, she could barely contain her own feelings. Nearby, Ken gave a low whistle, and she turned to look at him.

He tossed aside the book he wasn't reading and stood up, his arms open wide. "Welcome, Amanda, to the newest reality survivor show! On this week's episode: Will they be rescued? Will they be captured? Maybe they'll tear each other apart!" He chuckled to himself. "You'll hear this tape played over and over again till you can recite the lines yourself. Linda's favorite conversation piece is home. What she can't get through her head is that home no longer exists. Let's say, 'Boom!' All of a sudden, I can go back to my apartment. I won't call it *home* anymore. I remember once flying into JFK from out of the country and feeling that nostalgic joy of landing on American soil. Land of the free, right?" Ken scoffed. "Not anymore. Everything's changed. We can't go back to how it used to be."

A hard lump rose in Amanda's throat, and she rallied all her willpower to fight the burning tears blurring her vision. The very word "home" was loaded now, for with it came visions of that place of familiarity and comfort, the house that stored so many memories of her mom and now memories of her dad and sister, who might also be gone from her. … Ken was right: everything *had* changed. She couldn't go home anymore. There was no home.

That reality was more than she could handle right now, and she seized the first distraction that presented itself: "Is that the bucket you use for water?" Her voice shook, and she didn't wait for a reply from Ken. She grabbed the bucket and walked outside into the afternoon sunshine.

But no privacy yet: Bethany stood just a few feet from the doorway. She held some acorns in her hand and looked down at her daughter, who clung to her leg with a vise-like grip.

"*Please*, Mommy?"

"Rachel, I'm sorry, but we have to wait. Why don't you try to find some pretty leaves to go with your acorns? I'm sure they'll look beautiful in the loft."

"No."

"We could go for another walk."

"No! I'm hungry!"

Bethany, her eyes pained, reached down and stroked Rachel's back. "I know you are, honey, but Nasir is coming tomorrow."

"Isn't it dinnertime, Mommy?"

"Yes, we usually eat around now, but we can't help it—we just don't have any food left."

A chilling realization hit Amanda: the sandwiches and other food she had wolfed down just a few hours ago—that was the very last of their rations. How could she be so thoughtless, so greedy?

Her face grew hot as she said, "I … I had no idea. I'm so sorry. I never would have eaten as much as I did …"

"Of course you didn't know. You needed the food more than we did. And, like I said, Nasir should be here tomorrow."

"Are you sure?"

"No, nothing is a guarantee. That's just part of this kind of life. You have some shelter here and safety—for a time at least. But I'm afraid you aren't that much better off than when you were on your own."

"I think all of *you* were much better off when I was on my own."

"No one here thinks that." Bethany cocked her head. "Well … maybe Ken does." She tucked some hair behind her ear. "We always have to keep searching for a new normal.

You joined us today, out of the blue, and we have to acclimate to things. We all have to adjust, constantly, and sacrifice is always part of that. But you were led here somehow, and I'm sure there's a reason for it." Bethany reached down and picked Rachel up. Holding her in her arms, Bethany kissed her daughter on the cheek. "Rachel knows a lot about being brave and needing to make sacrifices."

Thumb in her mouth, Rachel hid her face in her mother's chest.

Bethany looked at Amanda, resilience in her eyes. "We all need to be brave and make sacrifices—for each other."

Amanda nodded wordlessly in agreement and then continued her trek toward the stream, feeling as empty as the bucket that she held in her hands.

A long night came and passed. She was warmer and more comfortable in the cabin than she had been for days—ever since she'd fled the city, in fact—but gnawing hunger and growing trepidation kept sleep at bay. Morning arrived, and the hours ticked away. Still, Nasir did not arrive. Would he come at all this time? She could hear that unspoken question and sense the unease that accompanied it.

The November sky had already turned dark, and the bare trees were mere shadows receding in the distance. In the depths of the Adirondacks, the night sky was clearer and the stars brighter than she had ever seen them. She and Ethan had sat in Central Park and gazed upon the stars together. Were these the same stars that looked back at her now? Was she the same person? Everything seemed different now.

The whole group gathered in the downstairs room. She assumed that no one wanted to go to bed. To do so would admit the disappointing truth that something had detained

Nasir and therefore the food they desperately wanted would not be coming.

Knock-knock-knock!

Amanda bolted up and stared at the front door. Next to her, Bethany gasped. Ken and Mark's conversation halted, and an immediate silence filled the room. Both men became still, watching and waiting. Amanda raised her eyebrows. Well, why didn't they answer the door?

Knock-knock!

"Nasir!" Joe burst out. "That's his signal!"

"Oh it *is* him!" Bethany's face relaxed with relief.

Ken crossed the room and opened the door.

There stood a somber, dark-haired, olive-skinned man, bearing two large paper bags. "Good evening, Ken."

"Nasir!" Rachel shouted. Awoken from her doze by the cool draft coming from the door, she jumped from her mother's lap and began clapping. "Mommy, let's eat!"

Food was the first priority. Amanda did her best to chip in and help with emptying the bags, passing around bowls and dishes, and distributing the contents of the late-night meal—a slice of bread, five crackers, and half a bowl of canned chicken noodle soup. As soon as everyone had his or her allotment, Amanda descended upon her own food. It wasn't enough to satiate her hunger, but at least her empty stomach wouldn't keep her up another night.

Next came the hunger for information. As she brushed the cracker crumbs from her lap, she eyed the visitor. What tidings did he bring?

"Nasir, what would we ever do without you? I don't know if we'll ever be able to repay you." Mark set his cup of water down on the back table. "Thank you again for coming and bringing us this food, for risking your life to help us."

"Were the roles reversed, there is no doubt in my mind that you would provide the same service, most willingly and generously." Nasir then looked at Amanda. "Yet it appears as though I have brought too little. Your numbers have increased."

"You're not the only one with news tonight." Ken stood near Nasir, his eyebrows raised and face attentive, as though he were about to conduct a deposition.

Nasir walked toward Amanda, and she stood to greet him. "Nasir Khalaf." He extended his hand, shaking hers.

Her palm was sweaty ... he probably noticed that.

"*As-salāmu ʿalayki.* Peace be upon you."

"Thanks. My name's Amanda ... Amanda Burrow."

"Burrow?" Joe had been studying the bottom of his chipped bowl for any remnants of soup, but now his head shot up, a look of shock on his face. "Your last name's Burrow?"

"The name rings a bell, doesn't it?" Mark cleared away Joe's soup bowl. "You must be thinking of Kevin Burrow. We used to see him every Sunday at church. Kevin was in charge of our local opposition group."

Joe still stared at Amanda, his eyes pondering undisclosed thoughts. "Uh-huh ..."

Nasir guided the conversation back to its purpose, and the interrogation commenced: "When did you arrive here, Amanda?"

"Yesterday."

"And how did you know about this place?"

"I showed her! It was me!" Rachel pointed at herself. "I found Amanda and Boots!"

"That's true." Amanda nodded. "The JPD followed me and I had to escape into the mountains. Rachel found me yesterday morning."

"So you are involved with the opposition party, then? That's why the JPD was searching for you?"

"Like Mark said, my dad led the local opposition group. I came home one day and found my family missing. Right after that, some JPD officers showed up at my front door and chased me with their attack dog. Somehow I escaped, with the help of my sister's horse—Boots, like Rachel said. I began wandering through the woods, and a few days passed. I had no food left. I didn't know what else to do ... I had just about lost all hope. And then Rachel found me."

Nasir started to reply, but Bethany interrupted, resting her hand on Amanda's shoulder. "It was a miracle you found us! I can't even imagine ... traveling all alone in this wilderness? That takes such faith!"

"Like mother, like daughter."

Amanda blinked in surprise at Linda's offhanded comment, made from the half shadows where she sat. "You ... You knew my mom?"

"I assumed you would have remembered. Julia and I ran the women's group at church together."

Unexpected warmth toward Linda surged within Amanda at that moment. Linda had known her mom. Strangely enough, that knowledge didn't bring pain or crippling sorrow. No, it was almost like hearing a soft whisper of her mom's voice in the room, reassuring her that she wasn't completely gone ...

Apparently satisfied with this initial questioning, Nasir had already moved on to a more pressing topic. He and Mark were conversing heatedly.

"It happened some time yesterday afternoon," Mark explained. "It didn't pass directly over the cabin, thankfully. If we'd had the fire going at that point, I'm sure it would have given us away."

Nasir frowned. "And this is the first helicopter you've seen in the area?"

"It is first, but not last." The normally taciturn Father Voloshin spoke in a deep, accented voice. "Our enemy draws closer."

"We must take even greater precaution. There is only one recourse." Nasir surveyed the group. "There can be no more fires during the day. The smoke will draw unnecessary attention."

So no more heat for warmth or cooking. Fire had become another luxury. Amanda cringed inside. She had brought nothing but harm to these kind people: first they sacrificed some of their food for her, now their fire.

"You're right, of course." Mark cleared his throat, nodding. "It won't be easy, but we can make do without fire. The alternative is much worse."

Linda stood, hands on her hips. "Not easy! How are we supposed to cook?"

"Food doesn't have to be served warm," Mark said. "Cold food is better than no food, right?"

Amanda interrupted any further argument with her own burning question: "Nasir, do you know anything about the people who have gone missing? Where can I find my family?"

"I do have news." Nasir's grim tone and pained expression stemmed any hope of *good* news.

"Nasir!" Bethany gripped the edge of her seat. "Please … what did you learn?"

"We have strong reason to believe that the NCP has detained many of the missing persons at a high-security confinement area, approximately a hundred miles west of here."

"A confinement area?" Joe cocked an eyebrow. "What's that supposed to mean? Like a prison?"

Ken's eyes narrowed. "A prison … or a concentration camp?"

Nasir frowned. "My apologies. We haven't been able to ascertain details regarding the exact nature of the facility."

Bethany placed one hand over her mouth, tears welling in her eyes. "And David? Do you have any news about my husband?"

Nasir shook his head. "I am sorry. We don't know the identity of any of the captives at this site. The opposition is working to formulate a rescue mission. It is highly complicated. The confinement area has the strongest defenses. When we act, it must be with a realistic expectation of success. Yet we don't know how much time we have, since there is a rumor that the NCP may be giving some of the prisoners the 'final freedom.'"

A weighty silence hung upon the room, and Amanda looked from face to face, the alarmed expressions making her dread the answer to the question she was now about to ask. "What's the 'final freedom'?"

Nasir turned toward her. "In the eyes of the NCP, these prisoners are a threat to society—and to themselves. Their steadfast loyalty to a natural law and moral code is their own self-inflicted prison, more harmful and terrible than any confinement area. The NCP views this mental imprisonment as especially grave, since the individuals are blind to it. When the prisoners refuse to reconsider their ideology, they are given the 'final freedom'—a once-and-for-all escape from their oppressive philosophy. To the NCP, it is an act of mercy because it is a release from pain; it is a merciful death because it relieves the prisoner's suffering."

Terror clutched at Amanda's heart and her voice shook as she said, "So they may all be executed."

Ken swore under his breath. "Yes, and it's awfully convenient for the NCP to be free of their loudest and most threatening objectors, isn't it? 'Mercy' is just a pretty name for slaughter in this case."

"We are making progress," Nasir assured. "Previously, we didn't know the whereabouts of the prisoners. Now that we do, we can begin to take measures to free them."

"Of course. Yes, that all makes sense." Bethany seemed to try to recompose herself, though her face remained ghostly white. "There's never a reason to lose hope."

"I do have another piece of news: there was an attack," Nasir said. "It happened last week, in the city, on the night that a large opposition meeting was taking place. We lost many talented, dedicated, and good people. No one survived the bombing." He took a deep breath. Nasir looked downward and his voice grew quiet: "I was supposed to be at that meeting. Yet I was detained: I came here first, and the traffic on the way back to the city delayed me. I never reached the meeting. You may say that I have saved your lives; yet you have certainly saved mine."

"Nasir … we're so sorry …" Bethany dabbed at her tears with the cuff of her sleeve.

Ken rubbed his chin. "Where was the attack?"

"St. Patrick's Cathedral. It's destroyed beyond recognition."

Amanda jumped where she sat, her chest tightening and her face hot with shame.

Mark began pacing back and forth. "Nasir, what can we do? People are out there risking their lives! You've risked your life! There must be *something* we can do to help."

Amanda's breath caught, and her eyes went wide as she stood up. "There's something *I* can do. Hold on a minute." Taking the stairs two at a time, she hurried to the upstairs loft and opened her book bag. Her fingers brushed against the cool, smooth metal of Ethan's laptop. She pulled it out and fingered the sleek, haughty *NCP* engraving in the corner. She had to be on the offensive now: she had to do everything in her power to help her family. Maybe this could save them.

She reentered the downstairs room, questioning eyes staring at her. She swallowed uneasily. "You've all taken me in, without question or criteria. But my being here has put all of your lives in danger by drawing the JPD closer. And I'm sorry because I haven't been completely forthright with you. I lived in New York City right before I came here. I didn't know what the NCP was doing with those who opposed the party. I was ignorant and stupid. My boyfriend turned out to be one of the leaders of the NCP, and ... well, it's a long story, but I decided to leave him. Out of anger toward him, I took his work laptop." She placed the computer in Nasir's hands. "Maybe you can give this to someone who could do some good with it."

Joe leaned forward on the wicker chair. "Awesome! Taking down the enemy with his own weapon! Cha-ching!"

Ken swore—this time much louder than he should have—and rubbed his hands together. "Talk about a smoking gun. Just picture all the plans and notes and maps that must be on that thing! And if we can hack into their internal network and sign in to all their accounts ..." He gazed ahead, a gleam in his eyes. "This has incredible potential."

"Man, they could even send a phishing email from his account to NCP staffers with top security clearance and use his influence to get in!" Joe's face glowed. "Think of the malicious ransomware we could infect their network with! Those jerks will be on their knees!"

"When did you learn so much about computers?" Mark cocked an eyebrow at his son.

Joe lifted a single shoulder and let it drop. "I dunno … messin' around on the family computer. You learn stuff."

Nasir stared at the laptop. "In light of this, I must leave immediately. But first, I will tell you that the NCP must be already suspicious regarding this location if the JPD is sending drone helicopters here. They are thorough in their work. They will be back here; of that I am certain. The longer you stay, the greater your peril. I think there is only one plausible solution: you must leave."

Linda stirred from her sullen state, her eyebrows raised. "Leave? When? Where would we go?"

"We will not wait a moment longer than necessary. But this new business will likely take me away from you for a greater period than usual." Nasir wrapped the laptop in one of the empty paper bags. "Also, I will need to send someone from the city to provide extra support for the relocation. I believe you will be safe for a little while longer. We shall pray that it is so." He walked toward Amanda and shook her hand again. "Thank you for this."

She gave a tiny nod. "Whatever I can do to help my family."

With that, Nasir bade them farewell. He exited the cabin and was soon swallowed in the darkness of the night.

"Good developments are happening out there. And, as always, we can do nothing but wait." Mark threw another log on the fire.

241

"We can pray." Father Voloshin stood up. "Let not forget: God gives opportunities, to battle against Enemy, so we overcome and be victorious. Even here, in isolated cabin, we can rise up against evil always lurking inside and find ways to conquer. Nothing shows good side of mankind better than individuals willing to stand up to evil. Make use of time we been given."

Bethany nodded. "Yes, of course." She looked down. Rachel slept once again, her head resting on Bethany's shoulder. "I'll put Rachel upstairs to bed and be back in a minute for prayer."

Mark walked over to Amanda. "You probably noticed that we gather for prayer each evening. Would you want to join us tonight?"

She cringed. She was a neophyte in the world of spirituality and could barely pray alone—how could she pray with others? "Well, I think it's past my bedtime too."

It was a lame effort at humor. No one laughed.

"Maybe tomorrow night, then. Linda, Joe, and I will take shifts tonight keeping watch. If you need anything at all, you can find us downstairs, okay?"

Amanda nodded, then walked upstairs. Ken stood nearby, holding the sole candle, which cast just enough light to distinguish object from shadow. Bethany tucked a blanket around Rachel and then, after a silent wave, returned downstairs.

Ken walked toward Amanda and held the light between them. "So you're not joining the Kumbaya circle either?"

"I'm more into private prayer, I guess."

"Yeah, you like keeping things private, don't you? You know, I haven't trusted you since day one. I knew that you weren't telling us the whole story, that you had something to hide. Never guessed it was an NCP laptop. Thanks for not screwing us over."

Ken blew out the candle, giving her no chance to respond, and then made his way to a pile of blankets on the other side of the loft. Amanda stood in the darkness, listening to the sound of Rachel's breathing, unhurried and tranquil. Father Voloshin's baritone voice boomed from below: "We pray for Your guidance, protection, and for help we need …"

Amanda lay down on a blanket, pulling her book bag nearby and resting her head on the loft floor. She extended her right hand, and her fingers fell upon familiar material: canvas. She sat up and groped around until she held the object: her painting. In the dark, she couldn't see it, but running her fingers across the surface confirmed it. The ripped canvas was unmistakable.

She visualized Ethan's face, his unrelenting gaze upon her, and the darkness around her became much more unwelcome. Whatever she did and wherever she went, he followed. Even here, miles and miles from the city, she could almost sense his presence—the ripped canvas reminding her of his smell, his voice, his touch …

Amanda clenched her teeth, cursing each moment she had spent with him. She fought the memory of that afternoon when she had wandered into the lounge and seen him for the first time. *Why me? He could have been with any girl. And yet … he picked me.* The bitter regret, like an infected wound, filled her.

Where were You when I went to Ethan's apartment with my painting? That's when I needed You the most. Why didn't You stop me? Are You a God of silence? Things could have been so different. But they aren't.

She lay motionless for a long while, trying to listen.

Was it me? Maybe You were there, calling out to me ... and I wouldn't listen. Maybe I shut You out for so long that when You tried to intervene, I couldn't even hear You.

She slept poorly, the image of Ethan never leaving her. When the first indication of light hinted at the eastern horizon, she lifted her blanket and rose, the canvas held in her arms. She tiptoed down the rickety stairs, trying not to awaken the others who still slept. When she reached the first floor, she spotted Joe. He was slumped on the small crate from which he sat guard, snoring. She grimaced. This was not the most ideal way to guard the cabin, but at least she could pass outside unnoticed.

It was a dismal November morning. Drizzle fell in sheets from a gray sky—in fact, the whole world looked gray. She walked for a while and then stopped beneath a bare maple tree to look at her painting one final time. The canvas, her treasured painting, had become nothing but a reminder of Ethan. He had irreversibly tainted it. ... Why even carry around something so irredeemable? Yet she couldn't bear to destroy it herself, to shred it or to bleed the colors indistinguishable in the stream. That was too violent. It just had to be out of sight, someplace where it wouldn't haunt her anymore.

She bent down and began digging in the soft earth with her hands. She never should have revealed her painting to Ethan. But it was too late for that. She had made her choice—a choice that could never be undone.

Why didn't I wait? Why did I give in to him?

She buried the painting and then covered it with a leafy blanket. No one passing by would realize its presence. And as for her, she wouldn't be able to retrace these same steps into the woods to this precise spot. It would be impossible for her to find this particular tree, the one that marked the burial place of her painting. Only the dirt smudged beneath her fingernails provided evidence of the deed.

With her eyesight blurred by tears, Amanda wiped her hands on her jeans and walked away. She had buried her painting and, with it, a piece of herself.

CHAPTER TWENTY

KNOW YOUR ENEMY

Amanda knelt on the floor of the downstairs room, sorting clothes and preparing them for cleaning—today's chore. She welcomed the task: doing something, as menial as it might be, was better than doing nothing. She didn't like the thoughts and memories that plagued her when she was idle. Almost two weeks had passed since Nasir had come and she'd given him Ethan's laptop. She struggled to go through each day, knowing something big was probably happening out there, yet having no idea what it might be. Now she did the only thing left to do: pray that her dad and Chiara were alive and safe.

Bethany, also helping with the laundry, called to Rachel, "Honey, please grab your dress and my sweater, okay?"

Rachel ran upstairs, and Bethany took a deep breath. She eased herself onto a crate, her hand holding her lower back, a look of pain on her face.

Amanda set down the clothes and watched her, troubled. "Umm … is everything okay?"

"The baby must be sitting right on a nerve." Bethany exhaled, her eyes closed. "Each week, laundry day seems to get harder. I guess that's a good sign: baby is growing."

"I can finish the rest. Do I take all of these to the stream?"

"Yes. But we'll wait for Rachel to come back. It'll take her awhile. ... She usually gets distracted whenever I send her on an errand." Bethany smiled at Amanda. "How are *you* doing? You must think about your family a lot."

Amanda gave a small nod. "Yeah, I do. And I'm sure you miss your husband."

"Every day." Bethany glanced down at her skirt and smoothed out the wrinkles, spreading the material straight and even. "It's been three months now, you know. Three long, trying months ... months where I've gone to bed at night willing myself to believe: to believe that there is a purpose for all of this and that there is a God who will bring justice and order back. Sometimes my feelings do nothing to help me. It's just a sheer act of the will: I believe because I must. If what I believe isn't true, then nothing is true. But I've been given strength."

Amanda unnecessarily adjusted the pile of clothes, avoiding eye contact. "It's hard to do that—to trust. The messages around us and the circumstances we find ourselves in seem to point to the exact opposite. Everything around us seems to say that God is dead."

"That's exactly what the NCP would like us to think. I've been given the gift to trust that something greater is happening. Through all this, God has been my Father, and Faith has been my Mother."

Amanda eyed her. "Faith is our mother? I never heard it described that way before."

"It makes sense, though, when you think about it. Faith guides and protects us in the darkest of times ... giving us rebirth into new life."

At that moment, Rachel came bounding into the room, arms filled with clothes. "Ta-da!"

"Oh my!" Bethany laughed. "I think you brought down a few more things than I asked for. Come here, you!"

Bethany reached out and grabbed Rachel, tickling her. Rachel's giggles and shrieks filled the room. Amanda watched, chuckling. Her mom used to do the same exact thing. As a little girl, Amanda loved being held captive by her mom's loving arms, wrestling to get free while laughing all the while and, once liberated, longing for her mom to grab and tickle her all over again. The memory didn't make her sad or pained, though; it simply made her smile.

Bethany stood up and kissed the top of Rachel's head. "Alright, little miss, time to go to the creek."

Amanda shook her head. "No, you should stay here and relax. I'll go to the creek. I don't mind doing laundry."

A male voice chimed in: "I got it." Joe, jumping off the staircase, came into the room and lifted the whole pile of laundry.

"Oh," Amanda said. "Okay, thanks. So we'll be back."

She held the door for Joe and waved to Bethany and Rachel. Then she followed Joe outside. They passed Boots, who nickered a greeting. Amanda paused just a moment and jogged over to him. She pulled an apple out from her coat pocket and held it in her palm. She had saved it from her lunch, figuring Boots would appreciate it. She was right: he took the whole apple in his mouth in one bite and then chomped on it, juice dribbling from his mouth. She gave him a quick pat and then hurried on, trying to catch up with Joe's long strides. The day felt chilly. As much as she liked to keep occupied, washing the clothes would be a brisk job. She appreciated Joe's offer to help her.

They worked for a while without speaking. Joe crouched down with his back to her. Scouring a pair of jeans, he broke the silence: "When did you last talk with your sister?"

Amanda looked up, taken aback by his unexpected question. "I don't remember exactly." She didn't want to admit the truth: it had been over two months. She missed so many opportunities to speak with Chiara, to hear the relatively insignificant details of her teenage life, which now couldn't be more significant. She would give anything to hear about Chiara's best friend's breakup or the new shade of nail polish she experimented with.

But Amanda had forfeited those conversations—perhaps never retrievable—for what? For a disillusioned drug experience and a man who betrayed her. How could it be so clear to her now and yet so clearly the opposite before?

"Was Chiara happy?" Joe stared at Amanda with a serious face and it clicked: of course … they knew each other.

"Yeah, she seemed like it. … You were friends with her, right?"

Joe took a dripping pair of jeans and began to wring them, clenching the material together, squeezing until his knuckles turned white. "I saw her right before we left. It was late August and we were hanging out together. I didn't know my family was leaving so soon. Otherwise, I would have asked her …"

"You wanted to tell Chiara something?"

He raised his eyes again, and even under his flop of brown hair, Amanda recognized a maturity she had previously overlooked. "There's just something about her. She was always so energetic and fun, even mucking out a horse's stall. It was like being around her made everything better." He swallowed and turned away, mumbling, "I was gonna ask her out."

249

"Oh."

"Yeah. I just hope she's okay." He left without another word, the finished laundry in his hands.

Amanda caught the look of utter sadness on his face as he walked away. She stood there, unmoving, watching his large frame until he disappeared among the trees. Joe shouldn't be hiding like some convict in the woods and Chiara missing, just one more among the countless others who had disappeared without a trace. *Why? What is the purpose for all of this?*

She finished up the last few items of clothing and walked back to the cabin. On the way to the front door, she spotted Father Voloshin, once again sitting on the tree stump in the backyard. Over the past weeks, she had observed that he spoke little and kept to himself most of the time. She had learned from the other residents that he was a Russian Orthodox priest who had been forced into hiding like the rest of them. She walked up to him now. He had numerous books piled around him and notes scattered about, scribbled in forceful penmanship.

He was flipping through what appeared to be a very old book, the sheets yellowed with age and the spine barely held in place. The priest seemed deeply engrossed in his work— either that or he was ignoring her—and didn't look up.

She stood there, debating how to initiate a conversation. Then she noticed a sheet of paper by her sneakers: a page must have fallen out of a book. She stooped down and picked it up. The writing was not in English. She couldn't understand a word on the page, but something about the characters looked familiar.

"Sorry … I don't mean to interrupt, but what language is this?" She held the page up for Father Voloshin to see.

He peered above the rim of his reading glasses. "Hmm?" He pulled the sheet from her hand, eyeing it. "Greek."

"Oh. … Excuse me. I'll be right back." Without checking to see if he heard her or if he even cared, Amanda ran into the house, emptied her arms of the laundry, and hurried upstairs. With her sketchbook in hand, she rushed back outside. She had at last found the answer to a question she'd long wondered about.

Beside Father Voloshin once again, Amanda opened the sketchbook. On one of her multiple evenings spent at Little Pete's, she had decided to copy the writing scrawled across the doorframe of the room. What did it say? Contrary to Ethan's claim that the writing was mere decoration, she felt convinced that words always carry some meaning and purpose.

Amanda turned the page so that Father Voloshin could see it. "These words are Greek, right?

Can you tell me what they say?" She had printed the letters: ἔλθε, κύριε δράκον.

He darted a glance in her direction and then took the sketchbook into his free hand. His eyebrows furrowed. "Did you write this?"

"Yes. Well, no. I mean, I saw it written somewhere and copied it down."

"It's an invocation."

"What does it say?"

He handed the sketchbook back to her and said, "'*Come, Lord Dragon.*'"

"Oh." She sat down on the ground, staring at the Greek words. The only other association she could make with the word "dragon" was the powerful mural painted on the exterior of Little Pete's. Maybe Pete had some sort of fascination with the mythical creature.

Father Voloshin put down his book and turned to face her. "I fear Enemy is seeking you."

"Yeah, I know. They sent the helicopter."

"No, you do not understand me. You do not know your enemy. Very few know."

"And you do?"

"You think this a persecution? No. It is war. And it is same war from very beginning of time."

Amanda shrugged. "Sure. Throughout history, evil people have persecuted others—for religion, nationality, race, for any excuse whatsoever. But that doesn't mean we don't have specific enemies now, in our time—people we can stop."

"Yes, but there is one Enemy. There always been one Enemy. Granted, he is cunning, works stealthily through lots of people, under mask of varied philosophies and ideologies. But he is one, and he we now face."

"And who is that?"

"He is father of lies, who convinces people of greatest lie: that we can be greater than God. That is what our persecutors believe, no? They are convinced they alone direct their own lives, that they alone are master builders of their own free world. If only they see the truth. They are not liberated from anything; they are captive. They are slaves to prince of this world. You know him too. We all know him because, at some point, he whispers his lies to all. He is accuser, evil one, adversary, ancient serpent, great dragon."

"So the members of the NCP doing these heinous deeds … you're saying that the devil made them do it, so to speak?"

"Each person is always free to choose their actions. But we do not do so in vacuum. God acts upon heart and so do cunning promptings of seducer. Many forces act upon human soul—not all good. And so here am I, praying for protection from deceit of our greatest Enemy."

A sudden gust of wind blew into the small clearing. They both looked up: Father Voloshin's pages of scribbled notes took to the air. Amanda set down her sketchbook, then jumped to her feet and hurried to collect the blowing sheets of paper before they escaped. She grabbed and chased the pages, only becoming aware moments later that Father Voloshin wasn't moving at all. Didn't he care that the wind was scattering his research about the mountain?

She paused and glanced back at him. Father Voloshin sat transfixed, his eyes locked on her sketchbook. Unbeknownst to her, the gust of wind had also advanced its pages. Now Amanda saw that the horrific image of her *Portrait of a Mother* lay exposed in front of him.

The priest never stopped looking at the face. He reached forward, picking up the pad. "Who drew this? Do you know what it is?"

Her cheeks burning, she snatched the sketchbook from him, her hands shaking. "I … I don't know what you're talking about." She hastened away from him, closing the sketchbook as she went. She rushed back into the house and to the isolation of the loft. Her heart racing, she sat down on the floor, trying to calm herself.

Was her perspective entirely wrong?

Perhaps she was seeing everything from an erroneous point of view. A persecution was unfolding all around them, but how encompassing was the struggle? Maybe, like her paintings, there was something beyond, another level of existence and reality. She had always perceived something of the sort when she painted, but maybe she had been too nearsighted and failed to see that this other reality extended beyond the canvas, into her own life.

Now she began to see that there might be something more—more than the here and the now.

Despite all her previous misgivings, she had somehow come to believe once again in the existence of God. Yet it couldn't stop at that. A necessary corollary of believing in *His* existence was a recognition that things exist beyond this sensory world of sight and touch: a supernatural world.

Amanda sat still, her mind whirling. *So then is God the only One who inhabits this supernatural world? And if there are other spiritual beings, do they have a hand in influencing what transpires in our visible world—for good or for evil?*

Sick to her stomach, she remembered the moment in Ethan's apartment when she realized that she had completed the demonic face on *Portrait of a Mother*. She had sketched that terrifying mockery by her own hand. But while acknowledging that truth, she also knew another force had been at work—an insinuating, luring nudge from something beyond. She felt it then; she felt it even now. It was a kind of persuasion. She had been under an influence, but not exclusively of drugs.

Maybe the greatest danger wasn't from *something* like a bomb or concentration camp; maybe the gravest harm was from *someone*—mysteriously beyond the human realm— planting rebellious, destructive ideas in the soul or keeping the soul chained through its own continued folly.

Could it be that the ultimate Enemy of freedom wasn't acting from without, but from within?

CHAPTER TWENTY-ONE

A PERSON OF LIGHT

Amanda finished the remains of her lunch: cold tomato soup. Everything was cold now. Though she wore multiple layers, warmth escaped her and she shivered, looking longingly at the fireplace, barren save for a pile of ashes. She couldn't wait until night came and they could again light the fire. In the meantime, she helped Linda collect the empty bowls. Above the clatter of dishes, the wind howled outside. November had folded into December, and the temperatures had dropped below freezing. An icy glaze covered the glass windowpanes.

Rachel now stood on a chair, drawing with her finger on the frosty window and breathing on the ice to make it melt. She stopped, peered closer outside, and began to wave her arms. "Somebody's here!"

Mark darted to the front window, ushering Rachel out of sight. They all waited in complete silence for a few tense moments, no one moving. Could this be the end? Had the JPD discovered them?

"It's Nasir, thank God." Mark relaxed his shoulders.

Amanda stood close enough to Linda to hear her mutter under her breath, "About time. Now we can finally get out of here."

Bethany put her hand over her heart. "Maybe he has news."

Amanda bit her lip, her breath catching in her chest. What would Nasir say? Was her family safe? Or would she hear the unthinkable?

Standing beside his father, Joe looked out the window. "Nasir brought another guy with him! I don't recognize him, though. ... Wait. It seems like they're friends with each other: they're talking ... and Nasir's smiling."

Mark opened the door, and everyone else crowded near the entry, blocking Amanda's sight. Mark greeted Nasir and then introduced himself to the newcomer, whom she still couldn't see.

"It's nice to meet you, Mark. I appreciate your kind welcome."

Eyes wide, Amanda swallowed. She knew that voice. With words caught in her throat, the sting of tears behind her eyes, she craned her neck, trying to verify what she already knew. Nasir walked into the middle of the room.

"Greetings." Nasir bowed his head. "I have much to tell you, but first I would like you to meet a friend of our cause. His name is Morgan."

Amanda dropped the glass bowls she held in her hands. They shattered into countless pieces all over the floor. Time stood still, and she saw that nothing had changed: the khaki pants, the crisp white dress shirt, the neatly combed chestnut hair. ... She stared, flabbergasted. He looked at no one else but her, his penetrating, sky-blue eyes locked with hers.

"You're ... You're here?" she said. "How? Why?"

He smiled back at her. "I'm here, Amanda. Would you like to go for a walk?" He gestured toward the door.

She stepped around the shards of broken glass. Ignoring her bewildered fellow residents, she left the cabin with Morgan, feeling unprepared for this. There was so much to say ... so much to understand.

"I don't even know where to begin." She led him toward Boots, who stood tied to the side of the cabin. "I still can't believe you're here."

"Nasir asked for some extra assistance up north, and I volunteered to help. Remember? I mentioned to you that my work in the city was temporary."

His serene demeanor and unhurried speech contained no element of surprise. Their unexpected meeting was apparently only unexpected on *her* end.

She cocked an eyebrow. "Did you know I was here?"

"I did."

"B-But I thought you never wanted to see me again." A lump rose in her throat, and she looked down at her sneakers. "You gave me no phone number, no address, no last name. I figured that you wanted nothing to do with me anymore— that it was easy to dispose of me and our friendship." She swallowed back the tears. She reflected a moment on her words, a heavy reality hitting her: "Yet ... I suppose that's what I did to you, isn't it? In Central Park. I wanted nothing else to do with you, all because of ..."

"I know why." He spoke gently. "Let me explain myself, if you will. I didn't prefer the way we said goodbye, but the peril was too grave for pleasantries and reassurances. If you had stayed a moment longer in the city, the JPD would have found you. They were actively looking for you."

Her head shot up. "What are you talking about?"

"Your roommate suspected you of infiltration and espionage. Nikki started having you tracked by the JPD early on."

"I was being followed?" Well, that would explain how Nikki knew her whereabouts. "Wait, you had that information all along? Why didn't you tell me about Nikki?"

"You wouldn't have believed me at the time."

She stared into the distance, considering his declaration. He was probably right.

Morgan continued, "Even as you and I talked there by St. Patrick's, Ethan discovered that you had left his apartment."

She startled at that: the sound of Ethan's name spoken aloud knotted her stomach.

"I assure you," Morgan went on, "it wouldn't have been long until he—or any officer of the JPD—found you. You were too involved, too much a part of them. You could only free yourself by leaving the city. Immediately."

"But it was so unlike you. I mean, not even to say goodbye?"

"Please believe me: I never meant to hurt you. I realized that your chance at safety depended on making that 1:00 a.m. train. When I placed the money in your hand and yelled for you to leave, I knew that any further dialogue between us would condemn you to waiting in that station for a train that would never come. I didn't say goodbye because I knew I'd say hello once again … soon. Besides, we were never truly apart. I think you realize that now." He gave her a meaningful look. "You've changed."

"Well, if I've changed at all, it's only because I've lost everyone and everything I had in life. That has a way of dramatically altering your perspective."

Morgan clasped his hands together. "For some, it's only when they are stripped of all they have that they realize the one thing that remains—that cannot be taken away—is all they truly need: God. I believe that you were meant to come here to this cabin, that He has a purpose for all of this. Sometimes the only way to safety is through the fire. For those whom God loves, He disciplines."

"I'll admit that I'm grateful to be here ... especially now that you've joined us."

"And I'm not leaving. I'm here for you."

He wrapped his arms around her, a warm hug full of assurance: security, friendship, familiarity. He was her touchstone: her link to the past, to Academy days when things were simpler. He was part of her transformation: not the corrupting pollution of the city, but the conversion that had begun there through their conversations. Now he was part of her future, a future unknown, but at least together.

"Thank you, Morgan." She took a deep breath. "And now it's time to hear Nasir's news."

She and Morgan reentered the cabin. The glass had been swept off the floor and everyone was silent, listening with rapt attention as Nasir spoke.

"I took the laptop Amanda gave me to the leadership of the opposition party. Some of our computer programmers successfully gained access to the NCP's internal network."

Ken rubbed his hands together. "I hope we hit those jerks where it really hurts."

Nasir nodded. "We acquired vast amounts of highly sensitive information, including the critical intelligence we needed about access points to the retention center. That was our priority, and we decided to strike immediately, before the NCP became aware of the leak."

Bethany fingered her wedding band, her face white. Amanda wanted to speak but couldn't. Thankfully, Mark asked the question she couldn't get out: "And you attacked the retention center?"

"Yes, three days ago. We had a group of about fifty armed members of the opposition. They surprised the JPD officers guarding the site. We took most of the officers as prisoners themselves. Our losses were small in number, though not without great pain in parting. We lost a good comrade of ours. Michael Williams died in the attack."

Amanda gasped. "Michael ... Williams? Do you mean the art professor at the Masters Academy of Fine Art?"

"Yes." Nasir nodded with a frown. "You knew him as well?"

"Yeah. He was my professor."

"Then I am sorry for your loss. *Inna Lillahi wa inna ilayhi raji'un.* To Allah we surely belong and to Him we shall return."

Nasir continued, but Amanda turned to Morgan, speaking in a whisper: "Michael assigned me the art project to sketch *Portrait of a Mother.* Through that painting, I confronted my own mother's death. Only by doing it did I reconnect with you. And that isn't to mention the painting itself, the mystery of its meaning. ... It's like he somehow knew I needed to do that sketch."

Morgan nodded. "There are no coincidences. God weaves a pathway of seemingly disjointed events, leading you down a road that you never anticipated and perhaps even resisted, but in the end becomes exactly what you need."

"... and about eighty captives escaped." Nasir proceeded with his narrative, and he at once reclaimed Amanda's attention.

"Do you ... Do you know who was there ... who escaped after the attack?" Bethany's voice trembled.

"Was Daddy there?" Rachel turned two brown eyes, full of hopeful appeal, in Nasir's direction.

Nasir spoke thick with emotion: "Yes … yes, he was. Your father is safe and well."

Bethany burst into sobs, her shoulders shaking. Rachel stared at her mother, then began crying herself.

Mark picked her up. "It's okay! Your mom is just happy. They found your dad!"

"He's waiting for you." Nasir knelt down beside Bethany, placing a hand on her knee. "I personally gave David your love and told him that you will be on your way to him shortly."

Shouts of congratulations and thrill filled the room, and the residents crowded around Bethany. Mark threw a now smiling Rachel up into the air, spinning her around.

Amanda backed into a corner, her stomach a heavy pit. She wanted to share Bethany and Rachel's joy, but Nasir hadn't said anything about her family. Maybe he didn't know anything about them. Maybe they weren't there. Maybe they weren't even …

She turned and began going up the stairs, unable to stand there a moment longer.

A hand on her shoulder stopped her. "Amanda, wait. There is more good news." Nasir spoke loudly, trying to make his voice heard over the rest of the noise. "Your father and sister are also safe."

Amanda's breath caught, then she half gasped, half cried, "They're okay? Really? Are you positive?"

Nasir nodded. "I saw them myself. I told them you are coming to them."

Her legs buckled and she sank to the floor, covering her face with her hands. She cried, heavy sobs racking her body, but joy poured out with the tears. They were alive! She could be with them again—soon. Her longing for her family, if even possible, became more intense. But at least they were out of danger.

Could they really have a happy ending to this nightmarish fate? Dare she hope for that?

A gentle touch helped her up: Morgan, smiling, gave her a hug. Soon everyone, Father Voloshin included, began embracing her and comforting her. Hands clapped her back or squeezed her shoulders; arms pulled her close. Joe gave her a fist bump. A long time passed before everyone became collected enough to bombard Nasir with questions.

Amanda asked hers first: "Where's my family now?"

"They and the other escapees are in Canada."

Amanda furrowed her brow. "Won't the JPD pursue them?"

"No, the NCP has their hands full at the moment. Once the opposition accessed all the information available, we determined that we needed to cause a complication for the NCP, to buy some time and distract the party so we could unfold further attacks. So our computer programmers went to work."

Ken burst out laughing. "They tore the crap out of that network, didn't they?"

"Indeed. The NCP experienced a complete breakdown of its digital systems. They won't be concerned with recapturing escapees right now; they are worrying about restoring their data and infrastructure."

"So what's the holdup?" Joe threw his hands up as he paced about. "We've got the location. Let's beeline it to Canada!"

Nasir gave a small nod. "I couldn't agree more, Joseph, but the trip must wait yet."

"Why? What's wrong now?" Linda sulked, her head resting on her palm.

Nasir glanced out the window. "It would be most imprudent to travel now. As we speak, a severe snowstorm is approaching the Northeast, with heavy accumulations predicted. There is no possible way for us to travel and navigate through those conditions. No, we must delay our escape for a bit longer. We will plan to leave two days from now, at daybreak."

The room broke out in chatter and excitement at the news, and once Nasir had completed his reporting, Bethany proposed a way to celebrate. She brought out a large chocolate bar that she had stashed away for a moment like this, much to Rachel's delight.

With the others occupied, Amanda drew Nasir to the side and asked, "Does anyone in the NCP know how the opposition destroyed their internal network?"

"In other words, do they know that it was through the laptop you stole?"

"Right. ... Can they trace the breach back to Ethan's computer?"

"I am no IT specialist, but I am almost certain that they can. Even so, you should not worry, my friend. In three days' time, you will be gone from here and reunited with your family."

She began to bite her nails, goosebumps running along her back. She wanted to believe Nasir. But the image of Ethan—goading the NCP on after learning how his computer had led to the biggest attack against his precious party—struck fear in her. He would want revenge, and as he once warned her, she had to be prepared for him to win.

Amanda turned to Morgan. "Every time I think of Ethan and the way he made me feel—the powerlessness, the addictive nature of my relationship with him, the things I did when following his suggestions—it terrifies me. He was ruthless in the pursuit of his desires. He never cared about me at all; he only 'loved me' in order to use me. What could he be capable of now, when his anger has been stirred so much and his precious political party attacked? Ethan participated in the bombing of St. Patrick's—he doesn't shy away from murder. I can only imagine what he justifies in the name of greater freedom. He knows I stole his laptop. He *will* come after me."

"Those with faith need not fear. Someone greater is in command."

She nodded and then smiled shyly at him. "And you're helping me too."

"I'm nothing without God."

Mark invited her to join them for prayers that evening. He had been inviting her every night, in fact, but for the first time, she agreed. She closed her eyes and listened to Bethany's heartfelt petitions and generous thanksgiving. Amanda had no lofty words to proclaim or memorized scripture to recite; she silently chanted the one phrase that dominated her mind and inflamed her heart:

Thank You!

God had answered her prayer: her family had escaped from the JPD. She wanted to give credit where credit was due.

It was interesting, though, the way it happened. He didn't rescue her dad and Chiara in a theatrical flash of miraculous intervention, but through the very people He'd placed around her. She had spent so much of her life—ever since her mom's death—in isolation. Even with Ethan and his friends, she was alone while together. Now she understood and began to internalize the beauty, grace, and gift of community.

In the tense and triumphant moments of the past weeks, these individuals surrounding her had become much more than mere strangers and fellow refugees. Under these bizarre and unlikely conditions, she had found her place. Besides with her family, she belonged here more than anywhere else—more than with her "friends" at Valor Academy or with the diabolical crowd at Little Pete's.

The refugees had taken her in and cared for her— starving, penniless, a drug abuser, and a dropout. To them, she had nothing obvious to offer except further peril. In short, *she* had become "unfit." Now she understood firsthand: the boundary line between "fit" and "unfit" didn't exist. Just half a step separated the two groups. It didn't take much for anyone to become poor or disabled or helpless. This community had looked past her outward condition and recognized her inner worth—a worth not measured by her contribution to society. They had helped her live with dignity.

And then there was Morgan. Amanda looked at his face, humble and true, the light from the surrounding candles falling upon his soft features. He was with her again. He had never rejected or abandoned her. As in the city, she could still consistently turn to him, regardless of the struggle or worry. He never failed to offer her the word of hope or guidance she sought. She needed him, more than she needed anyone else before.

This community in which she found herself was real and genuine: people offering themselves for the good of the other. This was real friendship, and now she was finally a part of it.

The next day arrived, the sky thick with clouds. The snowstorm continued to approach.

After breakfast, Morgan surprised her with a request: "Paint my portrait."

She had been watching Ken and Joe play a game of Rummy and looked up at Morgan, who stood beside her. "Paint your portrait? What's that going to accomplish?"

"Isn't painting your favorite pastime? And we all need good ways of passing time until Nasir returns."

"That's true. … I suppose I could sketch you …"

"I don't mean just a basic sketch. I want you to paint my portrait in detail."

She gave a pained frown. "My last experience painting wasn't a good one. I'm actually scared to open myself up to that again."

"You don't need to fear opening yourself up—as long as you are welcoming the right influence. I think this will be good for you. Come on!" He grabbed her hand and helped her up. "Where's the best place for you to work?"

"As if there are many options." Her gaze floated around the room.

Rachel, squealing with delight, chased Mark in circles. Nearby, Ken shuffled the deck of cards, about to deal the next hand to Joe. Linda and Bethany sat together, talking, while Father Voloshin occupied the back corner with his pile of books.

"We can pull a chair over there." Amanda pointed toward a window. "There's some light there at least. I'll go get my supplies."

She soon returned. Morgan sat in position, his back straight, a serious look on his face.

"You can relax a little, you know," she said, then pulled the supplies from her bag, grateful she had never gotten around to putting them away. She lacked a canvas, so a sheet of paper would have to suffice for watercolors.

It had been so long since she'd last painted in earnest. Had it not been such a crux of her previous life, painting now would have almost seemed foreign. Like smoothly diving underwater, she entered that world where everything else around her stood still. Her paintbrush began creating strokes she did not foresee. She followed her intuition, bringing to the paper the composition of Morgan's inner being. If there were conversations happening around her, she didn't hear them. If people came over to observe her progress, she didn't notice them.

She and Morgan stayed like that for the rest of the morning. He never complained and hardly even moved. She shifted often, not cognizant of the discomfort of the crate on which she sat. Only the portrait taking form before her mattered.

At last, she relaxed, resurfacing to the present moment, and they both stared at the image lying between them. Bright, intense light filled the entire sheet, top to bottom, corner to corner. Countless shades of yellow, intermixed with white, created the sensation of moving beams of radiance. Ever so subtly, in the center of the picture, was the faintest outline of a person. Certain waves of luminance curved together to form an almost invisible figure, hardly discernible from the surrounding dancing rays of light.

His face turned to her, awash in admiration. "You did it! You painted me."

"Really? It's that clear to you?"

"Undeniably. Just think about it! Tell me what you see."

"I was supposed to paint you. Don't ask me what I ended up doing."

"But you *did* paint me. You painted me more clearly than anyone else could."

"I painted …" She examined her work, struggling to find the right words. "It's a person of light."

His face beamed with a smile, animated with excitement.

She held up her hands in exasperation. "What does that even mean?"

Morgan opened his mouth to respond, but Mark called for everyone's attention: "Hey, listen up, folks. We need some firewood for our final night here. Should we draw straws, or do I have any volunteers?" Mark surveyed the room, rubbing his hands together—maybe in expectation or just to keep his fingers warm.

"I'll go." Amanda stood up, stretching. She needed to give Boots some exercise anyway.

"Well, since Amanda's going, that means we can count Morgan in too." Ken smiled wryly. "And I might as well go. I've stared at these four walls long enough."

Amanda followed Morgan and Ken over to the front door.

Mark watched them put on their coats, his eyebrows creasing together. "You guys be careful out there, okay?"

"I'll try not to get any splinters." Ken opened the door and left.

Amanda waved to Mark and walked outside, Morgan at her heels.

CHAPTER TWENTY-TWO

SHE OUGHT TO BE LOVED

"Why don't you two lovebirds go off on your own and I'll track eastward?" Ken jerked his thumb to indicate the woods behind him.

Amanda fidgeted with her coat zipper. "Shouldn't we all stay together? Safety in numbers, right?"

"Nah, three's a crowd. Besides, I'm not walking around defenseless." Ken lifted up his coat, revealing a black holster and the grip of a handgun. "Happy scavenging." With that, he stuffed his hands into his jean pockets and strode off.

She began to saddle Boots. Overhead, billowy, dark clouds covered the entire sky, blocking any sunshine. The barren landscape surrounding them added to the day's bleakness. Everything had died or become dormant. It would be months until life returned to these woods. She shivered inside her coat. Something in the air seemed different: the storm was imminent.

Amanda finished and then Morgan untied the reins as he said, "We'll have to ride or else we won't get there in time. Here, you go up first."

Seemingly without any effort, Morgan hoisted her into the saddle. He vaulted himself up onto the horse as well, wrapping his arms around her and grabbing the reins.

"Let's go!" he said.

Boots began an eager trot. Amanda smiled, grateful to be riding in the expanse of wilderness instead of being stuck in the claustrophobic cabin. Having Morgan here with her made it even more wonderful.

She turned her head, calling back to him, "What do you mean by 'we won't get there in time'?"

"You'll see."

They rode for a little while, and then Morgan slowed Boots to a walk, gradually pulling him to a halt in the middle of a large clearing. Morgan jumped down and, offering his hand, helped her out of the saddle. He walked a few paces ahead of her and then stopped in the middle of the empty space.

"Right … here."

Amanda eyed him. "Morgan? What's going on?"

"Just wait!"

She opened her mouth, hoping to question him further, but he turned around and placed his finger on her lips.

"Shh! Just watch."

She looked all around, staring at nothing.

"There it is!" He pointed upward.

"What? There's *what*?"

A few seconds passed. Then, like magic, she spotted it too: the first snowflakes of winter. The woods were silent as the snow began cascading from the heavens and down upon them. Slowly, before their eyes, the millions of tiny flakes, each one individually crafted, landed on the leafy carpet, transforming the browns and deep reds of dried, dead leaves into a blanket of purest white. They dotted Amanda's upturned face, their touch like many icy kisses.

Smiling, Morgan gazed at the white expanse all around them. "All things can be transformed; even the darkest scarlet can be made snowy white."

"Do you really believe that? Do you really believe that no matter how dark the depravity or how twisted the perversion, all people can be transformed? All people can be forgiven and deserving of love once more?"

"Of course I believe that, but regardless of what I think, it is who you are."

"What are you talking about?"

"You are *Amanda*. Your name literally means: *'She ought to be loved.'* You are always God's beloved. Nothing you have done or ever will do can change that."

He paused, his eyes assuming a distant look—he was praying. His focus returned to her once more, yet she couldn't read his expression.

"Amanda, I've been waiting to ask you something. And I think now is finally the right time."

She caught her breath. Whatever came next would obviously be serious. "What is it?"

"Did you buy a yearbook from Valor Academy?"

She laughed. "*That's* your question? You waited to ask if I bought a yearbook?"

"Just answer the question, please."

"Did I buy a yearbook? Yeah, my dad forced me to. What does that have to do with anything?"

"Did you ever look me up in it?"

"No, I never thought to. Why?"

"I wasn't in it."

She shrugged. "Who cares? There are lots of graduates who didn't bother to have their senior picture taken. Why are we even discussing this?"

"You don't understand. I wouldn't be in your yearbook because I never attended Valor Academy. I was never a student there."

She stared at him. "But you were at graduation."

"So were your family and many others."

"Morgan, it doesn't matter to me what Academy you attended. Or if you attended any at all! Why don't you just tell me what you're trying to say?"

"Did you ever ask me my last name?"

"Well ... no." She had never thought to ask him about that. It seemed strange, but also somehow natural.

"What about my family? Did you ever ask where they live, my parents' occupations, anything about my siblings?"

A warm flush spread across her cheeks. "No, never. You're right, Morgan: I've been self-absorbed. Most of our conversations have been entirely about me. I'm sorry ... I'm working on that and—"

"I have no family here."

"Wait. You mean your parents passed away?"

"You once said I never told you my address, right? Well, I don't have one."

"Hold on—what are you talking about? You're an orphan, an Academy dropout, homeless ... what, exactly, is your story?"

He put his hands on her shoulders, looking deep into her eyes. "Do you think a Father would allow His children to walk abandoned, helplessly alone while the Enemy prowls about them? Is anyone strong enough to fight these battles alone?"

At that moment, from somewhere off in the distance, came a reverberating, jarring noise almost like fireworks: a gunshot. Amanda jumped and then froze for a few seconds, processing the undeniable sound they'd just heard. She had no time to speak or question: a series of sharp *CRACK!* sounds filled the air. Boots snorted, the whites of his eyes showing. Amanda ducked to the ground, pulling Morgan down with her, and covered her head with her trembling hands. She had no idea where the gunshots came from or how close they might be.

And then, as suddenly as it had started, the gunfire ceased. Eerie silence filled the air.

Still crumpled in a ball on the ground, she whispered to Morgan, "Ken! He's out there alone!"

Morgan's face wore a grave expression. "Maybe not alone."

"We need to help him!"

"We should check in at the cabin first: the others will be wondering. Not to mention we have no firearms ..."

Her mouth dry, she nodded and followed his lead. In minutes, Boots had galloped back through the woods, Morgan guiding him with precision. Amanda clung to Morgan, expecting at any moment to run into danger.

To her immense relief, the cabin came into view.

Mark flung the door open. "What happened out there?"

"I don't know." Amanda dismounted and walked toward him. "We heard the gunfire, but we don't know where it came from. Ken isn't with us—he wanted to go off on his own."

Joe stuck his head out the door. "There were lots of shots. Is someone else out there?"

"Seems like it," Amanda said.

Morgan stepped forward. "We need to go find Ken— immediately."

"I'm coming too." Mark pulled on his coat and cocked his gun. "Joe, stay here with your mother and the others. Keep the door locked."

The last thing Amanda saw inside the cabin was Joe's pale face, pinched with fear. She walked Boots to the side of the cabin and secured the reins. She turned around and caught a glimpse of Morgan's back, entering the woods nearby. Without stopping to think, she ran across the yard and followed him into the dense forest.

She was careful not to get too close, just in case Mark should spot her and send her back. Thankfully, their fresh footprints gave her a clear path to follow. She had to do this. It was her fault that the JPD was here. She couldn't let the others get hurt on her behalf. She swallowed uneasily. But maybe Ken was already hurt. Or even worse.

Amanda kept walking through the swirling snow. It was hard to tell now how far behind she might be from Mark and Morgan. She started moving faster. The snow came down harder, the flakes thick and the wind picking up. What if she got lost out here? She stopped, peering at the ground to locate the footprint trail. They must have switched directions. She spun around, her head turning left to right, panic building. Maybe if she just retraced her steps? But the falling snow was quickly erasing even those footprints. Despite the cold temperature, sweat trickled down her back. Then, a few feet away, her eye caught it: a trail of crimson, splattered all over the snow. Blood.

She found footprints amidst the blood and followed both, until she came to a small stream where the trail seemed to stop. Just ahead stood a small landmass that rose above her head and formed a natural bridge over the stream. She walked to the overhang, and looking through its dark corridor, she exhaled in relief. Morgan and Mark were just ahead, studying the ground.

Standing there, Amanda watched them and wondered when to tell them that she was there. Her teeth began to chatter, and she rubbed her arms. A drop of warm liquid fell onto the back of her exposed neck. That wasn't a snowflake; it was heavy … more like a raindrop. Then another … and another. She wiped her neck and raised her hand, wanting to pull the collar of her coat closer. She glanced down at her hand and screamed: bright red blood stained her fingers.

Jumping back from her spot, Amanda stared with horror at the earth bridge above her. Almost indistinguishable, hidden among prickly bushes and accumulated leaves, a hand protruded forth, draining itself with a steady stream of blood.

Mark and Morgan arrived at her side, and Mark grabbed her arm as he said, "Amanda, what are you doing here?"

She pointed a shaky finger at the bloody hand. Together, the three of them scrambled up the landmass. She recognized the worn yet sturdy leather boots lying under some brush. They belonged to Ken.

Amanda could see his chest rising and falling. He was alive at least, half-hidden under the shrubs and dead foliage. He must have sought this cover. Why else had he dragged his failing body so far? His attacker, though, still loomed large—perhaps even closer now. She glanced over her shoulder but saw no one.

"Ken! Ken, it's me." Mark spoke near Ken's ear.

Ken breathed heavily and lay in an awkward position. His feet writhed in pain, and his eyes, open to see his comrades, screamed for help. A large, damp spot stained his coat where the blood seeped through. He had been shot.

Mark tried again: "Can you talk? What happened?"

"Bastard … shot me … JPD …" Ken gasped, clenching his jaw in torment.

"It's his shoulder." Morgan examined Ken. "He's losing a great deal of blood."

Ken went on, "Said there's … more coming … not him, though … I took care of him … he's not going anywhere …"

"We're taking you back to the house. We can treat you there." Mark stood up.

"Don't … freakin' pretend!" Ken's face looked gray and clammy with sweat. "I'm … dying. You can't … *treat* me."

"We won't give up until we've done everything possible to save you." Mark turned to Amanda and Morgan. "Let's get ready to move him."

Mark and Morgan carefully lifted Ken's upper body, but Ken still cried out in pain. Amanda carried his legs. They started through the snow, Morgan calling out which direction to go. She had no idea how he could remember the way. Ken seemed to waver on the verge of unconsciousness. She glanced down at his ashen face and found his eyes—once so piercing—now vaguely glancing at her … and beyond her.

"If I don't make it … tell the priest … put a good word in …"

"Open your heart." Amanda's quiet petition came from somewhere within her she didn't even know.

No response came.

They trudged onward, Ken's eyes now closed and his head bobbing from side to side with the movement. Amanda stopped worrying about the possible threat lurking around them; her sole concern now was to keep Ken alive.

It seemed like an eternity, struggling through the endless world of swirling snow, but at last, the cabin came into view. The others ran out, faces creased with worry and terror.

Huffing, Mark barked out, "Clear a space on the floor! Put down a blanket!"

With a flurry of motion, they scrambled to get Ken indoors. At once, the door was locked, a blanket set down, a fire kindled. Amanda rested Ken's legs on the floor, her arm muscles groaning and cramped from the long-held position. She crouched in place, gazing at Ken's still body, the bloodstain ever growing.

"Dad, can … can you help him?" Joe whispered.

"I straighten teeth. I've never worked on a bullet wound." Mark rubbed his tense face.

"Nasir is a doctor and he's coming in the morning. He can help us then." Morgan's steady words and calm demeanor seemed to quiet the whole room.

"And for now, we'll do what we can." Bethany walked over to Mark. "I worked as an RN before Rachel was born. We can do it together. We have to try at least. He'll die if we don't."

Mark took a deep breath and nodded. "I'll grab my equipment. Linda, start boiling some water. Bethany, you better have a look at the wound. Everyone else, go upstairs and don't come down until we tell you."

They filed up the stairs. In the loft, Rachel crawled into Amanda's lap. Chiara used to sit with her that same way, so many years ago. Morgan sat beside them, while Joe and Father Voloshin settled themselves by the other wall. The storm raged outside, the snowfall blocking any view out the window. Boots was out there, left alone and exposed to the storm. He saved her life and this was how she repaid him?

"Let us pray." Father Voloshin made the Sign of the Cross, swinging his hand from east to west, and held his hands in prayer. *Yea, though I walk through valley of shadow of death, I will fear no evil …*

Amanda tried to focus on the prayer, but Ken's words haunted her: the JPD officer said there were more coming. How much longer did any of them have? Was this whole venture just one long, drawn-out torture that would end in violent death? This was the severest of sentences: to be ripped from the possibility of being reunited with her family when the goal was so close, so obtainable at last.

Alongside fear came burning fury, all aimed at the one person who must have orchestrated this horror. For Amanda, that one individual epitomized all of the perverted philosophies and corrupted beliefs that had set this bloody persecution in motion.

How much more would be demanded of her? Ken didn't deserve to die. And yet, even now, he might have breathed his final breath. Hatred pounded in her heart and coursed through her veins.

Her vitriol stewed until she could finally whisper to Morgan, with the prayer now ended and Rachel asleep on her lap: "I hate Ethan … I hate him with every part of me. He's taken everything from me, ruined me. And now he's damned us all to an inescapable death!"

Morgan laid his hand on top of hers. "Hatred has become your prison, Amanda. You must forgive him."

She drew back. "What! … That's impossible."

"It is possible. And it's essential, in fact. An unwillingness to forgive is an unwillingness to be forgiven. Nothing is more like God than mercy: to forgive one's enemies."

"Well … I guess I'm not God then."

"And you can't be, but you can be *like* Him. But aren't you now just another devil? This is the real battle. It's not out there, against the JPD officers or NCP leaders. The greatest

278

struggle is within the human heart. Who will win? Who will claim it? Has your hatred locked the door to your heart?"

"What are you implying, exactly?"

"Don't you yourself want to be forgiven? Haven't you rejoiced in forgiveness freely given? Then forgive. Love ... love your enemy. Love Ethan."

"How can I? He doesn't deserve it! I can never get back what he's robbed me of. He's taken everything from me. I will *never* forgive him!"

"Somehow you've been rescued, delivered from your perdition. Can't you ask the same for another lost soul? Who among us *deserves* God's love? Shouldn't we all receive it, poured out for us?"

"Okay, God loves him. But Ethan is already halfway to hell, so why shouldn't I wish he finally gets there?"

"Because wishing his destruction will destroy you too. Forgiveness banishes the power of evil. It makes what is broken whole. It sets you free."

A creak arose from the darkness below: someone was coming up the stairs. All eyes turned in that direction, waiting. Mark appeared, the wrinkles on his face more prominent than ever and his silver hair disheveled. He sat down on the floor.

"How's Ken?" Joe looked at his father.

Mark sighed. "I don't know. He's alive ... for now. He lost a lot of blood, though, and we obviously can't give him a transfusion. Like Morgan said earlier, Ken just needs to get through the night. Nasir can help us tomorrow. Tonight will decide everything."

Amanda swallowed. "Is Ken awake?"

"Yes. And he's asking for you, Father."

Father Voloshin raised his eyebrows. "I come now." With that, he hurried downstairs.

"We'll stay up here, to give Ken space," Mark said. "Might as well grab a bite to eat and head to bed. ... Tomorrow's departure will begin early." He rubbed his chin, thinking aloud.

Joe glanced out the window. "Unless we're all dead before tomorrow comes. The gunmen can't be far from us."

Standing up, Mark ignored Joe's ominous statement and said, "Joe, come downstairs with me and help me get some dinner together. Morgan and Amanda, keep an eye on Rachel and try to pack up the final things remaining in here."

Stirred awake by the recent movement, Rachel helped organize the few cherished possessions that the fugitives had brought with them. Amanda reached for a small box that lay in the back corner of the loft and found it half-full of cigars. Padróns—Ken's favorites. She placed them in his bag.

"You should pack this too."

She turned around. Morgan, smiling at her, held out a package wrapped in plain white paper. She stared at him, mystified.

"It's for you." He thrust the present into her hands. "Consider it an early Christmas gift."

"You bought me a Christmas present? Here, in the middle of absolutely nowhere, you found a gift for me? Morgan, sometimes I can't understand you. And you know, we never finished our conversation from earlier. I didn't forget about it."

"We'll finish that conversation soon, but not now. Come on, open your gift!"

She gave him another searching look and then obliged him, ripping open the wrapping. It took three small tears to confirm her mounting suspicions.

"You buried it, didn't you?" Morgan clasped his hands together behind his back. "I thought it was time to be resurrected."

She looked upon her painting, open-mouthed in amazement. "But how … how did you know where to find it?"

Bewilderment and awe at Morgan's kindness filled her. She gazed upon the painting as though she were seeing it for the first time. She eagerly took in the falling raindrops and the three interlocking hands that served as an umbrella to shelter her. Yet tears blurred her vision: Ethan had butchered the canvas. … He had permanently destroyed the lady's face.

Amanda wiped the tears from her eyes. "It's ruined. No one could ever fix this. It's beyond repair. That's why I got rid of it."

Morgan shook his head. "No. *Behold, God makes all things new.*"

CHAPTER TWENTY-THREE

WHAT IS TRUTH?

The crackling and popping of the fire filled the downstairs room. Amanda sat near the source of heat, keeping watch for the others who slept upstairs. Just a few more hours until dawn. Just a few more hours until they could leave. No—to be more precise: a few more hours until they could *escape*.

She held her painting in her hands, mulling over Morgan's words. Could she create it anew? Maybe the destruction wasn't permanent, the damage not irreparable? *The lost can be found; the wounded can be healed; the weak can be made strong ... stronger than ever before.*

Perhaps none of this was ever really about Ethan. Amanda had searched for love and settled for a flimsy shadow of what it could be. With him, she'd emptied herself. She poured herself out for him, gave him everything in her heart. But her heart did not belong to him; God had formed her heart and only He could satisfy the longings inside of it.

Ken's shaky breathing grabbed her attention. She knelt beside him. His face looked ghastly pale, and beads of sweat dotted his forehead. The tight wrapping of the bandage covered his chest and shoulder.

She placed her hand over his and whispered, "I'm sorry, Ken. I never wanted this to happen."

Amanda then tiptoed to the front window and peeked under the corner of the curtain. The sky had cleared, the snowstorm having finished and moved on. A crescent moon illuminated the scene, casting black shadows across the drifts of snow. Nothing stirred. Everything seemed to sleep under a thick blanket of white.

She put on her coat and scarf and then grabbed her book bag as quietly as possible. Yes, it was the middle of the night. Yes, it was cold outside, and the snow would probably come up to her knees. But Boots was out there—had been out there the whole duration of the storm—and the least she could do was to check on him and take him an apple. This would take just a minute. No one would even need to know that she left the cabin.

Outside, her feet sank through almost a foot of snow. She turned the corner of the cabin but stopped short. Boots was gone. She glanced around. No hoofprints … no sign of him whatsoever. Maybe she didn't tie the reins as well as she thought? Her stomach was a heavy pit. That horse saved her life. He was Chiara's beloved pet. What if he was hurt or lost?

She started walking toward the stream. He might have gone there for water. "Boots!" she called, as loud as she dared, into the stillness of the night.

Amanda reached the stream, and in the cold light of the night, she searched for Boots up and down the bank. She saw no sign of him anywhere. Then a sound—a kind of rustling and crunching of snow—came from behind the trees. She stood, transfixed. The branches of an age-old pine shook in her periphery, toppling snow that had lain there precariously. A human figure appeared, stooped and shuffling through the brush. Her heart pounded at breakneck speed. At last, the inevitable had happened: a JPD officer found her. Her long and storied flight from danger ended where she'd started: cornered and alone. She had reached the end. ... She would never see her family again.

The man, free from the trees, fully stood. Looking around, he jumped and cried out, apparently taken aback by the unexpected sight of her before him in the moonlight. A heavy hood shadowed the individual's face.

"Amanda?"

A chill seized her. He let down the hood, his face revealed. But she already knew who it was the moment he'd spoken. His voice pierced Amanda like ice to her heart, a knife to a wound not nearly healed enough.

"Ethan." She could barely say the name, an avalanche of emotions surging through her.

He stood just feet away, staring back at her. It was him, but not as she remembered. He had changed: his face unshaven, his hair matted and in need of a cut, dark circles piled under his sagging eyes. But the change went more than skin deep. Those keen, self-possessed eyes looked dull. He seemed like a ghost of his former self.

She took a shaky breath. "Whatever you're here for, it has to do with me. So leave everyone else alone."

"The others? I don't care about them."

"Are there JPD officers with you?" She scanned the trees behind him, anticipating a growing force.

"There were three of us. You guys killed one of them. I took care of the other one."

"What? ... You ... You killed him?"

"It's nothing he wouldn't have done to me, first opportunity he got. I had to get to you first. Alone."

"And why's that? What do you want from me? Didn't you already take enough?"

His face became creased with fury, his nostrils flaring and a vein in his temple throbbing. "You owe me something—"

"I owe you *nothing*!"

"Listen!" He stepped closer, his jaw clenched. "I went through hell just to get here to you because I want the *truth*. I want an explanation from your own lips. Everyone around me is convinced they know what happened, and they've almost convinced me too, but ..." He stared wildly at her, his old confidence and self-assurance gone. "That night you left, I went back to my apartment. I needed you at that moment—more than ever before ..."

Her jaw dropped. "You can't be serious. You *needed* me? What did you think I'd do ... praise you for your work at St. Patrick's? For your murder of innocent people?"

"I didn't know about that, okay? I didn't know about the bombing!"

"And I'm supposed to believe you're telling the truth?"

"What is truth anymore?" He rubbed his eyes. "Look, I didn't know! When I first joined the NCP, no one ever said anything about killing people. And when they told me the NCP had a big, secret project, I never pictured murder! I knew nothing about the planned bombing or that people would be there at the time. I arrived at St. Patrick's that night, and Nikki told me what was up. I felt numb. I didn't want to be part of that. I'm not a murderer."

"Didn't you just tell me that you killed a JPD officer?"

"That's different! He would've killed me."

"It's still a life." Amanda crossed her arms. "But I forgot. Things aren't black and white with you, are they? You live in the world of gray, the world of shadows."

"I don't know. I've only seen darkness for a long time." He sighed and frowned. "After St. Patrick's, I felt shocked and alone. Everyone I knew belonged to the NCP. Except you. I needed you. You were the only one who wasn't part of this … this evil. Everything in my life was falling apart. I needed something to hold on to, something that was real. So I went back to my apartment to find you."

"Wait." She held up a hand, her mind spinning. He wanted … needed … her? This had to be just another deception.

But he continued, as though he didn't hear her: "You were gone. My office was totaled, everything destroyed. I couldn't find the most valuable item: my laptop. Do you want to know what my first thought was?"

"You were worried how much trouble you'd be in with the NCP, right?"

He stared at her for a long moment. "No. I was worried about *you*. I thought you were in danger. I thought the opposition party abducted you from my place, or took you for ransom … or something like that. It never occurred to me that the perpetrator could have been you."

"But you suspected me all along. That's why you had the JPD tracking me."

He shook his head. "No. Nikki did. She was positive you were an operative for the opposition. I told her that was impossible."

"Why?"

Ethan glanced away and ran his tongue over his dry, chapped lips. "I told her that you loved me." He hurried on, "But you were gone. The JPD trackers immediately alerted the NCP. Nikki blew the whistle that my work computer was missing too. The NCP held me as a suspect until they could verify the facts. The JPD found you at your family's home and then lost you in this wilderness. Still, I stood by my story. You must have been abducted. You *couldn't* have done it. I waited, convinced that I would hear from you. Then what seemed impossible became possible. The opposition ravaged the NCP's computer network and attacked one of the captivity sites. And they did it all thanks to my computer."

She swallowed. "So the NCP knew it was your fault?"

"Of course. The NCP put me in a private prison. The JPD interrogated me multiple times, usually using torture. They confiscated all of my possessions. Any phone conversations that could be retrieved, any messages, email correspondence—they reviewed and inspected everything for any sign of treachery. I have nothing left. I am now classified as an enemy of freedom."

She stared at him, then asked, "How did you end up here?"

"They gave me an ultimatum: my life or yours. They ordered me to find you and the stolen computer—or face the punishment of death. They didn't send me alone, of course. Two JPD officers were in charge of me. We tracked you to this mountain. Now they're both dead. It's you and me." He stepped closer, his fists clenched. "You've put me through unimaginable hell. I've been tortured, imprisoned, prodded along at gunpoint across this frozen mountain wilderness. I've lost everything: my apartment, my car, my career, my reputation, my friends ... all because a certain Amanda Burrow came into my life. And of course I lost you too. Or maybe I never had you. Now, before the end, I want to hear it from you: Was any of it ever true?"

Her chest was tight, and blood pounded in her ears. "*You* lost everything? Did *you* lose your family? Who cares about your car or fancy apartment or high-paying position? I lost my dad and my sister! They were in a detainment center, which is just a fancy word for a concentration camp. But you already knew that, didn't you? You probably helped put them there!"

His eyes widened. "They took your family? No ... I had no idea."

He was quite the actor. ... She almost believed his feigned surprise.

She glared at him. "I can't believe a word you tell me, not after what you've done and how you've used me."

"No—really ... I didn't know about your dad and sister. I heard they were being tracked, but your dad obviously had a huge target on his back. I think the NCP started withholding information from me, once Nikki alerted them. They kept me in the dark about a lot of things toward the end, especially anything having to do with you."

"Sure." She shook her head, sickened by his ever-spewing lies. "And how much did you withhold from *me*? That day I met you in the lounge, at the Masters Academy ... that wasn't mere coincidence, right?"

"Of course not. The NCP assigned me to you. It was my side job. I liked the game of trying to get information from our opponents without arousing suspicion while keeping an eye on possible spies. ... But why don't we just lay all the cards on the table right now? That's what you were doing too. The NCP is right, aren't they? You were working as an infiltrator. We played each other all along, didn't we?"

A lump rose in her throat. "No, I wasn't working for anyone. I wasn't acting. I would have done anything for you. I basically did."

"That's a lie!" His shout reverberated through the silent woods. "How could you have felt one shred of anything for me? If you did, why did you betray me?"

She drew back. "Betray! I was entirely loyal to you—to a fault. I cared about you so much that I gave you the one thing that meant the most to me. I stole your computer only because you stole something even greater from me."

His blank expression gave her greater fury.

"*My painting!* You destroyed the most precious, most valuable thing to me. You knew how much it meant to me!"

He pursed his lips, then let out a slow breath, the vapor trail drifting off as he said, "It's less painful to forget the truth, isn't it? ... You have it all wrong. I didn't steal it from you and destroy it; we did it together. You and I both shredded the canvas. I told you that I thought it was best—that the painting represented all your childhood fairy-tale dreams. ... Talk about grandiose fiction. That juvenile image was a yoke preventing you from moving forward in full freedom. Destroying the painting liberated you. I didn't do it alone. You may not remember all of this because of the drugs, but you and I did it together."

"That's ... That's impossible."

He scoffed. "It's very possible ... because that's what happened."

Amanda bit her lip, doubt beginning to seep around the edges of her version of reality. Perhaps her drug-induced state had in fact kept certain aspects of that night conveniently hidden. Perhaps she remembered what she wanted to remember and ran from all the rest. Her heart sank: deep down, she admitted the truth she had long denied. He was right: he hadn't done it alone. The blame fell on both of them.

She wouldn't abandon her cause this quickly, though. He couldn't be let off the hook as though he had done no wrong. "Even so, who were you to decide what was best regarding my painting? You had no right to determine what

I needed or what the painting represented to me. You may pretend to be your own deity, but you aren't my god!"

He shrugged. "At one time, you valued my opinion. I didn't force you to adhere to it. You were free to do what you wanted. You can't blame me for what followed."

"Free? I couldn't have been more a slave—a slave to my desires, to my passions, to pleasure, to the pill … to you. For all your great proclamations about total liberty, you and your political party have no idea what freedom truly is."

"It's not my political party." He growled the words, hatred laden on each syllable.

"Oh, so you renounce their ideology, then?"

"No, not the ideology. There is nothing wrong with the philosophy that I've lived by. It's how the NCP has gone about implementing it in society—that's where they went all wrong. I'm not to blame for the false execution of the truth."

Now Amanda scoffed. "You can't even see it! It's your philosophy that led to these actions. The ideology you've subscribed to for so long has caused all of this! This is their natural end. … You know what? You claim that you're free to do whatever you want, yet *we weren't even free to love each other*. We didn't know the meaning of freedom."

"And you do now?" Arrogant mockery tinged his question.

"Yeah, I do. … The battle isn't between the NCP and the opposition. It isn't even between you and me. It's here, within our own selves. The battle raging right now is within you, within me. … We are all fighting the same war." She took a deep breath and met his gaze. "And I'm not going to be held prisoner any longer. I forgive you, Ethan."

"*You* forgive *me*?" His abrupt, forced laughter sounded scathing. "Did you not hear the story I just told you? Did you forget the ultimatum placed upon me: my life or yours? Keep your forgiveness … your pity. I don't want them."

"So what are you going to do? Are you going to kill me?"

A long pause followed. Ethan stood perfectly still, as though listening. He turned his head, staring into the dark woods near them. "There's something over there. Something's here with us."

CHAPTER TWENTY-FOUR

IN THE LIGHT OF FREEDOM

Amanda stared into the pitch-blackness. From the recesses of the trees came the unmistakable sight of two burning red eyes staring at them, unblinkingly fixated.

"Go!" Ethan lunged toward her, shoving her forward. "Get out of here!"

Even with no idea of what she was running from, she obeyed, stumbling forward through the snow. A few yards on, she glanced back over her shoulder. The fearsome, stalking form of a mountain lion emerged from the shadows. It all happened in an instant: her eyes widened in recognition of the predator, her breath caught in her chest, her legs scrambled, pounding her forward in the thick snow. Her body was full of frenzy, but her mind blank, save one thing: flight. She could hear Ethan behind her, fleeing as well.

The snow had caged the beast, wrapped around his tree, yet the storm had now passed, leaving him starving and restless. The lion prowled about the mountain, seeking something to devour. Tonight it had chosen them.

Amanda raced ahead, pushing the limits of her muscles and limbs. Yet moments later, a horrifying bellow filled her ears.

A clear sound of struggle came from behind. Frightened and feverish screams, human and beast, mingled and filled the night. The sound of unadulterated pain stopped her. She turned around and witnessed the scene.

The agile mountain lion had leaped, its precision and power no match for man. Ethan was now the victim, held captive on the snowy ground, defenseless as the lion continued its attack.

Help me! she prayed.

She flung her book bag to the ground and rifled through it, searching for something she'd stuffed in there long ago. It had to be in there! … She'd tucked it away for a purpose … and … yes—yes! Her fingers closed upon it: the box of matches from home!

Amanda opened the box and tried to strike a match, her hands quaking. A feeble flame shone. She pulled her sketchbook from the bag. Then, dashing over to the nearest tree, she set the sketchbook ablaze and threw it deep into the many branches of splintered wood and brush that lay in a thick pile on the ground, kept dry by the dense overhang above.

The fire sprang to life. She grabbed a dead branch from the ground and immersed it in the mounting flames. Weapon in hand, she rushed toward the mountain lion, her torch of light growing in intensity and the flames behind her spreading from one low-hanging dry limb to another and then from tree to tree on that densely packed slope. With her free hand, she swept up her bag and chucked it as forcefully as she could, squarely at the animal.

The lion darted back, dodging the projectile, its sinewy body turning around to consider her. The persistent hunter roared, revealing a full set of razor-sharp fangs, dripping with blood that looked black in the glow of moonlight. Amanda edged closer, and they eyed one another. Now she sprinted forward, the fiery torch a sword before her, and plunged the inferno into the lion's side just as it braced itself to attack. Bloodcurdling screams pierced the air, and the beast bounded away from Amanda, veering past her. As it did so, searing pain shot up and down her arm, but with uncharacteristic willpower, she maintained her death grip on the branch. Her eyes remained locked on the wounded lion as it licked its chops, stalking about, hissing and growling.

I trust in You.

She stared into the burning red eyes. She charged again, letting out an echoing cry and meeting her opponent in the ring of fire that now encircled them. Aiming her fiery torch at the beast's face, she missed—it turned away just before her blow met its target. Still, the fire caught hold of its shoulder.

It proved to be enough. As silently as it had entered, the lion fled into the darkness, abandoning its prey.

Yet it would prowl again, until the end of the age, seeking the destruction of all.

She hurried to the place where Ethan's body lay prone on the ground. He issued forth no sound; the only noise was the gentle, almost soothing, crackling of the branches still kindling the light of the fire she had created.

Blood stained the snow surrounding Ethan. She crouched beside him, easily locating the source of the blood: a wound on his left calf, penetrating deep into his leg. A number of bite marks and gashes peppered Ethan's body, with little rivulets of blood flowing from them. One ragged cut even went across his cheek. Still, his chest rose and fell rhythmically.

"Ethan! Can you hear me?" She grabbed his cold hand, lying motionless in the snow, and held it between her hands, rubbing it.

He turned and looked at her. He stared, wide-eyed, panic and shock written across his pale face.

She clung to his hand—whether to comfort him or to steady her own terror, she didn't know. "I'm sorry!" Her tears began flowing, unchecked. "I'm so sorry for everything."

"You came back—why?"

"We can't just sit here talking. You're bleeding. I've got to do something … get help or water or …"

His focus became clearer. He tightened his fingers around hers. "No, Amanda … first I need to tell you something. I never believed them. I always thought there was … that what we had together was genuine. *That's* why I had to find you first." He paused again, seeming to gather his strength. "And I wanted to tell you that I'm sorry. I didn't love you in the best way … or even the right way. But I loved you in the only way I knew how."

Faded memories of a first conversation, a date in Central Park, and a kiss in the pouring rain floated before her. How many times had she gazed into those hazel eyes, kissed those very lips? How many times had she desperately wished for him to say the word "love"? And now he had, after he'd risked his life to save hers.

But how many times had he lied to her, manipulated her, kept information from her, tried to win her over to a political party that almost killed her and her family? Even now, he could still be playing her. He wanted to survive, to get himself in the most favorable position to claw and fight his way back to the top. Right now, he could only do that with her help. He knew just what to say and how to say it.

She dropped his hand and took off her coat. "I'm going to wrap up your leg and hopefully stop the bleeding."

He struggled to sit up. "Amanda, come on. It's a simple question: Why did you come back to help me? Just answer me."

Her throat constricted. She kept winding her coat sleeve around his bleeding wound, around and around. It was like her feelings for him, circling around her bleeding heart: from love to hate to … But, no, she wouldn't let him deceive her again. She wouldn't give him the satisfaction of knowing he'd won this round of the game he played, the puzzle he kept toying with.

She knotted the sleeves together and stood up. "I came back because it was the right thing to do."

He collapsed to the ground, looking away from her and not replying.

She opened her mouth, intending to say something, but didn't know what to say or feel. Nothing seemed clear anymore. "I'm … I'm going to get some water and wash your other cuts—there's a stream right here."

Unraveling the scarf from her neck, she hurried down toward the water. She used her boot to smash through the ice at the creek's edge. She knelt down and plunged the scarf into the frigid liquid, which intensified the pain of the cut on her arm. She yanked the scarf out, water and droplets falling from her hands. But something caught her eye and made her breath catch. Under the surface of the water, looking back at her, was a face. Someone looked up at her, through the water—a face as familiar as her own, but so superiorly different.

This woman's eyes were gentle and warm, yet contained a wisdom deeper than all the waters of the Earth. Her skin was the purest white, dazzling even when compared to the newly fallen snow. Her glance was captivating, life-giving, so much so that Amanda couldn't turn away. Yet her look was humble. Her exquisite features were singular, her radiance otherworldly.

It was the lady from her most precious painting, the sacred, mysterious image that she and Ethan had destroyed. The lady was here restored, here renewed. And more vivid, more beautiful, more burning with life than paint and canvas could convey.

Amanda stared, longing flooding her heart, her being. A profound peace swept into her, incomparable to anything she had ever felt, even in times of apparent security, pleasure, and contentment. Like the morning star, rising over the blackness of night, she filled Amanda with light and affection.

And then someone spoke ... perhaps within her, perhaps without ... a musical sound, like the voice of one thousand harps playing in the purity of silence. *"Thank you for helping him—he is my son too."*

Amanda glanced around her, hoping to identify the voice, but there was nothing. She returned her gaze to the surface of the creek, but the lady was gone. Had she just imagined it? Was it real?

Yet she couldn't deny the peace that reigned within her and the quiet, steady trust that filled her soul. She didn't know all the answers to her questions, and many obstacles still loomed so large ahead. All of that remained the same. But within Amanda, things had changed. The Mother, her Mother, had given her rebirth.

Somehow things would work out for the good.

Amanda began walking back and determined to let this moment remain in her as she returned to her work: saving Ethan.

She took the damp scarf and dabbed at his cuts. He gritted his teeth but managed to talk through the pain: "What happened to you? You look different." Ethan's voice sounded weak, but he stared at her.

Amanda moved the scarf to the slash that ran across his cheek. Her fingers brushed against his stubble. She held the Mother's message in her heart: *Thank you for helping him—he is my son too.*

She met his gaze and took a deep breath. "I want you to know the joy that I know now. Come with me … come with us."

"Where are you going? … And do you even know the way?"

"We're headed to safety, to freedom. Others know the way and are guiding us. My family is there already. Will … Will you come with me?"

"You *want* me to come with you?"

She looked down at her hands. "Yeah, I do."

He narrowed his eyes for a moment. "Alright, I'll come along. But how do you propose I get there? How can you even get me out of *here*? We're completely alone in this wilderness and you're not strong enough to—"

At that moment, the sound of footsteps came from behind them, and a lone traveler appeared. Amanda sighed, relief filling her: Morgan. He walked toward them, smiling as naturally and calmly as if he had been crossing a parking lot or joining her at a table in some corner coffee shop. She watched him approach, and it seemed like she observed him with new eyes … eyes of faith. Her portrait of Morgan, her earlier conversation with him in the falling snow, the ease and familiarity of their connection—the pieces clicked together. Maybe she had always known the answer, deep down, but, until now, she didn't have the faith to voice it.

During all those solitary hours that she'd spent painting by herself and enjoying the company of no one while growing up, she had somehow never felt alone. And neither was she now, in this hour of need. Someone had been sent to protect her. Morgan had been there all along.

"I see you need help." Morgan stood beside her.

She didn't need to say anything about her revelation; Morgan already knew. So she simply nodded, amazement and gratitude overwhelming her. "And you're always here to help me, aren't you?"

Morgan put his hand on her shoulder. "Always, Amanda."

"This guy again? What the hell is he doing here?"

The furious outburst interrupted her thoughts. She looked down at Ethan, now propped up on his elbows, his eyes bulging and head turning from Amanda to Morgan and back again.

"I told you, Morgan's just a friend. I mean … if you had any idea how impossible it is for him to be anything else … it's nothing you have to worry about, okay?"

Ethan scowled. "Sure doesn't look like nothing. Looks like something pretty serious, actually."

"No." Amanda crossed her arms. "But what is serious is your leg. We need to get you back to the cabin."

"May I?" Morgan knelt on one knee and held out his hand, offering to help Ethan up.

Ethan nodded, avoiding his gaze.

"I'll support you on the other side." Amanda took Ethan's arm and put it around her neck.

Together, she and Morgan helped him stand. Limping and stumbling, the three of them walked back toward the cabin. Ethan stayed silent the whole time, his face white and tense with pain.

Back at the cabin, Mark stood in the front door, staring wide-eyed. "What's going on? Who's this? What happened out there?"

"He's hurt, Mark. Maybe we can just get inside first?" Amanda tried to catch her breath, the last few steps trying her strength.

She and Morgan guided Ethan to a nearby chair, where he sat clutching his leg with his hands.

Amanda looked around the room. To her surprise, everyone stood there, except Rachel, who she supposed slept upstairs. Bethany held a tissue in her hand and tried to stifle a sob. Joe's eyes looked red, as though from crying. Linda let her tears run down her cheeks unchecked.

With her stomach now turned to lead, Amanda whirled around and looked down at Ken. Father Voloshin knelt beside him, whispering prayers and making the Sign of the Cross over him. Ken's breathing was no longer labored; it had stopped.

"No. No!" Amanda rushed forward. "He was alive when I left! And now he's …?"

Father Voloshin stood up. "He went to God. … God called him home."

She stared at the dead body. It was Ken, but it also wasn't him. It was his body, but not the Ken she remembered and had come to know. Ken had entered that other world, just veiled beyond this one.

Father Voloshin picked up his Bible and held it to his chest, his arms crossed. "Ken fought final battle. Many believe God comes to soul three times at moment of death. He is great Beggar who knocks on door of the heart. No sin is beyond His love and mercy. But Enemy also makes final offensive, his last strike to claim a soul for eternal punishment, one final *'Non serviam!'*—'I will not serve!' We do not know how Ken chose in end. But we will continue to pray for him and to hope."

Amanda nodded woodenly, the lump in her throat preventing her from speaking.

"Amanda?" Mark called to her. His face looked exhausted, but he took a deep breath and straightened his shoulders. "We're all grieving. But we're still fighting the battle, and you have to give me some answers and explanations."

"I can answer for myself." Ethan sat back in the chair, adjusting his leg and wincing. "My name's Ethan Ramsey. I worked for the NCP until they said I was an informer for the opposition, which—for the record—I was not. They condemned me to come here, the equivalent of a death march. Two JPD officers accompanied me, both of whom are dead now. I was trying to get to Amanda, to make sure she was okay."

"Whoa, whoa." Mark held up a hand. "Why would the NCP choose to send you here? Why wouldn't they just kill you flat out? Why risk a mountain expedition where you could possibly escape?"

Ethan shrugged. "They have their ways. It was probably a sick pleasure on their part. I'm sure they derived some kind of amusement from the idea of Amanda and me dying here together."

Mark glanced from Ethan to Amanda. "So you two know each other?"

"Ethan's my ... I mean, Ethan was ..." Amanda caught herself, her cheeks burning. She looked at the floor. "We knew each other in the city." She cast a sideways glance at Ethan, who cocked an eyebrow at her.

Mark rubbed his chin and peered at Ethan's leg. "And your injury?"

"A mountain lion attacked," Ethan said.

Morgan nodded. "Ethan saved Amanda's life."

Amanda caught Ethan's look of surprise at Morgan's defense of him.

Mark glanced around the room at the others, as though seeking their input.

Bethany stepped forward. "Amanda, it sounds like you know Ethan pretty well. Can we trust him?"

Amanda sensed everyone staring at her. Bethany's question was the very one she kept asking herself: Could *she* trust him?

Joe scoffed. "There's your answer. If you gotta hesitate before answering that question, it's already a big fat no."

"Joseph, run upstairs to my bag and grab my rope." Mark pulled out his gun and cocked it. He turned to Ethan. "You can come with us, but you're coming at gunpoint."

Amanda's heart sank. This was not going to warm Ethan up to the opposition group.

Joe ran back downstairs, the rope in his hands.

Mark kept the gun aimed at Ethan. "Go ahead, Joseph. Tie his wrists. ... Mr. Ramsey, you make one wrong move and I'll shoot."

Amanda gasped. "Mark, please. He's not going to attack us."

Mark continued to stare at Ethan. "Look, Amanda, I've got women and children here to protect. We already lost someone. I can't take any risks. This guy worked for the NCP. Who knows what he could be doing here? I don't buy his story."

Ethan raised his eyebrows. "Ironic, don't you think? Being bound to go to freedom?"

Mark ignored him. "Bethany, can you get the bandages and take a look at Ethan's leg? That should be wrapped better before we leave."

Amanda started chewing on a nail.

Morgan touched her arm. "Let me take care of your cut too."

She'd almost forgotten she even had a cut.

Morgan took some gauze and tape from Bethany's supplies and led Amanda to the back corner. "It already clotted, but it's still better to cover it." He worked serenely, his face placid.

She watched him tape the gauze in place. "Hey, Morgan?"

"Yes?"

"Does anyone else know that you're my—"

"No. You're the only one who needs to know."

"You're not going to suddenly disappear now that I know who you are, right? I just can't imagine doing any of this without you."

"I'm always with you. But I can't always be with you in this way. It isn't natural for me, you see. It's not how I was created. There are times of exception, of course, but that time will soon end."

She nodded. "I understand. I wish you could stay like this always, but I'm grateful for what I've already been given. I need to ask you something else too. I went outside tonight to check on Boots, but I couldn't find him. Where is he? Is he okay?"

Morgan smiled. "He's safe. You didn't tie the reins tightly enough, so he escaped."

"So it is my fault after all."

"It's better this way, Amanda. You couldn't have brought him with you. He's free now."

Knock-knock-knock!

Amanda jumped and held her breath.

Knock-knock!

She exhaled: Nasir. Joe hurried to the front door and opened it wide. Nasir came inside, stomping snow from his boots. Amanda gathered around him with the others. What news would he bring? Was it time for her to reunite with her family?

"Nasir! It's so good to see you!" Bethany hugged him.

He nodded, his mouth turned downward in a frown. His eyes roved about the room. He had enough to observe: the expressions of worry and grief on those surrounding him … Mark's gun pointed at a newcomer whose face Nasir couldn't see … Ken's lifeless body on the floor.

Nasir stiffened. "Ken! What happened to him?"

Bethany's lips trembled. "He died about an hour ago. A JPD officer shot him yesterday in the woods."

"Someone who came with *him*." Mark jerked the gun in Ethan's direction.

Nasir's eyes widened. "Ethan Ramsey?"

Eyes slit, Ethan looked Nasir up and down. "How do you know me?"

"I work in the city. I'm well-informed of what's going on."

Amanda stepped forward. "I can explain everything, Nasir."

Linda stood up, her face red. "My gosh, haven't we done enough talking? Can't we just get out of this miserable place before we're *all* lying dead on the floor?"

"Linda." Mark shot her a disgusted look.

"No, she's correct." Nasir nodded. "We all must leave—now."

"Like *now* now?" Joe glanced out the window. "It's the middle of the night."

"No, dawn is coming. I have a moving truck parked along the dirt road, about half a mile from here. There are large packing crates inside, which you can hide in. The opposition group has an in with a gentleman on border patrol. He's one of us. We've arranged with him to let us through to Canada, but we must do it now. His shift will end in four hours. If we don't get through by then, it's possible we never will. We have adequate time, but we have to go immediately."

"I'll get my bag." Linda took the stairs two at a time.

"But what about Ken?" Bethany glanced behind her at his body.

Mark tightened his lips. "We can't bury him. There's a foot of snow out there. Not to mention the ground's frozen ..."

"He taken care. I prayed over him and sprinkled with holy oil. We place his body outside under tree. God willing, one day we return and bury him properly." Father Voloshin adjusted his glasses.

"That is the best we can do." Nasir nodded in assent.

The next few moments passed like a dream. Amanda watched Nasir, Father Voloshin, Joe, and Mark carry out Ken's body ... a small funeral procession. She wiped tears from her eyes. She still couldn't believe he was dead.

Then they made their exodus. Nasir carried a sleepy Rachel in his arms, leading the way. Linda and Bethany followed. Morgan and Joe supported Ethan on either side, while Mark walked behind them, his gun pointed at Ethan's back.

Amanda came last of all. She closed the door to the cabin a final time. No reason to lock it now. She stepped into the snow, following the others. Far on the eastern horizon, she perceived the slightest lightening of the dark sky. Dawn was indeed coming and, with it, the promise and hope of being reunited with her dad and Chiara.

It came to her on the journey that in the battle between freedom and sin, between manipulation and love, between demons and angels ... we must struggle.

But we are never alone.